Short and racy…..Jo Nambiar's debut novel draws a fascinating picture of the cult-like thugs who made killing with the *roomal* or cummerbund almost an art form.

- Juliana Lazarus, Bangalore Mirror

The novel begins with a hair-raising folk song….. Nambiar explores a forgotten era of mass murderers of Hindustan. If you enjoy stories set in India, you've found your next must-read with Nambiar's *Phansigar.*

- Sonali Shah, JetWings in-flight magazine.

Phansigar

Jo Nambiar

PARTRIDGE

ISBN:	Hardcover	978-1-4828-7440-2
	Softcover	978-1-4828-7441-9
	eBook	978-1-4828-7439-6

The story and characters in this novel are fictional. A few historical personalities have been included to embellish the story.

Print information available on the last page.

To order additional copies of this book, contact
Partridge India
000 800 10062 62
orders.india@partridgepublishing.com

www.partridgepublishing.com/india

This Work Is Dedicated to My Parents

To Bridgette
If it was not for your immense patience, tolerance and support
I could not have remained occupied in the varied lunacies
you are now hopefully acclimatized to.

Special thanks to Liza Varghese and Niloofar Ahmed
for their encouragement.

I wish to record my gratitude to Late Mr. Sohan Lal Dutta for
prompting me to publish this work.

Song Of The Phansigar

If you will part with an anna
And squat under my peepul tree
I'll tell you of Rakt-Beej-dana
A monstrous demon was he

When Brahma our Lord and Creator
Sent man to live on this earth
He blessed them all with virility
And of happiness there was no dearth

But alas, not a man or a woman
Not a newborn child could be saved
From the ravenous Rakt-Beej-dana
For their flesh and blood he craved

This voracious predator of mankind
Could wade the deepest ocean
And with every meal that he would find
Put an end to Brahma's creation

There was great consternation in heaven
Lord Shiva lamented to Parvathi
"Dear consort, who is this demon?
For I am the destroyer, not he."

She saw her Lord was crestfallen
"Wherever Rakt-Beej-dana might be
I'll go as Kali - The Black One
And murder the fiend", quoth She

If you will part with another anna
I will tell you of Her defeat
At the hands of the demon Rakt-Beej-dana
It costs money to be replete

Kali cut in twain with Her sword
She sliced and quartered like a lemon
But from drops of blood this giant spilt forth
There sprang to life a new demon

Waxed hot and weary with Her endless task
From the sweat of Her arms there did fall
Two mortals whom She blessed with a mask
And a cloth She called a ruhmal

She commanded them to strangle the demons
Not a drop of blood should She see
Mere mortals, sir, like you and like me
With élan they served Her decree

The demons gone, they knelt before Her
They placed their ruhmals at Her feet
She blessed the men, She returned their cloth
"Your needs by this ruhmal shall you meet."

"This cloth now serves you my good men
For the next generation and a hundred
For prosperity favours the ruhmal when
You efface those not of your kindred"

Farewell, you've heard my tale for a fee
Now my sacred ruhmal do you dread
You sir, who sit under my peepul tree
Neither are you of my kindred

I will tell again my story of yore
After I've consecrated your body to Her
Another traveller to my tree I will lure
To listen to the Song of the Phansigar.

Prologue

It was a night of omens. As the riders spurred their horses and camels up to their rendezvous on a rocky knoll overlooking the highway, each man was beset by an uneasiness he could not understand.

The night was creeping over the hills, deepening every shadow on the bluff they negotiated. The light of the feeble moon transformed the pale sun-bleached surface of the rising uplands through which they rode into ethereal silver. Silver and black. Only the flame-of-the-forest forced a differing hue occasionally on the horizon, as if to land-mark the riders' erratic and rambling route.

Raghubir was the first to notice a lone wolf darting up the broken terrain on their left, and disappear among the thistles ahead of them. He pointed a finger to indicate the animal to the rest of the group.

They halted.

"By Bhawani, should we proceed any further, my brothers? That wretched animal is a time-honoured harbinger. This could spell disaster to our plans. If Veeru Mahasaya were to lead us tonight, he would certainly have us abandon the expedition."

A turban-less rider of the group, a wild man with long matted hair and beard, halted beside him.

"As we have come this far, Raghubir, let us ride on. It requires a thorn to remove a thorn. Perhaps we will meet with two better omens ahead! Besides, even Veeru Mahasaya expects us to strike a *bunij* tonight to gift his wife when she arrives tomorrow. He has not seen her in over nine months."

"You are right, Panditji," added Gafoor. "We have come far. It is the eve of Muharram. There will be plenty of hapless *bunij* on the highway."

Two riders at the rear of the group chuckled, but fell silent at a cold glance from Raghubir.

"We are breaking more traditions tonight than ever before, you fools," he chided them. "Did I not beg of you two to let go of the liquor just for tonight. Sober up, or we run a terrible risk here!"

After some hesitation they urged their animals forward again. A crisp cold wind blew wisps of vapour from the muzzles of the animals, as they laboured up the incline. The long robes of the men fluttered noisily in the wind. Not a word was spoken till they had reached the top.

This time it was Farookh who broke the silence.

"Listen, can you hear jackals barking and baying? Hai Allah, on this night there appears to be more than one omen that have cast an unfavourable shadow upon us."

They now halted on the edge of a precipitous slope.

"Veeru Mahasaya would not have allowed us to seek *bunij* under these circumstances," Raghubir repeated. "Brothers, shall we take the road back home?"

"Muharram does not come everyday," Pandit, the unkempt haired man responded. "And to a city of this greatness! We have travelled far to reach here tonight. Could we not just wait a while till a favourable omen indicates an auspicious moment? By Bhawani, I'll wager those ruts on the road have been caused by rich traffic."

Below the crest upon which the nine men sat mounted, a narrow ribbon of dust, rutted by cart-wheels, indicated the treacherous road from Bidar and Puttancheroo, winding through craggy piles of rock as it entered the outskirts of the city. They could see the lamps of the *dargah* of Hussain Shah Wali built upon a tank. Further, the tombs of the Qutb Shahi rulers of Golconda loomed high, the magnificent domes catching some of the pale light from the sky.

Far on the horizon, Hyderabad, the pride of the Deccan, prepared for the annual celebration of Muharram. It was 1815, the middle of the reign of Mir Akbar Ali Khan Sikandar Jah, Asaf Jah the third, Subedar of the Deccan, known all over the continent as the Nizam.

It was that time of the evening preceding a festival, when the exhausted traveller reached near the end of his journey. Hope and apprehension writ large on his face, he would now be anxious to reach the safety of the city. There would be stragglers too. Either burdened by the old and infirm members of his family, or the tired women and children that travelled along. Either due to being heavily laden with goods and wares, or having lost a pack animal or two on their journey. These stragglers, small in number, and often travelling without escort, were always the weariest, the least resisting and the most vulnerable.

Simultaneously pathetic and terrible to behold, the scene that waited to unfold, had been enacted time and again on the outskirts of every great city on the sub-continent, but with continued success and unfailing precision especially on the Deccan Plateau and the Central Provinces.

The predators of this night's drama dismounted on the hillock, and waited silently for a sign that would reassure them that all was well. They lived in a world of meticulously observed rituals and superstitions. But tonight, the absence of their leader had divided their ranks to a state of indecision and uncertainty.

After waiting nearly half an hour, their eyes detected a movement on the dusty trail. It appeared over a ridge where the road met the horizon. Stragglers perhaps?

But they were soon disappointed. It was a large and well-armed camel-caravan loping towards Hyderabad. The cameleers out-weighed their numbers three to one.

Pandit cursed, and ran his grimy fingers through his hair.

"Look. There go some of our best prospects," Raghubir declared pointing regretfully at some heavily laden camels that trailed at the rear of the caravan. "I'll wager those two *baniyas* don't belong to the group but have sought their protection! Those bags might well be full of gold jewellery"

"By Bhawani, don't look for sherbet when you die of thirst!" Pandit responded reproachfully. "If we are destined to strike *bunij* tonight, they will come down this road with our names written on their foreheads."

Two of the younger members guffawed aloud, drawing an angry glance from Raghubir again. "Silence *bewakoofon*! Idiots! Haven't you heard it said that voices carry far in the night! Are you both still intoxicated?"

They fell silent. The caravan having passed, the road lay desolate before them. The cold wind blew relentlessly on the band, now huddled in discomfort on the rocky crag.

Then there came down the road two figures, clothed in saffron robes, walking unhurriedly, musical instruments in hand, singing a haunting and melodious song.

"Miserable beggars," Raghubir remarked. "No *bunij* here either. I have the inclination to roll down a boulder or two to scare them off."

"Baul singers," Pandit interceded. "Wandering minstrels. Let them pass. We gain nothing by taking their lives. They are as good as dead already."

They silently listened to the eerie strain of the music, played on a two string instrument.

Oh ameer, oh fakeer, why can't you see eye to eye
The gold is here forever, but all of you will die
Who is ameer, who fakeer, I will then ask of you
Death does not know wealth, and what is due to whom

"Bakwas!" Raghubir exclaimed. "The idiots pretend wisdom!"

Oh ameer, oh fakeer, if you could see eye to eye
Give a loving hand, when a brother lies down to die
Who is ameer, who fakeer, I will then ask of you
Only Life knows mercy, and what is due to whom

"Why don't they just shut up and move on quickly?" Raghubir murmured impatiently under his breath. "Shall I send a rock down on to their loving and merciful heads?"

The duo however passed unharmed still singing in a high pitched tune till they disappeared from view.

Another half-hour wore on.

Farookh was the first to hear it. "Hai Allah! A lone cart! A carriage of two horses."

"A handful of miserable beggars by the look of it. Either they have a damaged wheel, or a sick horse," commented Raghubir. "Observe how they plod."

"Or heavily laden, by Bhawani," Pandit whispered, his white teeth eerily visible on his bearded face as he smiled. "Brothers, we cannot be blessed with a better situation tonight. They don't have escorts, and the road is clear both before and after them."

"Let me send those two drunks to scout the *bunij*," Raghubir suggested. "That will sober them up. If the *bunij* is worth our while, let them deliver the *jhirnee*, the signal, to us. We will then descend upon the cart. Come on, Imran. And you Motiram. Go for it, and by Bhawani, don't you bungle, or Veeru will have both your necks when we return, I promise!"

The two young men mounted their horses.

"Cut their animals loose to immobilise the cart, and drag everything off the path," Pandit instructed them. "Remember, that we must finish them behind the many boulders on the side of the highway. We cannot leave any evidence on the road. We don't know what else comes riding on this road tonight."

As Imran and Motiram took the path descending on to the highway, Gafoor whispered aloud. "Jai Bhawani! Allah hafiz! If there is trouble and we need to take flight, we will congregate at the usual point at Naubat Pahad with Veeru."

The duo disappeared. Now as the darkness deepened, the rest of the group on the crest could barely see the road below. Clouds were gathering in the wind, and the pale silver light of the moon was suddenly replaced by a discomforting blackness.

They waited in readiness. The sound of clattering wheels grew louder as the carriage approached. They breathed slowly, ready to pick up the sound of the familiar whistle that had heralded so many ambushes before.

A minute of uncertainty followed. The unhurried rattle of the carriage wheel, as it laboured on the uneven road now continued without interruption directly below them.

When the sharp signal finally rent the night air, it was followed by the sound of a struggle, a grunt and a loud moan. The men on the crest were galvanised into motion in an instant. With stealth that belied their numbers, and the fact that they rode a mount each, they slipped down the path the scouts had taken, urging their animals skilfully down a winding gully, between piles of boulders, until they suddenly arrived upon the well trodden highway.

Raghubir was the first to descend upon the road. He dismounted even as his horse galloped helplessly, caught in the momentum of its descent. The night was as black as hell, but the *bunij* appeared to have been effectively ensnared.

He could discern the shadow of the crooked carriage, thrown askew when the horses had been cut loose and caused to panic. A wheel lay trapped in a deep rut, beside which the driver lay in a gruesome position, his broken neck at an impossibly oblique angle to his body. A most horrible scream of despair rose from behind a boulder on the opposite side of the road, and for a moment Raghubir wondered if it might be heard as far as the *dargah*.

The party now filled the road blocking the path of anyone in the carriage who might make an attempt to escape.

Gafoor tore open a curtain behind the carriage and dragged a woman out by her hair. She tried to scream, but her voice stuck in her throat. A young boy seated in petrified silence inside broke into a hysterical cry, but Pandit struck him viciously with the palm of his hand and dragged the near unconscious boy out of the carriage. Once again a pathetic scream rose from behind the boulder.

"Hai Bhawani! Shut that infernal sound!" Yelled Raghubir, and would have walked across to see what it was if his eyes had not caught another man crouched in the darkness under the carriage. But before he could reach him Motiram had located the man, and was dragging the struggling traveller into the midst of the group. They pounced on him, kicking him in the belly and genitals even as he begged and sobbed. Farookh silenced him with a length of cloth thrown around his neck, while two of them pinned his legs to the road.

The woman Gafoor had dragged out of the carriage died without resisting, as the *ruhmal* in his enormous hands lacerated the flesh of her delicate neck.

Pandit did likewise, his *ruhmal* suspending the helpless boy in mid-air. Following a violent spasm, he dropped the lifeless body on the ground.

They rummaged about. A sizeable quantity of gold and silver were found in a small hand-sewn bag amongst the clothes in the carriage.

"Search the bodies," Raghubir ordered. Then he turned when he saw Imran emerging from behind the boulder dragging the corpse of a young girl he had just strangled. From her disordered and dishevelled appearance, even in the darkness of the night, he could tell what had been the fate of the girl previous to her death. Raghubir slapped Imran so hard that the younger man spun wildly before falling on the road.

"Dog that you are! Has that liquor not satisfied you? Was it necessary to seek pleasure in a mere child? Hai Bhawani, this *bunij* has been presented to us by Her grace, despite bad omens. Do you wish to defile it?" He kicked the young man's side in disgust. "Be-*aklay!* Wait till Veeru Mahasaya hears of this!"

The search of the two female bodies fetched a few more gold ornaments, one of which was of exquisite design and had a jade pendant of a very rare kind. The two men carried some silver on their person. The boy had died in vain. He carried nothing.

"It has not been an altogether disappointing night, my brothers," Pandit remarked. "Let us make haste. This region is too rocky. Shallow graves will have to do. Then we need to break this carriage, and throw the pieces behind some boulders off the road. Leave no evidence here, for it becomes difficult to use the same spot to ambush a *bunij* in the future. The world must believe this family disappeared after entering the city of Hyderabad."

They prepared to offer a ritual to Goddess Bhawani, a sacrifice to consecrate the bodies to Her.

When all was done, they would eat the consecrated sugar or *misri*, "the *goor* of the *touponee*", and ride to Naubat Pahad where awaited their great leader, Veeru Mahasaya.

* * *

Veeru Mahasaya, bathed and anointed, sat in prayer in the shade of a neem tree, even as the first light of dawn barely glowed in the horizon. A gentle breeze blowing from the Hussain Sagar cooled his damp body. His long hair still dripped, sending droplets down his broad back. Veeru's mind was in deep contemplation though his eyes were only half shut. While he awaited the arrival of his brothers, he breathed with the ease of a large feline in slumber. Far in the distance he could hear the strains of wandering minstrels singing a heart-rending and melodious tune.

He had been told by his dying foster-father that he was the child of a brahmin couple who had been accidentally waylaid and killed at Indore, many years ago, along with two Gujarati *angadias*, or gem couriers. Veeru had noted the difficulty with which the dying man had pronounced the incident 'accidental'. Showing dubious mercy, the man had raised the four-year-old to learn the only vocation he would ever know. Veeru, a religiously inclined individual took to his vocation dutifully and efficiently, just as an obedient son of a butcher would after his father.

He derived no particular joy from this vocation, and would have preferred any other, except for the fact that he had been sworn into this trade outside a Kali temple by his foster-father, and he had known no other trade or skill in his lifetime. He however believed in destiny, and if this were his, he was scrupulous in the dictates of its doctrine, and rigorous in his fidelity with the traditions of the trade as initiated to him by his foster-father.

The men in his charge arrived one by one riding around the Naubat Pahad. Veeru had been unable to accompany them the night before for he had yet to complete the mandatory forty days of abstinence and prayer for the souls of those he had killed in their last expedition.

Raghubir and Pandit greeted him from afar. He could see from their disposition, that the night's hunt had been successful. Farookh, the stout Muslim and Motiram rode some distance behind them.

"Jai Bhawani!" Raghubir greeted him, as he dismounted. "You were right Veeru-bhai. That pass on the highway is a fearsome place."

"And a rare one," Veeru smiled. "It is my favourite entrance to a city, save the one outside Bhopal."

"But a very rocky region to conceal the dead," Pandit complained. "The animals of the night would have furrowed and feasted before the sun is up."

"Is the road clean?" Veeru enquired.

"As clean as we found it," Motiram reassured him as he dismounted.

By now all nine men dismounted and assembled around the neem tree.

"We cannot be seen in counsel here for long," Veeru remarked, his ears picking up the wandering minstrels' song again in the wind far away. "Our group is too visible. It would be wiser to enter the city and mingle with the crowds on this day of Muharram. Now show me the takes of the night. The *bunij*."

Veeru nodded appreciatively as the sewn bag of gold *mohurs* and silver were exhibited. "A good haul for the trip back to our homes. To Jhansi, Gwalior, Rewa and Bilaspur."

"Now take a look at these. Fit for a princess. Pieces of jewellery you will be proud to present your wife when she arrives here today," Pandit held out his *ruhmal* displaying among others, the necklace with the rare jade pendant.

A wild animal-like howl emanated from Veeru Mahasaya. His scream echoed all around the Naubat Pahad. It was a heart-rending wail of a man sobbing in utter despair.

He clutched the wet hair on his head, and broke into a demonic laughter. A strange hysterical laughter that ended with a cry of intense pain.

"Oh God! Hai Bhawani! Oh Kali Ma? What have you done to me?"

He fell over and dashed his head on the ground.

"Brothers, your *bunij* was my family," he cried. "My wife, my daughter, my son! Hai Bhawani, I must see the end of this!"

In the dazed silence that followed on the Naubat Pahad that day, only the minstrels could be heard in the distance.

Oh ameer, oh fakeer, when you see eye to eye
Gold will lose is lustre, with life then you will vie
Who is ameer, who fakeer, I will demand of you
Did you not realize your wealth, and what is due to you?

It had indeed been a night of omens.

* * *

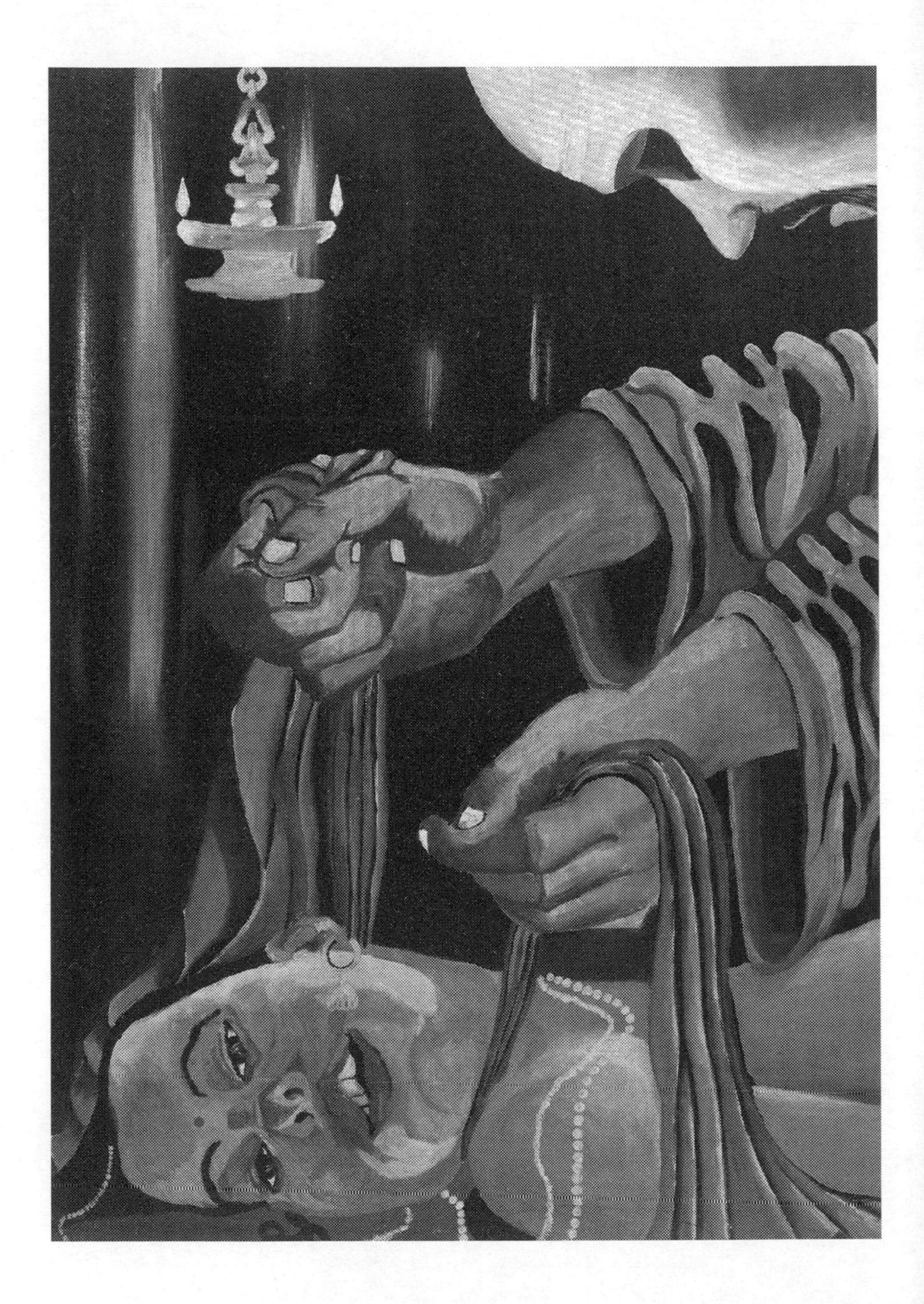

Part I

John Penmarric travelled out of a quiet Cornwall in the spring of 1825 to be part of the prodigious London of those times. At twenty-one, on that sunny morning, he knew that the journey he was beginning was to become the watershed in his life as there was no turning back to St Ives.

In those days a private hotel, called the Sailor's Bell, was the fashionable rendezvous of all the young idlers of Newquay. Fashionable, because even the English gentry visiting this region often rested here. St Ives, Cornwall was John's home, the only homeland he had known these twenty-one years. The Sailor's Bell at Newquay was homestead. These young loungers of the Bell were mostly his native bunch of eager Cornish boys, fairly affluent by local standards, though none of them having been any further east than Plymouth. Except Bob Pendarrow perhaps. Bob's arrival at Newquay and their subsequent acquaintance at the Bell was to result in John's keen desire to travel and see for himself the great metropolis of London that Bob spoke so much of.

At twenty-six, Bob Pendarrow was not just older but the more accomplished of the lot. It was Bob who first described in creditable terms new-fangled concepts like those of the new steam driven machines and hot air balloons. He boasted of a friend, a Mr. Babbage, who had won the Gold Medal of the Royal Astronomical Society for his invention of an engine for calculating mathematical and astronomical tables. Bob had also worked in the West India Dock Company for a few years where he had acquired a small fortune and a characteristic dockyard arrogance. This apart, he was a genial fellow and had accumulated a vast, albeit unrelated, store of information about the world; of the kind that have enticed the English schoolboy seaward for generations. The boys of the Bell, especially John, held him in awe, and gazed enthralled when he expounded his knowledge of rich kingdoms and idyllic islands visited by English merchants. John had little hope then of seeing the world the sailors saw. Bob had him understand in no uncertain terms that the authorities at London at the East India Company's office recruited men of a more impeccable breeding than he could boast of. It might have helped if he was not Catholic, if he had learnt an Oriental language, or at least if he had been born into the isle's noble, landed aristocracy, whose lesser accomplished sons had found the means of attaining "Nabobhood" in India. "The rest of us could otherwise live barely better than a native," he would say.

The coach John boarded had only three passengers, headed for the towns of Exeter and Salisbury. Further east the turnpike offered a more comfortable journey than the Cornish country roads. But the traffic to London swelled at every mile. At Exeter two passengers alighted to be replaced by a shy and modestly attired couple; French Huguenots who spoke better English, John noted, than the thickly accented Cornishman back home. They were headed for the Spitalfields area where the silk industry flourished.

Bob Pendarrow's eulogy of the great prospects London held for him made the journey less tedious than it might have been. A letter of introduction from Bob, a box, a portmanteau, his first- aid box and a modest education was all that trundled along with him that day. And a small fortune in savings to keep him buoyed till he chose to return to Newquay; "If 'ee chose to," Bob had said. "But 'ee never can live in these parts again, Johnny. It'll be a wisht ol' job to go back to pilchard hauling and tin-mining. 'Tes proper to think o' finding some gentleman's job at the dock yard with the education 'ee have. Take this letter o' recommendation to one Mr. Charles Hutchinson at the West India Dock Company. If 'ee ever feel the need for a job, it will serve you well."

At the Salisbury toll the dust stirred by cattle being driven to Smithfield stung the nostrils. Coaches, carriages and men on horseback were aplenty. The lodgings and accommodation at Salisbury seemed squalid when he recalled the modest elegance of the Sailor's Bell at Newquay. However his mind continued to dwell on the prospects of a better London coming to fruit at the end of his journey.

But with Salisbury was also the beginning of a sense of apprehension and foreboding.

John Penmarric's parents were dead. His mother when he was just nine. His recollection of his mother always brought to mind a pretty smiling face, large soft hands and a distinct warm kitchen odour. His father had been a prosperous fisherman, whose fortunes were not entirely wrought from the pilchards he netted in the bay along St Ives in his impoverished later years. He had helped John's grandfather smuggle tea and French claret into Newquay in the days when the trade had been lucrative and safe. This prosperity had led him to farming and mining and put John through an education of sorts. John learnt French and for a year worked as an assistant to a country physician. At Newquay he worked at a chemist for a meagre income to keep himself occupied.

John's anxiety as he broke journey at Salisbury was, he believed, stirred by memories of his father. Of those moments, more than a year ago, as he lay resigned to his fate with severely congested lungs. A kind of asthma he had contracted during his mining days. Wincing in pain as he laboured to breathe, he was propped up on a large pillow. Staring out of the window, he had said, "I've nothin' to pay for my debts, son. These freebooters 'll have 'ee runnin' and borrowin' before I'm gone." John could see he was plainly distressed.

"You started with nothing, father," John tried to console. "Besides, I have an education. There's always something to do up-along Newquay."

How he liked to believe his confidence put his father at ease! He watched his father's drawn face nestled in a shock of yellow hair that had lost their lustre and appeared more grey and silvery now. For a long while the old man stared out of the window onto the seafront where the seagulls screeched unceasingly and flew in great arches.

"It's a funny world out there, John. You do somethin' 'cause you're sure 'tis good for 'ee. 'Fore long a wrong wind blows by an' nothin's the same anymore. Always watch the waters these days son. There's somethin' bewitched wi' our times. I have these frightful dreams John. 'tis due to these debts I reckon. This appalling dark lady keeps beckoning you, my boy. Like a black banshee, I see this woman calling out to you, John. Long bloody tongue like some oriental nightmare…"

His last words. John could never forget his final ranting over the growing debts. It loomed large over the frail bed-ridden man. His helplessness worsened his condition. He died unhappily. Following the funeral, John lost not a moment deliberating over his father's debts. Selling the farm and the boats, something his father would not have allowed, left him a handsome sum, even after making good the debts and paying off the creditors. His soul could now rest in peace, while he, John Penmarric, was a free man. Within the month he was off seeking greener pastures at Newquay.

The large town offered an exposure one didn't experience rusticating meaninglessly in the Cornish countryside around St Ives. He chose the somewhat hopeful existence of the educated in the bustling business centres. But Newquay, he discovered to his discomfiture, offered only second-rate jobs. Not the kind of fortune a recently disinherited young man would be contemplating. John was in search of a largesse at short notice and vying to quickly regain the kind of assets he had to relinquish to satisfy his father's creditors.

It was on such a winter of uncertainty that the smiling enigmatic figure of Robert Pendarrow strolled into his life one January evening in the precincts of the Sailor's Bell.

His father's last words, like those of a soothsayer, lent the journey out of Salisbury a certain caution and melancholy that was inexorable. It however prepared him for the realities of a London even Bob's descriptions had failed to emphasise sufficiently.

London reeked. It reeked of slush and garbage. It stank of horse dung. Rattling along in the coach, as they entered the city, the bustling metropolis closed in on him like some dark and sordid forest of humanity. For many years to come this first ride in the streets of

London in the approaching dusk would remain deeply etched in his memory. Well Bob, is this the city that rules the world, John brooded. Never in the villages of Cornwall or even at Newquay, Plymouth or Torquay had he seen more wretched specimens of street arabs, urchins and scoundrels than those that idled the arteries of this city. The suburbs they left behind them were in fact somewhat cleaner; the half-rural villa lined roads were roomier than the heart of the metropolis. Elms grew copiously interspersed with almond and cherry trees.

Evidence of a city in the throes of change was perceptible everywhere, a constant reminder of increasing prosperity. There was construction work on every street. Wheelbarrows, muck-carts and carriages of every description jostled unceasingly among horsemen, livestock and coaches. Even the bollards erected to protect pedestrians had heaps of garbage and waterspouts pouring around them water-logging entire street corners. London's streets were dangerous. Even the river Thames was a nettle of masts, not quite spared from the crowd, noise and odours of the city it drained.

It was dusk when he alighted in front of a private hotel in the Strand to seek accommodation. While the manager dispatched his personal effects to his room, he let his eyes rove over the chandeliers and the exquisitely attired people in the parlour. Only now was the London of Bob Pendarrow's commendation suddenly pulsating all around him. It was Bob's idea that he should seek quarters here. The Strand was a fair beginning to imbibe the city's social graces and begin his intercourse with the place. The hotel itself presented a confusion of taste in architecture, carpeting, upholstery and woodwork. The society responsible for this provided an even more bewildering spectacle. One had only to peek out of the window to see specimens of the most bizarre fashions that London's nouveau riche flaunted, as they flashed and flitted about the Strand.

Dinner was an expensive affair. London's grouse and gravy and her white wines were meanly priced. The port was steeper. John was sufficiently tired on his first evening to sleep most of the night in a deep and dreamless slumber. A hot bath and clean sheets, he discovered, were matchless tranquillisers at the end of a journey.

But he stirred at dawn, as one was apt to do in the style of his Cornish upbringing. And he thought he heard his father's sonorous voice once again," there's somethin bewitched wi' our times son..."

And for a fleeting moment he thought he saw the seagulls again over the peaceful bay outside his sleepy village in the country.

* * *

It was not until about a week's residence at the plush London hotel that John found himself making any meaningful acquaintance. In the meanwhile he had procured for himself a modest wardrobe of London's latest trappings. It gave him confidence to don in the style of the genteel and the decorous he saw around him. John Penmarric was tall and lean. He possessed considerable strength of limb, and often wondered if his broad shoulders and muscular arms made a rather rustic impression on the learned and the prosperous. However, he preferred to retain a clean-shaven face which, coupled with his long black hair and sharp nose gave him the quiet demeanour of a scholar. Over the fortnight he gravitated towards a layer of society that would, he thought, perhaps be better able to give direction to his own ambitions. Young and recently prosperous, they stood out like bright cherries in the dark greyness of the city. Wealthy traders of every large and minor colonial enterprise mingled about the Strand for reasons he found obscure. Often they appeared to have worked their years in remote corners of the empire only to make their grand presence in the Strand every year. They kept the London tailors and chefs busy. They were generous with the wine. Stewards and girls in waiting fell over each other to oblige them. Doors opened for them when they stepped forward. Seats emptied wherever they entered. The best wine cellars were only unlocked on their arrival. Bankers were indefatigable and sleepless men at these times. Even London's women were busy dispossessing young "nabobs" of most of their strength and wealth.

And it was one bright Friday morning over a bacon, eggs and kippers breakfast, as John had good reasons to remember, that he first met Lucy. Beautiful daughter of a London merchant, Lucy Polgarth had returned after a two-year stay in India where she managed some of her father's affairs. Her light brown tan, exquisite silks and a copious vocabulary of colonial jargon first drew his attention. Then he was completely captivated by her smile, - frank, unpretentious, almost adventurous. Aware of this, she would playfully, if discreetly, spare no opportunity to convey to him that she enjoyed his heed.

He courted Lucy for much of that beautiful season, till the state of his finances became alarming. She seemed to possess her father's enterprising intuition, for she seemed aware of his dwindling purse, try as hard as he would to hide the fact. The bravado of a twentyone year old amidst all this benevolence and mutual generosity, especially when in the company of an enchanting lady, can be hard on the purse.

His good sense prevailed, for rather than be forced out of the metropolis and out of Lucy's life, he decided finally to take Bob Pendarrow's advice and look for work in the dockyard.

It was not until autumn that he found work in the West India Dock Company on the Thames as the youngest assistant of the pier-master to oversee the dockers unloading tea, indigo and cotton. Hutchinson the pier-master was a dour and portly individual with yellow hair, a lantern like jaw and beady eyes.

"I have great respect for your friend Pendarrow," Hutchinson said. "You have been highly recommended. You know what we pay, don't you, my boy? You will find we pay among the best there is on the seafront."

"I have no complaints about my salary," John replied, seeing it was almost twice as much as any he had heard offered anywhere in the city for a similar position.

"You will be briefed by Preston in the morning with regard to your duties should you accept this job." The dourness suddenly vanished. "Why? You will, my boy! Accept you will! I've spurned many a young lad who lacked integrity and ambition. You hear me, my boy! Ambition! Well-fitted that you are, I see you have known some wealth and good life. It ain't worth alosing, is it, my boy." The beady eyes smiled. "Now here's a key. Good friend Preston has his ways. I have mine. And so does Pendarrow. Now you walk in these doors, all highly recommended and all, by none less that our good friend Pendarrow. That makes four of us for the task in mind. And I look at you. What do I say? Here's a lad. Seen a wee little of life. But full of energy. Oh! And ambition! You get to earn here, John. I dare say, you get yourself a tidy sum if you play by the rules. You learn your job, you do your job and you'll end up loving this place here."

Suddenly Hutchinson seemed almost amicable, if only a little too keen to recruit him. John wondered about the letter Bob had sent, the contents of which lay folded on the table. Highly recommended! Indeed, Bob's word seemed to carry some weight with the dour Hutchinson, for he seemed quite elated now. John also wondered what the nature of this job was to require all this inducement.

The pier-master seemed to have read his thoughts. "For the regular work here, my boy, you will understand that I have the choice of employing a number of our London lads. But I have my special reasons for letting you in. I have been awaiting this long while for one recommended by Pendarrow to walk in these doors one day. The lantern jaw leaned forward earnestly over his desk. "A matter of confidentiality, John. There are some delicate affairs you will learn to handle here. Extremely delicate, you understand?" He looked at John keenly and ran his tongue over his lower lip three times in succession. "You look like a bright young man to me. And sensible enough, I dare say! And for such a man there are some special errands on the yard." He paused.

John remained silent waiting for him to finish. The pier-master stood up and walked around to his chair. "Let me be a little more precise," he continued, running his fingers through his thick yellow hair, keeping his beady eyes riveted at the young lad's face all the time. "This empire of ours is a large one, and many are the suitors to her spoils. Rich merchants, John! Who makes rich merchants? What nation makes the wealth we do? Why, I ask you, are we riding every sea on the globe? Let me tell you my boy, I have seen more vessels dock here than you have seen pilchards down about St Ives. And in all these years I have seen not a dozen - nay, not a handful of consignments that was not ill-procured in some fashion or other. That is what we handle every day a ship berths here." He paused.

John waited. Was he expected to respond to this?

"And my job is…" he began.

"Yes, Your job! Your job, my boy, I'm coming to that. Now, you hear me - "he continued "Your friend Pendarrow sat on that very chair you sit on now, my boy. Three years ago, I remember. He sat there listening to these very words. Young Pendarrow came here with half your education, and perhaps even less to speak of in terms of money. But he listened to everything I've said to him. He trusted me, you hear. He trusted me! He worked by the rules. He's rich today, son, rich!" He paced the floor of the office slowly, watching John all the time, hands folded behind him. "And all because he stayed with the team, and played by the rules. Your job, I daresay will be simple enough. Initially, that is. We have George Preston on the yard to brief you in on the details. He's the senior customs house Officer."

When it seemed apparent that Hutchinson was still not forthcoming as to the exact nature of the job, John decided he had to be blunt.

"Sir, with due respect, may I venture to ask, am I required to do something illegal or immoral?"

For a moment the dour countenance returned. He paced to and fro. "You have a poor choice of words, Mr Penmarric. I was just beginning to explain to you the nature of the world around you. I'll have you understand this job for what it really is. But first let me tell you that your dear friend Pendarrow was sent by me to Newquay to recruit fresh talent. You were not in the Strand by accident, my boy. We wished you to look around you. Feel the comforts of a civilised society before wondering to yourself how so much wealth could flow around you without being able to touch it. What you saw around you was pelf, my boy. A sane and civilised society showing off its lucre. The emoluments of subjugating a raja somewhere. The remuneration, the winnings, the pickings of an empire, gleaned by the routing and bondage of some idyllic society somewhere. Many a chest-load of private consignments - spoils, if you please, make their way through the yard to every fine home and mansion that stands in

London." Hutchinson's eyes narrowed, looking straight at John as he spoke again. "Our duties lie in this area my boy." His face was stern. "For a price, we overlook the surplus, you understand? For a handsome commission, a very handsome commission, we let pass the poor man's fortune. We are not here to question his sources. We shall not concern ourselves with the opulence. Only its passage, you understand? We provide the safe conduit that makes the Englishman's overseas enterprise lucrative. Nothing illegal here, my boy. It's down right patriotic! Now we do keep books, and require our clients to pay an affordable tax to the crown. That I ensure, my boy! You see there's nothing immoral here, as you put it. Our clients are the best of citizens - doctors, engineers and soldiers from afar as India, Burma and Africa. These poor souls have toiled their entire lives in the most inhospitable places. The least we could do is provide a safe passage to their earnings. John, what's a commission, offered in good faith and earned by us to see this empire prosper? And this commission, you will learn, is shared fairly when it comes around. Your salary in due course will be of little consequence." He returned to his seat behind his desk. His beady eyes narrowed again. "Can I depend on you?"

John looked straight at the pier master's eyes. He wasn't entirely convinced of the dignity or respectability of the job, but he wasn't entirely unhappy either. Here was finally a prospect of some money. For the ambitious dreamer that he was, the fortune hunter, he felt sufficiently tempted to accept the offer. Anything similar in bounties, he believed, was only wrought out of some adventurous gambol overseas.

Hutchinson seemed to read his thoughts again. "Not all of us might consider it worth our while to become sailors and soldiers; to spend a lifetime in some sweltering forest to furnish his London home. Your life would have been spent! That's why we hold the keys to an important function. The hazardous road home from the King's dockyard to their stately houses in London. There are good many Englishmen who would not think twice to the parting of a fraction of his spoils to see them safely home." He leaned forward and whispered. "A little help to our brethren. And a fair commission for our effort. That's all I ask. A matter of trust, you understand. Robert Pendarrow is a trustworthy man. Look where it has got him. And you, my boy, are one of his carefully chosen recruits."

John had no doubt about that. Bob couldn't have chosen a better man than a recently disinherited fool, who had been unwittingly led to squander much of his wealth about the Strand.

Hutchinson waited for a moment patiently, allowing the impact of his proposal to sink into the young man's mind. "I have here this job for you. I will speak no further on the matter, since what you know so far is not sufficient to damage my enterprise. But I must have your decision."

John wondered about Bob Pendarrow. The Bob he knew at Newquay had obviously taken great care not to draw any undue attention to his recent prosperity. But his confidence, nay his arrogance, and his ever-so-content smile had always stirred a sort of envy at the Sailor's Bell. Only now did John understand. And as he thought of Lucy, he was prepared to hazard his cards to go Bob's way.

The following morning he found himself in George Preston's office at the custom house. Preston was an enormous man with a ruddy face and a monocle on his right eye. He was amicable and brief. "You will learn on the job, boy. As of now, you will be required to accompany specific goods on behalf of the customs house to the home of their owners in the city. You will be paid the due portion of the promised commission whenever you do these specified errands. As with all such good fortune, there is an element of risk. Let me not be guilty of not forewarning you. And when not detailed for special duties, you will assist me in overseeing the unloading of merchandise. Tea, Indigo, Cotton and such other cargo: This, in fact, will remain your normal duty, your official detail, for which you will receive a salary." He smiled wryly. "True, there's little else here. Fortunes still come by the shores." He placed a heap of files and a ledger before the young man. "Here, go over what there needs to be learnt, boy. We shall be off on our rounds on the yard in an hour."

That winter was a prosperous one for John Penmarric.

In the weeks that followed his first meeting with Hutchinson there was little to do. He supervised and recorded the innumerable chests of tea, boxes of indigo, and bales of cotton that emerged out of every clipper, sloop and brigantine that found berth on the pier. He mingled with the staff on the yard and acquainted himself with their various duties and functions. Following Preston's instructions, he noted discreetly and with minuteness the change of shift and the period of lull on the pier. It was not long before he gained a clear insight into the periodicity and rhythm of work on the docks.

One dreary afternoon, quite exhausted after a strenuous spell on the pier, John was seated in his cabin, with little to engage himself with. He was idling his time making sketches of seagulls flying across the back cover of an old ledger when he was startled by the trim, smiling and well-groomed figure of Bob Pendarrow standing at the doorway. Bob was holding his hand up, a gesture John could only infer as something oscillating between a weak apology and a greeting. He had not seen Bob since leaving Newquay, and much as he wished he could censure and castigate him for his present fortunes, he was speechless. Bob had, after all, only shown him the road to London. Treading the path to penury was his own doing. Above everything, he owed Bob a little gratitude for the job he now held.

"You could have told me, Bob," he finally broke the silence between them.

"It doesn't work that way, Johnny." Bob said slowly walking up to John, now holding both hands up. He found a chair. "What goes on here cannot be spoken of any place else. Certainly not at the Bell." He smiled a disarming smile, extending his hand. "How are you doing, my good fellow?"

John could not help a faint smile in response as he shook his friend's hand. "Financially in the doldrums, if that's what you're asking. Otherwise the job promises a good salary." He regarded Bob's fine cut clothes and the smart silk hat he placed before him. Even his accent was distinguishably changed. It almost didn't sound Cornish anymore. "And you, Bob? Of course, I needn't ask you, need I?"

"On the contrary, Johnny, I'm not as rich as Hutchinson or Preston makes me out to be." He paused and eyed the younger man to gauge if his confession was believed. "I've had my measure 'o privation, believe me. I've seen the low water, took me awhile to make good my debts. I certainly am not impoverished today; you could say I'm just 'bout comfortable."

"You expect me to thank you for recommending me for this job, don't you Bob?" John asked.

"Not unless you have reason to." Bob sounded nonchalant. "Take your time, Johnny. The truth is we needed a man here. My job was to find one. And to that end I was not required to be candid. Even to a friend! This is the real world, Johnny. Any intrigue in your present circumstance has been explained to you by the pier master. The choice of acceptance of these duties is wholly yours. Come Johnny, look back awhile! You could still be lying in languor at the Sailor's Bell as the rest of our boys there do just now. Ambition isn't greed. Every job has its indelicacy. But the rewards are substantial."

"All I've done since I've been hired is the humdrum…" John began.

"That's why I'm here," Bob interrupted. "We have a special consignment tonight."

A silence followed. Bob looked pleased as he saw John's eyes light up. He swept aside the ledger with the seagulls.

"A very special consignment from a distinguished client has arrived on the yard. It lies there among the hundreds of packages you unloaded this morning. It must be located tonight and delivered with discretion to the family of the client at a London address."

John tried to recall all that he had unloaded that day. There were chests of tea from China, indigo and jute from India; parcels of various sizes and shapes from all corners of the globe constituting mostly mail and inexpensive artefacts. The Englishman has a penchant for picking up the most novel knick-knacks of native and tribal art to impress his family and friends at home. There was no duty levied against these items. The Port authorities trusted the package by its weight and the description as declared by the consignor. While John was left wondering, Bob continued, "You need not worry yourself till it is time for us to do our little errand, Johnny. You are, I believe, in a position to assess the situation on the yard tonight?"

"It's Saturday. The yard will be empty but for the guards." John replied.

"Some of them are in on this. We await the eight 'o' clock change of guard. Preston will be here at a half past eight. You are required to be here at the same time to clear the consignment. Except for the time we choose to carry out the task, everything is official and legal. We are the port authority, remember?"

"Then why choose this irregular and inconsistent hour?" John enquired.

"There are problems associated with the passage of such goods as these that you know very little about, dear fellow. The cover of darkness will be used to extricate the port officials, which includes you and me from the responsibility. Any charge of improbity, should we be discovered, will be explained away as a case of a break-in or burglary on the yard. There are details, fine details John, that I cannot be very explicit with. Our methods have always worked before. It will work for us tonight."

John nodded despite being a little dumbfounded.

"I shall now take leave," Bob declared, standing up. "We shall meet as decided. You will come in as you usually do, past the guard. They will not question you. The rest will be detailed to you as we progress with this task." He paused, and seemed to gauge his new recruit. "So go over in your mind everything we have just discussed while you doodle those birds. I promise you that from this day on, life will not be - what did you call it? Humdrum? Good day, my dear fellow."

He smiled in his enigmatic fashion and left the assistant's cabin as suddenly as he had arrived.

* * *

It was close to half past eight.

John looked in the direction of the vessels that lay at anchor across the pier. The smell of crates of fish unloaded that evening drifted in the black night air. He had entered the yard and walked past the guards without incident. It was an unusual hour for a port official to be around on the docks. The quayside was deserted, but he strolled out to it in the manner of an official making an impromptu inspection. Then with an affectation of bored indifference he strolled to his cabin at the far end of the warehouses. A few lanterns hung on the wall of the warehouse throwing long shadows of the balustrade along the yard. It was another five minutes after he had unlocked his cabin that Bob and Preston joined him.

"The keys," grunted Preston.

John removed the large iron ring from his bureau.

"The bill of lading register," he snapped again.

John obeyed his orders mechanically. In the light of the lantern placed on the table Preston opened the large register to the day's entries. He placed his monocle on his eye and ran his index finger down the list. He produced a letter from his coat pocket and consulted it for a moment.

Turning to Bob he said, "John here, has unloaded it in storehouse number five. Convenient enough, but judging by the sequence of the chest numbers recorded here, we may need to remove a few boxes off the top to get to it." He turned to John. "Don't let that worry you my boy. You were not to know. In due course of time you will get the hang of it. Now come, let us locate it. There is still work to do. You will watch and learn."

The three men proceeded to storehouse number five some yards from John's cabin. John unlocked the large doors and pulled them ajar. Preston walked down the aisle separating the rows of tea chests, holding the lantern aloft to read the numbers on them. He indicated a box at the bottom over which were stacked at least six large chests.

"That will be our quarry," he said, turning to Bob. Bob lifted the chests of tea one by one, till he was able to reach the object of Preston's attention. Silently the two young men carried the chest to John's cabin while Preston locked the storehouse door behind them. The chest, though heavy, did not betray in type, marking or weight whatever its dubious contents were.

While the boys caught their breath, Preston spoke. "The special contents of this chest are to be packed in these bags here." He produced four course cotton bags with drawstrings.

The sides of the chest were prised open without difficulty. The chest contained dry, black tea leaf, which as it poured out, filled the room with its aroma. Bob delved into the chest and produced four completely sewn leather pouches.

Preston examined them, squeezing, patting, and prodding them with his enormous hands as if they were alive. "Precious stones and gold coins by the feel of it!" he exclaimed. "However, the contents are of no consequence. A good commission awaits us on their delivery." He proceeded to place them in the bags he had produced for the purpose.

Unseen to either of them, John noticed what he thought was a fifth little bag, slightly protruding out of the heap of tea dust that had spilt on the floor. He picked it up. To his surprise it was a cloth doll of a kind he had never seen. It was embellished with real human hair, black in colour, topped by a strangely twisted black turban. Its face was a neatly stretched brown cloth ball and it wore a finely embroidered red tunic. A finely painted, terrifying and bearded face stared up at John.

"A native plaything?" John wondered, but neither Bob nor Preston appeared interested in the strange little toy that had inadvertently sailed the seas to reach London in a tea chest.

"Some child's prank perhaps, or accidentally packed by a native in the colonies. This tea from China was gapped and repacked at Calcutta." Bob did not bother to evince anymore.

"Now John," he instructed. "You and Bob here will return this chest to the storehouse. As for you John, against this particular chest you will make a little note in the register which says - Damaged-in-transit-and-handling."

The instructions were carried out without any delay. Preston once again produced the letter from his coat pocket and read out a London address. "See these bags delivered tonight and take a written acknowledgement for the same. For then only shall we be a few pounds richer in the morning."

That winter was indeed a prosperous one for John Penmarric. With slight variations, often as result of clients' instructions, the pattern of transition and carriage of the goods they smuggled out remained much the same. Goods varied in size and value, as did their destinations. In the months that followed, John could never quite get over the excitement involved in these special errands. Every time they were required to locate and deliver a consignment, he relished the drama and furtiveness of the act. Bob Pendarrow took John into his fold as they developed mutual trust. As the weeks passed, John saw little of Preston, who rarely came by in the night; except when the pattern of operation changed drastically, involving special risks or large volumes. It was Bob who received instructions from the customhouse officer and relayed the nature of the night's operation to John. As for the dour Hutchinson, he remained irreproachably above board. To the extent that John wondered where the man fitted into the scheme of things. There was also this strange underlying decree, this immaculate, sometimes ludicrous code of conduct that John found marvellous. Never in their transactions did anyone even remotely suggest defrauding a client or pilfering his goods. A thought, which every-time it crossed his mind, John felt ashamed of. There was some honour among thieves here, so to speak! It somehow made him feel noble. Above all else it brought about a certain respectability to what they were doing. John, who received perhaps the smallest proportion of the commission, found he had already saved several hundred pounds by the new year. And his savings multiplied despite shifting lodgings to a very decent ward of the city.

He saw more of Lucy Polgarth now. And Lucy intuitively seemed to know John was prospering. For once even her father seemed to notice him. The swarthy cotton merchant had more or less ignored John on their first acquaintance at the breakfast table on the Strand, and had seemed content to make conversation with others at the table. The man now often expressed a desire to meeting John.

"Do you visit Cornwall often?" Polgarth asked one evening over a dinner of oysters and grouse at the Golden Cross on the new Trafalgar Square.

"Not since my father passed away," John replied.

"And what do you consider of your present station? You said you worked at the dockyard didn't you?"

"Oh well, that is only a temporary situation. I have a fair inheritance," John lied, "which I hope to invest sometime in a worthy enterprise. Until such time I have a desire to remain employed and learn the intricacies of commerce. A dock company is erudite in this regard. Perhaps at a later date I might attempt a worthy position with the East India Company."

"Well said, my boy," the merchant exclaimed. "As for Lucy here, she has learnt a fair deal since she joined hands with me. Why, I would leave her alone to parley with the financial representative of Rothschilds and Lazards as easily as I would with the wily *shroffs* and *sahukars* back in India."

Lucy blushed modestly, looking more beautiful than he had ever seen her look. Her light brown hair was radiant in the flickering candlelight. John could smell her French perfume, and her silk dress looked ravishing on her supple frame.

John often paused to contemplate and thank his good fortune. Unlike Bob, whose lack of education resulted in a characteristic demureness in the company of affluent society, he could hold his own and sound convincing. He could lead a comfortable existence among the upper gentry of London's business community with ease. While Bob could be arrogant, even pompous, with close acquaintances, his coterie was still commonplace. This prevented him from exhibiting wealth without provoking suspicion. John, on the contrary, found himself dining among the elite and fashionable of Kensington Square and Pall Mall. He could even boast of once having been invited to dine at the elitist Athenaeum Club, one of whose patrons was delivered an exquisite tiara by him one night.

John was at the same time a mute witness to English upper class covetousness and propensity for all that was wealthy and bizarre that made their way into the country from exotic colonies abroad. For every week that winter he conducted the passage into the richer wards of London, untold wealth in gold, jewels and artefacts the likes of which belied, ironically, the dirt, poverty and destitution he saw all around the great capital. It was the most awesome demonstration of avarice. He often doubted if he was being compensated sufficiently, but for the moment his savings far exceeded anything that he had ever possessed.

* * *

The wheels of fortune are inextricably cogged to the machinations of destiny, as John Penmarric was soon to discover. From as early as the 1770s when Robert Clive, the great general and Indian adventurer was exonerated by parliament for his turpitude, English middle class morality frowned upon the concourse of misappropriated and unwarranted wealth. Though undue attention to this impropriety was largely avoided by methods such as the means Hutchinson and Preston provided, the lucre and flamboyance seeping into English society as never before became more and more apparent to the many watch dogs of social decorum and accountability.

At about the same time legislation was attempting to keep pace with the changing social environment in London and the empire at large. The Home Secretary Robert Peel was enthusiastically promulgating the reorganisation of the police system and a large-scale reform of the penal code. This would, it was rumoured, sooner or later replace the foot and horse patrols, or the Bow Street Runners, created some decades ago. As a natural consequence, the existing patrols tried hard to establish their efficiency so that their worth was not ignored. They hoped to form part of the new police force, and were set to impress the Home Secretary. Their informers were many in the city, and intelligence gathering, albeit unreliable, led to increased scrutiny on both banks of the Thames. Preston pronounced caution, and often required them to shift or transposition sensitive consignments to a safer location in the city for long periods of time before their delivery.

One evening in early spring John awaited Bob Pendarrow's return at a pre-appointed spot at the corner of St. James Park not very far from Westminster. Near Charing Cross they had parted ways, as they often did when Bob decided it was not necessary to expose both of them to these intrusive custodians of the law. Bob would pick up the consignment from its hiding place kept in a store of some acquaintance only he knew among the many book sellers, law stationers, seamstresses, wig makers and dealers of small toys and wares in the Charing Cross area. He would deliver the package to its recipient at the address of a lawyer on Belvedere Road across Westminster Bridge, and return in an hour to the park.

It was still cold, the spring not having entirely liberated the city. The first faint shoots of green showed upon the Elms. As the sky darkened, a gentle wind drifted through the park.

From where John stood he could see the street leading north to Charing Cross and east to the bridge.

John waited for over an hour and a half, now anxious for Bob's return. It was rare for Bob not to keep to his schedule, especially in the business they were in. To kill time, he had strolled from the park to the Charing Cross junction and back twice, and again this time to Bridge Street and back. He paused hopefully at the Abbey, as they had met at that point before. He was now impatient to get the business of the night over with. He would stop and look earnestly every time a carriage trundled past. In his anxiety every passenger began to resemble Bob.

He felt ridiculous when on one occasion a carriage that rattled up the dark street appeared to carry a passenger who even seemed to beckon him, waving a drunken hand. But as it grew closer, the life-size figure seated within looked like the native doll he had once picked out of a tea chest on the yard. Long hair, a black turban, frightful countenance and a bright red tunic. John frowned at the figure. As it passed him by, he wondered if it might not be an actor from some minor theatre in London, who had too much to drink and didn't bother to return his costume to the green rooms. But the coincidence of its semblance to the Indian doll gave him a chill. It also strangely made him laugh in apprehension.

Another half-hour slipped by.

To add to his distress, two patrolmen passed him by as he paced down the road once again. He was not unduly alarmed, for there were a few people about, and he had quickly thought up a convincing excuse for his presence there. But with the delivery underway and Bob's undue delay he could not unhitch the fear of the police.

Was everything going as planned? The question vexed him.

It must have been another ten minutes into the night before he heard a lone four-wheeler draw up near the park a few yards behind him. John pivoted around expecting Bob to step out. Instead two men disembarked from either side. Removing the side lamps from the carriage, they walked purposefully in his direction.

John was not certain whether he should remain nonchalant or flee. His posture must have betrayed that indecision, for the men suddenly broke into a run. In the light of the lantern he noticed one of them, a well-built figure, in a grey cape and cravat, removing a monocle from his eye. It was none other than Preston. The other man he could not recognise.

"It's okay boy," Preston called out in a voice that barely signified any composure. And the stranger accompanying him betrayed their intention by darting sideways to cut off any attempt by John to escape.

Instantly he knew something had gone drastically wrong that night. He spun around and shot off in the direction of the park, clearing a wrought iron gate in a burst of energy only his years could do with such ease. In a confusion of irrepressible doubts, his mind racing to understand the contingency, he tore through the darkness of the elms in the park. He was on the far side in less than a minute when he heard a sharp whistle. A shot was fired from a firearm in his direction. It grazed a tree and ricocheted off a bollard on the street. God! They were trying to kill him! He turned to run again.

Suddenly he was aware of the two patrolmen he had seen walk past him earlier, appear from the opposite direction to cut him off. For a desperate moment he felt trapped, but he heard the sharp whistle again.

Some instinct caused him to pause. The sound of the whistle came from a doorway that opened onto the opposite kerb of the street. A lantern hung crookedly outside, and in its light he could see a figure in a workman's overall and leather apron fervently gesticulating at him.

Despite his apprehension, John made an intuitive decision to bear up to this only hope. He raced across the street and dived into the doorway just as another shot shattered the lantern outside. Another crooked and smoking lantern hung on the wall inside the doorway as he stumbled in, clenching his fists. He had no recollection of ever having known this apron-clad man before but the man appeared unruffled. In the brief moment of respite, the man slammed the heavy door shut and barred it with an iron cross beam.

In an effort to immediately allay his fears, the man exclaimed "Pendarrow's man I am, good sir. But he is in a spot of trouble. Hastily dispatched me to warn you. You have walked into a trap. I'm here to help you out. Soon there will be a mob outside to help the police break in."

John noted that the man had a shock of silver hair, a fine moustache and a beard, and looked like an ostler or a stable hand. Beneath the silver hair he stood young, small built, poised and extremely agile.

The door now creaked and heaved with the effort of the crowd outside. They were pounding at the heavy timber, which did not seem capable of resisting them for long.

"Now what?" John exclaimed.

"Quick, make your way out through the back and on to the roof."

They rushed through what looked like a saddlery, out onto an enclosed courtyard hemmed in by decrepit walls all around. John could hear the commotion at the door, which a notoriously spontaneous London mob would soon help demolish.

Grabbing at every ridge and projection their hands could purchase they scrambled on to the roof. The rooftops were awry, asymmetric and extremely slippery along much of their gradient, but the duo ran through the labyrinth of smoking chimneys in the moonlight, often skidding dangerously towards the guttering at the low end of the roof. On suddenly reaching the edge of a building, they came upon a yawning gap, dropping vertically into an alley. The silver haired man leaped, almost impulsively, sailing through the air like a bird in flight, landing precariously on the roof on the opposite side, but with an ease that tempted John to try the same. It nearly killed him, for when he jumped, he fell short of his intended landing-point on the roof, and would have plunged down into the dark alley had he not been grabbed with an acrobat's precision by the stranger. They scrambled on, and by a circuitous and convoluted route to escape pursuit, they dropped onto a narrow street, devoid for the moment of any human form. Still running, they found themselves in a broader street lit up by gas lamps. John could not recognise the street in that instant. It was that hour of the evening when the continuous stream of four wheel carriages were rattling up discharging their cargoes of the prosperous and nocturnally inclined into the many sacrilegious quarters of the city.

The duo now tried to walk more casually and inconspicuously. John was shaking violently, adrenaline pumping feverishly in his veins. A few women, dressed in tawdry finery, tried to attract his attention, startling him violently. He felt cold sweat in his collars as his anxiety rose again.

His companion waved, and a four-wheeler arrived. He briefly instructed the coachman, who mounted to the box, while he ushered John inside. As the driver whipped up his horse John peered out to see if they were being followed. For in a short while he expected to see their pursuers spew into the street behind them and obstruct all traffic in an effort to ferret them out. However, everything appeared normal and he began to breathe more easily.

But as they rattled off John found his companion huddled in the manner of a man crying. Which indeed he was, John discovered, for the man was hunched over and held his face in his hands. For a man who had so adroitly rescued him from his recent predicament, this disposition was unexpected and rather alarming. He appeared to have been seized by some unspeakable despair.

"They've got our friend Pendarrow, sir," the man whimpered sinking back in his seat. "Poor Mr Pendarrow! Took a musket-load on his thigh. He was screaming like some lamb at the butcher's where he fell."

John recoiled in shock. "God be merciful!"

"And you sir, have very little time on your hands. I can only explain briefly, for I had little opportunity to speak to Mr Pendarrow."

John did not know what to expect, but he prepared himself for the worst.

"He was off to this address on Belvedere Street. That fact you perhaps know already. The authorities and their informers have apparently been tailing him for sometime, I would guess. However the goods he was wont to deliver was in dispute. I am uncertain of the parties involved or the nature of the dispute, for their origins are in some obscure place overseas. You should know perhaps that these goods in question were of exceptional value and men would kill to possess them."

John remembered many consignments of that nature which had been delivered on so many occasions, and wondered how many had died or been killed in their wake.

"Well, to prevent them from reaching the consignee, it would seem that a great many people had been enticed, bribed and blackmailed," continued the man. "While the consignee, as you know is a lawyer on Belvedere Street, the real recipient has chosen to remain aloof and unnamed. There are men and women of exceptional power and influence involved here. Even Mr Pendarrow was not to know. You meet me today for the first time under these extraordinary circumstances, Mr Penmarric. But I owe Mr Pendarrow a great deal, a great many favours," he barely muffled a sob, resting his head again in his hands. "Poor Mr Pendarrow!"

John did not wish to ask the man his name at this point. He would tell, John believed, in his own time.

"Well, the bribing and intimidation, or both, appear to have transformed your employers. They have switched loyalties, for they now stand absolved of any acts of corruption. While they gained from all this strange business over the years, they now see circumstances working against them and are in the process of wiping their slates clean. Tonight it seems, was chosen for a demonstration of their fidelity with the law, and you sir, along with our friend Mr Pendarrow, are to be the sacrificial lambs."

John sat there shattered, shocked beyond belief.

"What is to become of Mr Pendarrow?" John inquired, "Is there enough evidence against him?"

"Much worse," the man replied. "Much worse than you might expect. Did you know Mr Pendarrow carried a pistol?"

John shook his head. He had never known Bob was fearful enough of his life to need one.

"Well, in the melee that followed the ambush that was sprung on him, he was forced to fire his pistol to keep the hounds from reaching him. He killed a man. A patrolman, I believe. Yes, a young Bow Street boy. This will be considered a serious crime even if all other evidence against him is obliterated. It is heinous enough to attract capital punishment." He paused again in an effort to keep his composure. "Mr Pendarrow did manage to scare his pursuers sufficiently to break free and hide in the Olcott Mews between Lower Lambeth Marsh and Oakley Street where I have contracted some work. I know he ran to the mews because he was sure he would find me there. He was flushed and gasping for air when he came in. He carried the consignment in one hand. Looked to me like a casket of some sort. He was almost delirious with fear and brandished his pistol. He declared he had been compelled to shoot someone, but seemed to believe he had given his pursuers the slip. He was frantic to tell me whatever he knew and to dispatch me to St James so that you would be warned in time. That is just like Mr Pendarrow! A heart of gold, the man has." He sobbed again.

John sat in numb silence. They were now being jostled by the four-wheeler, which seemed to have turned into a poorly cobbled street.

"It was not a minute after I left Olcotts that I heard Mr Pendarrow scream in pain. They had surrounded the building which I had barely departed from. On hearing the scream, I returned and mingled with the crowd of curious onlookers while they dragged poor Mr Pendarrow out injured and screaming. He was overpowered and there was nothing I could do but carry out his bidding. Oh God! I do fear for Mr Pendarrow, I do." He sighed and closed his eyes.

John peered out into the street. The carriage they were riding was coming to a halt. John noticed that the coach stood outside the notorious rookery of St.Giles. Dilapidated buildings, overpopulated and dirty, from where vice, crime and often cholera spread to the rest of London.

His companion alighted and held out his hand. John took it. The hand was leathery, calloused and coarse.

"Dawson is the name, Jack Dawson. I live in these parts and don't care for your judgement, sir. I am a teacher in the only school in these parts – a wretched school, if you saw one. With a vile entourage to help me run it. But I am a good man, I am. And a good teacher of physical education. If Mr Pendarrow was here he would tell you. One day I hope to join the staff of a better school - somewhere in India or perhaps Africa."

John looked upon the shattered and grieving man standing below him. His eyes were those of a kind and frank man. He was ashamed of his long held opinion of the company that Bob Pendarrow kept. He could not think of a single acquaintance among the eloquent and the flamboyant that he wined and dined with who could remain so trustworthy and dependable in a moment of crisis.

"Rest assured, sir" John replied in earnest. "I am grateful; extremely grateful for the service you do me now. I will not forget this night of your generosity. God only knows I am still well and out of harm's way only by your act of courage. I am grateful to you Mr Jack Dawson."

"Then be gone, sir. Mr Pendarrow's last advice to you was, stay away from the dockyards, away from one Mr Preston and all other of the guards and officers of the yard. They will all be on the watch for you. They are turncoats. If you ever need me, alight here and ask for Dawson of Olcotts, the school master. Someone will lead you to me."

He was gone, like in a dream, before John could say another word. John peered out of the coach for a few moments longer. The dismal street outside made him shiver. He signalled the coachman who whipped up his horse once again.

John Penmarric took solace in one thing at least tonight. Not Preston, not even Bob was aware of the whereabouts of his new lodgings in the city. For some obscure reason he had not mentioned it to anyone. He had only now to make haste and vacate the place along with his belongings and find accommodation in some less pretentious locality and lie low.

Above all, he needed time to think.

* * *

In the weeks that followed, John Penmarric drew up a list of possible sailings out of London, out of the British Isles, and perhaps to India where he believed he could remain untraced and forgotten. He had enough money on him to pay for his passage and to last him for some while. For the fugitive that he now was, there was no going back to Newquay, and London was too dangerous to live in anymore. This was a city he had travelled out of Cornwall to witness and be a part of. Ironically, it now appeared to him that the whole of London was hunting him down.

He moved into a modest suite of rooms venturing out only in extreme necessity. Making only short forays, and always after dusk had fallen and when the crowds thronged the streets. He had not dared to even peer out of a window. And his mind would always remain burdened with worry about Bob; and also of Lucy, whom he had not seen since the tragedy.

It was over two weeks before he found the necessary courage and temptation to venture as far as the infamous rookery of St.Giles once again. The solitude was becoming unbearable and he believed he could learn something from Jack Dawson, perhaps even seek the services of this maverick of the mews. If he could convince the man to become his agent, his eyes and ears about the city, he could perhaps fathom what was going on in the world about him and what course he should take in his uncertain existence. His world had become a void and his situation so hopeless, that when he reached the rookery he could not help envy the laughter and the carefree banter of the drunk and the destitute. He had barely pronounced the name of Jack Dawson before he found himself being led through a maze of narrow alleys by a rabble of street urchins who pranced about him unceasingly and tried to pry into the pockets of his coat.

When he saw Dawson he let drop a handful of coins in the alley and was quickly ushered through a door by the man.

"Good to see you sir, and in fine shape too, if I may add."

"I need your advice to procure a permit and papers to sail out of this country," John declared without ceremony. His desperation must have shown in his abruptness, and he felt ashamed for it. "Indeed, Dawson, it is a relief to see a friendly face," he added honestly.

John looked around. The room that presented itself belied the meanness and squalor of the slum outside it. It was clean and well lit and could boast of a few fancy portraits on its painted walls. There were numerous books neatly stacked on a mahogany table and stuffed book-racks ran along an entire wall. There were hand-drawn sketches of pugilists, price-fighters and gymnasts above the bookcase. A drawing, unmistakably of this agile man Dawson doing an acrobatic act – a leap from a trapeze - hung above the door. A rich Oriental rug of deep maroon draped the floor. Dawson waved in the direction of a wicker chair and sank down into one himself.

"The permit to board a ship which you seek will not be easy to obtain. But it is not impossible if you are prepared to travel under a pseudonym. When you set foot in the Colonies, assume yet another name if possible. Break all ties with your present identity. If you are comfortable with such an arrangement, I do know of some gentlemen who might be inclined to help us for a price."

John then inquired after Bob. What Dawson had to tell him made his heart sink.

"Pray for his soul, Mr Penmarric. There is little else we can do."

John learnt that Bob was at Newgate on death row. The trial had been speedy and the evidence damning.

"We don't know how much he has spoken, or if you have been named in the trial, Mr Penmarric. But if Preston or Hutchinson has been called to give evidence, be sure you also now stand condemned. They will be on the lookout for you. Do forgive me for what I have to say sir, but I feel less and less inclined to have you visit this part of the city. I trust you understand my meaning. The wretched souls that live in these lanes have enough troubles of their own than to be menaced by another affliction. I will associate with you for as long as it takes to obtain the papers that you seek. For Mr Pendarrow's sake, I am prepared to go that far for you. But for your own sake, be gone from these shores. The likes of Preston will pay for their deeds in good time. We may trust God for that, sir."

As John left Dawson's quarters, he felt more blighted than the depraved inmates of St.Giles.

* * *

One evening, a month later, he met Dawson, who furnished him with the permit and the papers he required to sail to Calcutta.

He was also informed that Bob Pendarrow had been executed in public outside Newgate prison. John fell to his knees and sobbed like a child on Dawson's maroon rug. For a long time, he remained there on the floor, as wave after wave of uncontrollable despair and guilt swept over him.

Dawson sat in the wicker chair in his characteristic style, face buried in his hands. His unkempt silver hair looked greyer than ever.

They sat there for a dark and sombre hour, each man trying to come to terms with his torment. When at last, he was able to, Dawson spoke, "I need you to know that the unjust jury that delivered the verdict was hand picked and composed of Preston's friends and well-wishers. I have identified most of them. At least fifteen of them. They are from London, Sheffield and Liverpool. By God, I wish I possessed some power to put the fear of the devil into them. Some morbid way that I could affect their lives for the casual and callous manner by which they could snuff out a person's life. I saw others in the jury box who were Hutchinson's close friends and clients. I recognized them. His rich associates from Kensington, Hammersmith and Ealing. What sort of English justice is this? Those treacherous thieves from Stockwell, Brixton, Camberwell and Vauxhall; so many times has poor Bob served them, and faithfully too! How could they have turned so cold and unsympathetic? How I wish I could cast a spell to make it impossible for them to sleep a single night peacefully in their beds."

John was silent, numb and unable to compose himself.

"Mr Penmarric, I'm afraid your arrival on the coast of Hindustan will not be any less dramatic than your hastened departure from these shores. For I have also heard it said about the dockyards that both Preston and Hutchinson have resigned their positions for a situation in India. They have utilised the influence they enjoy with some of those rich and powerful clients in Lewisham and Blackheath to extricate themselves from the present discomfiture they face in London. They have been absolved by the court of any charges, but quite obviously the remuneration of these dockyards are not attractive to these men any longer. Watch your back Mr Penmarric, for this menace awaits you there in India too."

John stood up, leaning his tall weary frame against Dawson's painted wall. "Gone to India, have they?"

"So I have heard," Dawson repeated, "So I have heard."

John gathered his papers and stuffed them into his coat pocket. He stretched out a grateful hand, placing the other on Dawson's shoulders. His face was grim but a strange light shone out of his eyes. Without uttering a word he left Dawson's quarters.

Outside, Jack Dawson watched the young man retreat slowly down the alley in the gathering gloom. His head was held high, his stride resolute. And he did not look back.

"God be with you, dear friend!" Dawson whispered sadly. "Neither can I bear to live a life here any longer. Perhaps destiny will provide some reprieve for us both."

Part II

With his eyes firmly shut Veeru could hear the clear feminine voice, reverberating with a timbre of awesome authority. The words were kind, but they pulsated with a pronounced finality in his ears.

"I have tamed the animal in you. I have driven you like a slave till you have learnt to live in searing pain as serenely as you had suckled your mother's breast when you were born. The invariable chanting of the sacred mantras has elevated you to a higher plane of endurance. But never in all this did I ever wish you to forget the two tenets of Tantra. Remember them well. One must rise by that by which one falls, and the very poison that kills becomes the elixir of life when used wisely."

She led him to the edge of the forest above a wellspring and spoke to him again.

"The boon of Siddhi that I bestow upon you, *para-kāya praveśanam*, is now complete. Do not be frightened, my dear Veeru. Great are the mortals and the forces that I have summoned to put a halt to this evil that has befallen this land. You will see many a trial in the days to come, but the forces of Siddhi that you command will aid you through. Your soul can now enter into the body of another person. And for the purpose, behold I have just the person for you. He is an innocent individual without parents. Take him now while the moon still shines. I promise I shall never be far from you. For I shall prevail upon his sister whom you will meet tonight. When all is over, I shall release you in the waters of the Ganga, in the holy ghats of Varanasi from where you beckoned me."

As she spoke, from along the narrow mud path that divided the paddy fields came a young man carrying some empty vessels, headed for the wellspring. Veeru opened his eyes for the first time that night to find the light of the moon unbearable and blinding. He covered his brow with his hands in pain.

He heard the inspiring voice one last time. "Go now, for the time is near. For the horseman from the distant land that we have summoned has arrived, and is awaiting in these very woods to do his bid. His horse has already sensed me and is ill at ease. The stage is set and I must be gone."

* * *

Clambering up from the mud path, Shambu placed an empty vessel under the bamboo runnel of the well spring and secured his *dhoti* to withstand the strong breeze blowing from the paddy fields behind him. As the water reverberated against the brass he gazed up at the stars. The night promised to be cool. He shivered as the wind found its way through the holes in his shirt. He could smell the fresh green paddy and the faint whiff of smoke that rose from the huts beyond the fields. A dog howled somewhere in the night. It was the first hour of the moon. He was alone. The cooking fires in the huts would soon ember. The noises of children would fade away. The flame of the oil lamps would be lowered. And the tired village behind him would sleep another night.

Shambu lifted a heavy cudgel that he had concealed in the tall grass near the spring. He held it high above his head with both hands and swung it about in morbid rehearsal, startling a couple of partridges in the paddy before him. He was ready to carry out a mission, which he felt was long overdue. Lord Shiva give him strength tonight! He stood awhile holding the club and stared in the direction of the village. With a deep sigh he contemplated, his eyes focused on a light flickering in his village. The act at hand held a special fascination for him. But he thought of its consequences, and wondered how this peaceful village would quake when the morning dawned on his deed.

Shambu's village, Bijaipura, was situated on a sleepy sun washed plain, with a few barren hills and a forest on either side. He could not help but notice the contentment that each day brought with it. There was always work to do here. The precious cattle provided a substantial income while the paddy ripened. He thought of his sister Salmi's beaming face outside his hut every morning drying dung cakes on the walls before leaving for school. He was proud she could read and write better than the sarpanch. Even her guruji was immensely proud of his only female student. Would all this remain the same tomorrow? He liked to believe his people had the resilience to ride the tide should misfortune befall the place following his act. They had survived the famine a decade ago. The Pindari wars that followed raged in the district around them but by some miracle had spared their village. Shambu who had volunteered to defend the village had learned to ride the only horse in the village. Even the sarpanch's son envied his ability to gallop and scout about in the hills nearby while they prepared for the war. His people had secretly transported food grains to the hills and hidden them there in anticipation of another famine. But the crops had ripened year after year...

The dog howled again in the wind. Shambu removed the brass vessel and replaced it with an earthen goglet. He secured his *dhoti* again. A gust caused the water to splatter out of the narrow mouth of the pot and he bent over to rearrange its position. The water was cold tonight, and like the wind, it made him shiver uncontrollably. An uneasiness crept up on him like an oncoming fever. Was he afraid? Was he being watched? He fought back the familiar wave of panic about to seize him as had occurred on the previous nights. He looked towards the forest, almost certain some shadow stood in vigil watching his every movement. For Salmi's sake he must not allow himself to become overwhelmed by this feeling again. Somewhere in the distance he could also hear the high pitched singing of a wandering *Baul* minstrel.

Listen to my tune, I have been singing since you were born
You have no time to listen to my music, chant or call.

The melody will remain in the winds when you are gone
No hurry, for in another life, you will listen to this Baul.

He dropped the wooden club and scoured about the grass beside the spring, picking up a small earthen pot of *mohwa*. He breathed deeply, holding the pot to his face and letting the pungent fragrance assail his nostrils. The moon shone like deep amber in the liquor he held in his hands. Then holding his breath he poured the entire contents of the pot down his throat. He shook his head violently, and then stood still. The *mohwa* would require some time to hold his nerves together.

Listen to my tune, I have been singing since you were born
Your lives are all entwined and your fate was cast afore
You think you do as you had wished, waking up each morn
What has to come, what has to pass, was decided long ago

The water gurgled slowly at a rising tempo and he heard the goglet fill up to the neck. As it overflowed, he raised the brass vessel on to one shoulder and lifted the cudgel. Placing it carefully under his armpit he lifted the goglet. He then stepped away from the dribble and walked along the mud banks separating the paddy fields.

The silence of the night suddenly enveloped him. Except for the wail of an infant, the village slept soundly. The uneasiness had not left him entirely and beads of perspiration still stood on his forehead. The light he had seen flickered dimly again and again, and as he watched it he felt a deep rage well up inside him. He also felt grateful, for the anger dissolved his fears.

On reaching the village he placed the water on the edge of the path leading to his hut, and cudgel in hand, strode purposefully towards the large house, set apart from the huts, from the window of which shone the only light he could see in the sleeping village.

"Shambu!"

In the darkness he heard the lilting voice loud and clear. It was his little sister.

"Salmi! What are you doing here?"

"Don't do this, Shambu," her voice trembled in earnest. She was standing across his path, her tall lissom frame attempting to cut him off. He could vaguely make out her silhouette against the house. She was carrying a small cloth bundle.

"Be quiet," Shambu hissed, brushing past her as he reached the thorny fence erected to keep out cattle from the premises of the house. Salmi ran up to him and held his arm.

"I saw you remove this piece of wood from the *gaushaal*," she whispered aloud. "You looked angry, and I sensed what you were setting out to do." She was trembling.

"I had gone to fetch water," Shambu explained in anger. "Do you understand, Salmi! I did nothing tonight except fetch water."

His sister wasn't listening. "But this..." she began, trying unsuccessfully to wrest the cudgel from his arm.

"You are not to know of this. Get back to the village." He commanded. "Get back home."

"Shambu, listen to me just this once," she implored. "Why do you not care for what will become of us? Me? The child?"

His eyes flashed. "You! Look what has become of you! Tonight you do not even have a *duppatta* to cover your modesty," He whispered hoarsely. "What has become of an innocent girl?" Tears welled up in his eyes. "I care for you, and I care for justice!"

"But he is the father of the child," she wept.

"But not your husband!" Shambu retorted. "He is a white man. An English saheb. You are a mere servant in the house. You will never be given refuge in his home! Don't you see that? He has used you for his pleasure, that is all!"

Salmi wept uncontrollably. "Shambu, oh Shambu! I am ashamed of what has happened. But I am afraid we will not be able to live in this village after tonight. Please Shambu! Isn't there any other way!"

Shambu breathed heavily. He looked down at the little girl who had squatted at his feet. She looked small and vulnerable. He thought for a moment of the three-month-old foetus in her womb. He wondered what colour it was.

"This village will not forgive you when this child is born," he remarked hoarsely barely hiding his anguish. "How long can you hide your abdomen? You know very well how much they envy and tease you for going to a school. They will ridicule and blame your education for this. What will Guruji say when he sees you with child?"

"We could run away somewhere for a while…" his sister began, waving the little cotton bundle at him.

Shambu sat down heavily on the ground resting his chin on the vicious instrument of his night's mission. "Look Salmi," he said, and for a moment seemed to gain control of his anger. She crouched before him tear streaked and miserable. "The famine took our parents away when you were just a child. I can barely remember them myself. If we leave the village today without giving a reason to the elders, we will lose what little we have, the land, the house, the paddy, and the cows. We belong to nobody! Nobody knows where our parents came from. Nobody will marry you do you hear? Nobody!"

Salmi sobbed quietly. "God, what have I done? Oh Shambu, kill me! Kill me! But please don't go to jail for assaulting the saheb. If the saheb is destined to die by the hand of a man, it will not be yours Shambu!"

Shambu squatted uncomfortably still watching the window through which the oil lamp shone. "No one is to know that," he whispered. "He will die in the first blow."

Salmi uttered a muffled cry. She was terrified.

But now Shambu doubted if he would succeed at all. Even if he took the white man's life, his sister would be so distraught that every villager would read the deed off her face. And the child? What of the child?

They sat there on the cold path for a long time. A half moon shone on their sombre faces. In the distance somewhere Salmi could hear the rhythmic beating of a *dhol*. Nomads who visited the district every year were camped not very far away. The sound of the drum seemed to calm her tormented brother.

"Let us go home for now, Shambu," she said softly. "Come, I'll help you with the water."

Shambu stood up slowly, crestfallen and sad. Would tomorrow bring any solace? He picked up the cudgel and threw it into the thorny fence. They walked together down the path till they reached the containers of water. He picked up the brass vessel and let her carry the goglet.

Back in his hut he lay awake on his charpoy for a long time. Sleep came but slowly. He could hear Salmi on the other charpoy, awake and restless. Poor Salmi, how could he ever be angry at the only living human being he could call his own. Perhaps he should try and talk to the English saheb again. God! Curse the day he allowed her to work in the bungalow!

As he fell asleep he could still hear the *dhol* reverberating in the wind from the direction of the river a mile away. Soon the *mohwa* drowned the sound away.

From the moment Shambu fell asleep, Salmi felt less distressed. She slid off her charpoy and stood over her sleeping brother. As she looked at him she felt her head swim as if the fumes from the *mohwa* had somehow gained hold of her senses also. She didn't quite feel like herself. An extraordinary entity seemed to have silently stolen into her being.

"We both have a few more trials and tribulation, my dear Shambu," she whispered in a trance, unable to control the words she uttered. Her eyes flashed. "We are mortals. When it is all over, we will wash them away in the holy waters of the Ganga. I promise."

When he awoke the sun was streaming through a gap in the door Salmi had left ajar. He was not to know that she had stood beside him laughing for a while after he had fallen asleep, and left their home in the darkness of the night.

He was not to know that she had no intention of returning to their village again.

And not till later would he learn that the English saheb Salmi had prevented him from assaulting had been murdered by someone that very night.

* * *

Sitara Devi stepped down from her caparisoned elephant on to a platform erected to help her disembark. Her beautiful palanquin awaited her below carried by four uniformed men in starched turbans. Armed guards stood before and after, wearing swords and carrying loaded muskets.

Her head was uncovered by an obliging gust of wind, exposing copious black hair, groomed to perfection, the waves flowing over her shoulders. Her striking oval face and pale wheat complexion was enhanced by her slender neck and upright chin. She was aware how erotically the fine silks and muslin that she wore clung to her tall and supple frame. She took pleasure sensing the discomfort the men in the gathering felt as she slowly and very sensuously climbed down the steps of the platform. Then after a deliberate pause she gracefully extended her long and sinuous leg to slip onto the *palki*. She drew the curtains shut slowly, but not before leaning her pretty head out leisurely one last time to infuse an air of curiosity in the crowd. And as the *palki* bearers gingerly carried her across the lawns to her *haveli*, a mansion no less arresting than the lady herself, she left an air of perfume in her wake.

Now at thirty, she had already lost two husbands successively without bearing either one of them a child. One died mysteriously within a few days of her marriage while on a hunting expedition, presumably from a stray Pindaree bullet. The other was accidentally trampled upon by an elephant before the disembarking platform was constructed. Both events bequeathed her a large fortune in estates if not too much money. But it gave her office, and the power to exert authority over more than any one of her late husbands could have ever done in their lifetimes.

Arriving home, Sitara Devi languidly stepped out of the *palki* and shooed the bearers away. She lost some of her deliberate composure as she hurried into the *haveli* calling out to her maids as she divested of her delicate strapped sandals in the hallway. "Panna! Paro! Where are you two? Bring me some sherbet. Or I will drop dead of thirst."

The sherbet arrived in the hands of a giggling Panna.

"What are you so happy about?" she asked gazing through the lattice of a window at the small gathering at the far end of the lawn.

The delegations that awaited her audience this morning included a few minor noblemen of her clan, some officers of the local army, representatives from two villages with tax liabilities, Kashmiri carpet vendors who were here to deliver carpets she had ordered, and an assortment of jewelers and cloth merchants who frequently visited her.

"What a motley crowd we have today!" she exclaimed, savoring the flavor of the drink. "And what in heaven do those officer's of the Raja's army want?"

Paro burst into the hall, also giggling. "Oh Malikin, I have news for you. Kunalji is here."

"You devils!" Sitara Devi shouted in mock anger. "So that's what the giggling and the silly laughing is all about! Go, instruct the male attendants to put out the chairs in the lawn. They have a long wait in the sun while I'm done with that lad Kunal."

This provoked another round of giggles which stopped at a stern glance from the Malikin.

Bare-footed she raced up the winding stairs to her private quarters upstairs. She pushed open the door and indulgently fell into the arms of a smiling Kunal, waiting expectantly for her in her bed-chamber. The boy staggered back on to her bed as she playfully nudged him over, sprawling over him.

"Kunal, you idiot! I hope nobody saw you coming in here. I'm a widow twice over, and I don't want to lose you!"

Kunal breathed deeply, the scent of her hair permeating his brain. He kissed her neck and nuzzled in the falling cascade.

"Speak up!" she whispered, "Other than Panna and Paro, did anybody see you?"

He didn't speak. Instead he rolled over her and kissed her on her beautiful lips. When she tried to speak he kissed her again, this time deftly dropping a pebble-like object into her mouth. She looked surprised and immediately removed it from her mouth, holding it up between her thumb and forefinger. Her eyes lit up as she beheld the glittering red stone.

"You found them!" she gasped. "You found the Manar rubies! Oh my dear Kunal," and she gave his young genitals a gentle squeeze. "Sitara Devi, the prize every man sought in this province, is finally yours!"

Kunal shook his head playfully, teasing her as she yielded up to him. “The Manar rubies are a cache of forty pieces, each the size of this pigeon egg here. This is just one of them.”

“And where are the rest?” she enquired assuming a hurt expression, as she felt his hand climbing up her thigh.

“In good time,” he answered mischievously, feeling areas of her soft skin he had never touched before. “It took me months, since I first spoke to you about them, to hunt, locate and smuggle this treasure out. It was a dangerous and risky task.”

“So?”

“So very time you permit me into your bed-chamber, I promise I shall drop a piece into your mouth.”

She understood; and acknowledged the full import of his statement with a helpless smile. She spread her thighs in resignation.

“There are only thirty-nine more,” he whispered, a roguish smile transforming his boyish looks. Feverish with anticipation he pushed into her violently.

Outside on the sunny lawn, the small gathering would wait a long while that morning before they would see their *Malikin*.

* * *

“A cumin-seed in the mouth of a camel!” exclaimed Pandit, running his fingers through his matted hair, and squeezing a drop of perspiration from the tip of his straggly beard. “A drop in the ocean of time and tradition. That is all Firengee’s existence will mean to *Thugee*. He can neither change the dictates of our goddess Bhawani nor alter the age-old methods of our forefathers.”

“And yet the wandering bards have started composing songs in his glory,” remarked Manohar, seated beside him, watching their new companion attempting to fly a large red kite. “Saleem-bhai, why don’t you try trailing it behind you while you run? That way you might catch some wind. Or are you worried that your absurdly bound turban might unfurl and join the kite?”

"Unfortunately a bard does not make a lucrative *bunij*," Raghubir shook his head sadly. He paced up and down in front of the seated duo, diverting his attention between the young man trying to fly the kite and his two seated companions. "Or I would have liked to wind my *ruhmal* around his melodious throat and put an end to his singing. He neither contributes wealth nor earns any."

"Like a washer-man's dog," agreed Pandit. "Neither useful to the house or the river."

"But they now proclaim Firengee the prince of phansigars. Did you hear them sing in the bazaar this morning? In all my years I have not heard such *bakwas*!" Raghubir retorted, twirling the end of his graying moustache.

The four of them were gathered north of the town of Shivpuri, outside a dilapidated Kali temple, abandoned a few centuries ago when the Mughal emperor Aurangzeb had marched through the district. Desolate, overgrown and remote, it would perhaps remain so a few centuries more.

"There is a particularly disgusting song they sing about how Firengee was born," Manohar, the youngest of them remarked. "That he was born while his mother, a rich and heavily pregnant *bunij* was being strangled by one of our singularly mad *burthotes* many years ago. Literally squeezed out! Now tell me brothers, by Bhawani's decree, would a *burthote* ever strangle a pregnant woman?

"There are those among us who have," reminded Saleem sourly, catching the wind in his kite and watching it rise above the ruins of the temple. His long robe fluttered noisily, as he struggled to re-tie his black turban.

"One rotten fish pollutes the entire water," Pandit remarked in his characteristic style. The gang had aptly nicknamed him, for he was full of aphorisms and pithy metaphors.

"That goes for Firengee too," Raghubir shook his fist as he spoke. He spat with exaggerated vigour. "He is the rotten fish among us. For centuries, the existence of our sect has been a closely guarded secret. Even our own families do not know of our activities. None of us has aspired for fame in this line of work;

even less have bards in the country sing about it. Firengee will be our undoing."

"The English will be our chief concern from now," Manohar corrected him. "The authorities. They have woken up to our existence. They have weapons, and the necessary resources to track us down. In the good old days of Veeru Mahasaya did we ever care or worry about the English? Saleem-bhai, you will lose that kite if you let it go in the direction of those trees."

"Yes, but don't forget, Firengee rides alone," Pandit reminded them. "Our phansigars will never co-operate with him. He is his own undoing."

"Firengee is a betrayal to Bhawani and all of us," Raghubir remarked. "In the eyes of the authorities, no act, however heroic, can justify murder. That is why we bury the dead and keep our activities wrapped in secrecy. Firengee's notoriety in his treatment of his own brethren is bad enough. But to have himself identified by name outside the *thugee* fold, and achieve this kind of popular infamy, is bound for self-destruction."

"As you sow, so you reap," sighed Pandit. "That *kumbukt* will meet his match one day. Have you heard of his doings at the Sind-mori ravine?"

"We have all heard various fragments of that incident," Saleem spoke with disdain, twisting a loose end of his turban back into place. As he had expected, the kite had risen now high above the tallest trees in the vicinity. "Much has been made of it. I would not be surprised if Firengee has applied all the *masala* to that story himself. It is too fantastic a tale to believe."

"Like the story of his birth," Manohar interjected. "They say the *burthote* who finished his mother, died for his sin instantly of a violent fit. Born-of-the-ruhmal, they call Firengee. A *burthote* by birth! By divine grace, he has been given the ability to operate without a gang. They even say that Bhawani sends him his invisible assistants and *lugaees*!"

"Hai Allah!" exclaimed Saleem, stretching his tall frame to guide the kite higher. "Then why doesn't he seek his *bunij* among travellers and merchants? Why does he target thugs if he is a divine thug himself! Tell me my brothers, does this make sense?"

"Nothing about Firengee makes sense," exclaimed Pandit. "Everyone fears him. The English authorities are wary of the strange tales their bungling informers feed them with. And society holds him in awe. We dread him because he disregards us as fellow-thugs and preys on us whenever it pleases him."

"Curse him," Raghubir spat again. "At least, dear brothers, let us recognize a simple fact. That he is only another human being, prone to disease and pain, one who could easily die in our hands as we could in his. Besides, the rumours and the stories about him are ludicrously discrepant. In Narsinghpur they describe him as eight feet tall. What is he, my brothers? A camel?"

They burst into laughter. Saleem listened to them in amusement, as he edged towards the horses to retrieve another spool of string from the saddle. The kite was now high in the sky.

"Did you hear this one," Manohar called out to him. "That the *ruhmal* he possesses is an enchanted one. It is believed to have a life of its own. It requires Firengee, to only cast the *ruhmal* into the air. The cloth finds the intended neck on its own accord and strangles the *bunij* while Firengee looks on. I have not heard even Veeru Mahasaya from our good old days to possess such power."

They laughed louder this time. Saleem only smiled. He raised his forefinger at the others. "Let us not laugh. For none of us have seen Firengee. I don't think any thug has seen Firengee with his own eyes. For all our talk, he could just as well be a common thief or a Pindaree. Even among the thugee there are doubts if he really exists." He beckoned the young man seated beside Pandit. "Manohar, hold on to this spool, will you? Look, I have cleared the trees, haven't I?"

Manohar rose to his bidding. "Saleem-bhai, if he doesn't exist, why is his name whispered among so many of our own sect? In Narsinghpur the *Angraez* have puppet shows in the cantonment that acknowledges his existence. The *kathputli* artists have sung his name at all the *melas*."

"It is easy, my brother, to play foul with your own gang and place the blame on a fictitious Firengee," replied Saleem, tying the string from the spool to the end of the kite-string to give it more length.

Everyone fell silent. They solemnly listened to him. Manohar now held the spool while Saleem faced the thugs he had recently got himself acquainted with.

"Though I don't mean exactly that, my brothers. All I am saying is, if Firengee exists at all, he is certainly not as great as we collectively make him out to be. I have collaborated with other bands of thugs when the *bunij* was too big to handle. And I have noted that after a successful day's work, the band would rather have people believe that Firengee masterminded the robbery or killing. It keeps the authorities on the wrong trail. When foul-play is suspected, or when bodies are discovered, spreading rumours attributing their own deeds to Firengee has become a practice with these bands." He turned to Manohar, "Don't pull at the string when the nose of the kite points down, *bewakoof*. You will then most certainly bring it down into the trees."

Manohar pranced about enjoying the tug and drift he felt in his fingers. The kite rose higher as the new spool unwound.

"What you have just informed us only works to increase Firengee's greatness," Pandit remarked, scratching his unkempt head. "Are you saying that we have no reason to fear him, Saleem?"

Saleem ran a finger through his beard thoughtfully. The end of his black turban lay unwound on his shoulders again. "I really don't know Panditji. As I was saying, how can we judge this faceless creature whose reputation and whereabouts are always a matter of conjecture?"

"Then why are we sitting here making a mountain out of a handful of mustard seeds?" Pandit sighed. "Firengee, Firengee, Firengee! I wonder where he got that name?"

"He must have some peculiarities of manner, like you," Saleem replied. "Why else do you think everyone calls you *Pandit*?"

They burst into laughter again.

"Saleem-bhai," Raghubir interrupted. "We have yet to strike a *bunij* since you joined us. When we do, you must watch Panditji at work. He even recites verses from the scriptures while his *bunij* is gagging and choking!"

Manohar now barely managed to keep the kite at an even keel. He was laughing until his face contorted, and tears rolled down his face. "Hai Deva, you must listen to this one. A *shaer*. A couplet for the dying! Hai Deva, I nearly died laughing that day when I saw that *baniya*'s incredulous face. Can you imagine listening to profound poetry while someone is strangling you from behind? You should have seen his eyes popping out. There was more surprise in them than pain!"

Saleem laughed for the first time. "Manohar, you wretch! Don't you let go of my kite. Hai Allah, who was this lucky *baniya*?"

"Lucky!" exclaimed Pandit, making a mock pretence of anger. "I broke his fat neck with my *ruhmal*."

"Lucky for having died so quickly," Saleem teased him. "Rather than be subject to your couplets! Say, who was this fortunate *baniya*?"

"Badrinath Seth, the fat imbecile!" Manohar cried, laughing uncontrollably nearly letting the kite-string slip from his hand. "And his fat brother..."

"Don't take names, for Bhawani's sake!" Pandit shouted, suddenly looking solemn. "Don't you know it is inauspicious to take the names of the dead?"

Saleem twisted the end of his turban into place again and positioned himself squarely in front of Raghubir, who now convulsed with laughter.

And as Saleem had expected, the position was very convenient. For when he delivered a violent kick into Raghubir's genitals, the man fell silently to the ground, knocked unconscious. In a quick motion, he dragged Pandit down by his long matted hair, driving the bearded face into his own raised knee. There was a dull thud, as the mouth that issued couplets spewed blood. The man they called Pandit joined his companion, motionless on the ground.

Manohar had not quite recovered from his engaging fits of laughter. He looked comical, kite-string in hand, as the shadow of shock began to overwrite the laughter-lines of his face. In incomprehensible panic, he dropped the spool and pivoted around to run towards the horses. The taller man was at his heels in three easy bounds. Casting his *ruhmal*, he twirled it skillfully around the young thug's ankles. He then jerked it violently up, catapuling Manohar's feet into the air. Manohar fell, his face striking the ground before the rest of his limp body collapsed in a cloud of dust. He tried but failed to raise his throbbing head as the *ruhmal* was pulled free from his ankle.

"The bard was right, Manohar," the man they knew as Saleem said. "My ruhmal is enchanted, and sometimes possesses a life of its own."

He walked leisurely to his horse and pulled out some lengths of rope. He tied the fallen men securely one by one, their hands and legs immobilized by a number of complicated knots. He glanced towards the sky where the large red kite now drifted without restraint. Once again he twisted the reluctant end of his turban into place.

Mounting his horse, he hoped the men would not find the time to free themselves.

For, if his message had reached its destination the day before, at least a dozen *sepoys* of the English authorities now combed the area seeking the three men who lay bound. And if the kite had been noticed, three more thugs were going to make a long journey to their trial at Saugor, where an English magistrate held court.

He spurred his horse towards the east to make his getaway. Firengee could not risk being seen by the English authorities.

* * *

Nandakumar, fondly called Nandu, the guru of *kathputli*, the champion puppeteer in the troupe engaged for the entertainment of the English ladies of Saugor was an innocuous man. But today he could hardly contain his resentment at the English school master's choice of subject and the medium of communication employed to tell a story utilizing his puppets. The show was due to start at the English clubhouse, less than half a mile from the penitentiary that housed the largest horde of thugs, dacoits and criminals in the province. The single-partnered dancing that this white race was so fond of was nearing its end in the ballroom, and dinner, an elaborate affair, was soon to begin. It had always been a custom to provide some form of light entertainment at dinner time.

It was about 10 O'Clock when the ladies assumed their seats, dinner plates held informally in their hands, some gingerly placed on their laps, in the *shamiana* constructed on the lawns of the clubhouse. Native entertainers were not allowed inside the club, and so the *shamiana* was the final frontier for the local population to share some of the English gambol.

Puppetry was Nandakumar's forte. It was an occupation, other than the seasonal farming in his village that absorbed all his energies. He was born in the Malabar region, a small kingdom in the far south of the Indian peninsula along the Arabian Sea. He had been performing since the age of six, under the doting eye of his father and two uncles, all of whom were acclaimed *kathputli* artists. Except that in his home district the traditional puppetry was called *pava-kuthu* (glove puppetry) and *thol pavakuthu* (leather puppetry).The colourful puppets in his village were modeled to resemble Kathakali actors who wear heavy and mask-like facial make-up, headgear and bright costumes. The shows were traditionally performed as a ritual worship in temples equipped with a permanent stage or drama house.

Following Tipu Sultan's invasion of Malabar, Nandakumar, then a boy of twelve, his father and two uncles were captured and imprisoned at Srirangapatna, Tipu's capital near Mysore for a year. In the meanwhile, word reached the young Nandu's father that most of their clan had died fighting and that the women were forcefully converted to Islam. When Srirangapatna was stormed by the English, someone forced open the prison doors, and the inmates at great risk fled the land. They entered the Maratha territories in the north and joined a group of Lambadi gypsies headed further north into the Central Provinces. When a year later the elders chose to return to their home in Malabar, or what was left of it, Nandakumar was fascinated by the colour and pageantry of the theatres of the North, and decided to stay for some time longer, having quickly mastered the languages of the Marathas and the Gujaratis. He soon put together a troupe and took pride in his ability to match and outmaneuver the local puppeteers.

Among the nobility of the entire Ganges plain of North India and even in many princely states of the Deccan, Nandakumar's troupe became an essential component of many festivals celebrated in the year, instantly recognized and applauded by the very soldiers on the borders to the sentries that guarded the forts of the kingdoms, ere they sought audience with the rulers of the place.

Most of their performances were abridged versions of the ancient mythological Hindu epics, the Ramayana, the Mahabarata, the Krishna-Katha and Puranic literature; and among more liberal audiences, the Buddhist moral tales of the Panchatantra and the Jataka. Nandakumar was particularly fond of the baby-Krishna legend, especially the music that accompanied the telling of Krishna's stories. In all his travels, never had he heard a Krishna-song in any language that wasn't melodious, compelling and apt to the theme. He held a personal belief that for all time to come, songs relating the tales of lord Krishna would touch the human soul even if the listener wasn't a Hindu or was not able to comprehend the lyrics. The melody miraculously acquired that quality.

In the art of construction and design of his puppets, he was a master craftsman. In the many years he had been a puppeteer he had experimented with all the traditional forms - glove, rod, string, string-rod and shadow puppets. He had mastered the art of dyeing costumes, carving dolls, painting elaborate backdrops and engineering complex manipulation techniques to convey his style of theatre.

But tonight was not ordained to his favourite *Krishna-Katha*, or for that matter to any of the ancient Hindu epics. The English school master had seen to that. The foreign rulers of the land were yet to grapple with the Hindu aesthetics of the Ramayana, the subtle morals of the Mahabharata and the profound philosophy of the Gita. They were here at the clubhouse for light entertainment, something only a few pints of beer, some whiskey or a glass of sherry could comprehend. Nandakumar was sure even the simpler Panchantantra and the basic morals of the Jataka were conceivably misplaced in this environment. While the native audience elsewhere could be held in rapt attention, and moved alternately to laughter and tears with the telling of his story, the English ladies at the clubhouse had unfailingly given a standing ovation to Ravanna the demon as vociferously as they had raucously censured the deeds of Rama the hero of the Ramayana.

Tonight's was however a popular puppet show created for and catered to the English audience. A contemporary performance that required some of Nandakumar's puppets to wear legs. In most of Nandakumar's theatre, the absence of legs was never noticed due the long trailing skirt and tunics made of colorful cloth. Be they kings, clowns or dancers, they were traditionally clothed in long outer garments. But the author of today's performance, the silver-haired school master whom Nandakumar detested, had insisted on uncharacteristic changes to the puppets' costumes to please his English audience. Even Nandakumar's singers were muted for this evening show, for a choir of English children had taken the stage for the accompaniment.

The story of the play and the puppet-characters were drawn by the school master from the recent incidents of arrest and detention of natives from various corners of the Central Provinces, whose real life counterparts on that night were languishing or awaiting trial less than half a mile away at the English penitentiary.

But unknown to Nandakumar, the visual art form of puppetry was tonight designed to be used for conveying a meaningful message to the English audience by the school master, Mr. Jack Dawson. Since his employment at the catholic school at Saugor, he had been teaching music, theatre and gymnastics to the boys. He had encountered Nandakumar at the local fair during the Dussarah festival and enticed him to perform occasionally at the clubhouse for the English residents. However, the native language, music and stories of the puppeteers were met with lukewarm reception, until Dawson began to introduce innovative themes and techniques that would hold the attention of his English audience. However, this was not without resistance from Nandakumar, who would often and without warning change the course of the story by a nifty twist of his puppeteer wrist.

The Death Of A Tiger, a parody on the fall of Tipu Sultan, the Tiger of Mysore, written and choreographed by Dawson, was performed a month ago. Nandakumar and his troupe had taken great pains to manipulate the puppets in the battles of Sedaseer and Malvelly where both Stuart and General Harris won successive battles against Tipu despite incessant rocket fire by the Mysore rocketeers. But much to the school master's infuriation, the guru of *kathputli* was disinclined to show Tipu's soldiers fleeing, crying and begging for mercy as Dawson had choreographed.

Things took a turn for the worst when, at the final battle of Srirangapatna, when the charge led by Wellesley breached the fort walls, Nandakumar - much against history - deliberately allowed Tipu to escape death by a deft manipulation of strings. The incredulous English audience at the clubhouse gasped at this distortion of recent history. Tipu had just managed a spectacular leap over the walls of the fort of Srirangapatna, right into the waiting arms of the guru backstage.

Taken to be a parody, the audience perhaps found light entertainment in watching the Tiger of Mysore vanquished and turn turtle, but not to the deeply embarrassed school master.

"Don't you know that marionette should be lying dead?" Jack Dawson had yelled at Nandakumar, wishing he could somehow wrest control of the puppeteer's troupe.

"We don't know who the English buried at Srirangapatna," Nandakumar declared innocuously. "A body believed to be that of Tipu's was located and identified by his own people. I have heard it said that they all had their tongues in their cheek when they did it."

"Fine," Dawson yelled again, not wishing to prolong the agony of trying to discuss history in the little Hindustani he knew, with a puppeteer who told mostly mythology in his performances. "But the leap? For God's sake, what kind of leap does a mortal do over the walls of a fort? This isn't your monkey god Hanuman! It is an ordinary man, for Christ's sake!"

"Ah ha! I can show you an ordinary man or two in my village in Malabar who could do a leap such as this," countered Nandakumar.

A one time acrobat, now a teacher of gymnastics, Jack Dawson glared at the guru in disbelief and scorn.

From that battle of Srirangapatna fought in the clubhouse a month ago, each beheld the other with a degree of disrespect and ridicule, if not outright hostility.

Tonight as the ladies found their seats in the *shamiana*, the familiar clouds of war were once again gathering over the puppeteer's stage.

As the wicks of the stage-wing lanterns rose to bounce their lights off the many reflectors positioned on the stage, silence fell upon the *shamiana*. In the eerily growing incandescence, the gathering beheld a group of gaudily dressed Hindustani merchants shuffling in an exaggerated style only puppets were capable of. They were traveling on a road against the backdrop of a forest carrying their wares. A tense Dawson gave the cue for a small overture to begin playing on the piano, keeping to the rhythm of the hobbling men. At a crescendo, a new group of ghoulish creatures in dark tunics dropped from the tree-tops on to the travelers. While the music now took on a fearsome note, the travelers died one by one in the hands of the ghouls, strangled and kicking for life, till the music faded away.

The thugs quickly searched the bodies and disposed them in little holes on the floor of the stage, and were now making preparations to share the merchants' wares that still dangled visibly against the green backdrop. On a cue from Dawson, drums began to play to the beat of galloping horses as a detachment of pink-faced puppets with smart redcoats swayed into view, horses pinned firmly between their legs. The struggle that now ensued between the thugs and the English soldiers held the audience in awe. Thug after thug, the sinister gang was subdued, and on a cue from Dawson the piano began to play a familiar English marching tune to the applause of the audience.

But that was when the whimsical guru did a turn. With a nifty twist of his wrist followed by a heave, he freed a particularly macabre looking thug from the row of prisoners, and with the merchants' wares in tow, had him leap spectacularly over the soldiers and spirited away behind the stage. A spontaneous rapture from the audience for this comic relief ensued. The intended message, the moral of the story, was lost in the instance of this commotion. Jack Dawson was livid.

In the squabble that followed that night, Nandakumar had only one simple explanation for his conduct.

"The English were never totally victorious, Masterji. Let us not misrepresent facts. Haven't you heard the wandering minstrels singing? Firengee, the prince of thugs has always managed to give the soldiers the slip."

* * *

Hugh Trenton ran across the dockyard jostling the coolies who had the misfortune of colliding with his enormous frame. He held an in-land *dak* message in one hand and his hat in the other. Scrambling up a wooden stairway that creaked under his weight he burst into the port office. Behind a green desk sat the only other English man in Calcutta who matched Trenton's size and weight.

"George! God George!" Yelled Trenton. "Hutchinson is dead. Hutchinson! Charles Hutchinson!"

"What of?" George Preston enquired, slowly recoiling from the news. "Sit down for God's sake, Hugh."

"Strangled to death by a native."

"God, no!"

"In his sleep too. The fool slept with his window wide open. The poor fool!" exclaimed Trenton.

"Show me the message," asked Preston placing a monocle against his right eye.

"The funeral was conducted by Tucker, the chaplain at Saugor". Trenton handed over the piece of paper and wiped his forehead with his sleeve. "They have cordoned off the village. Preliminary enquiries have revealed nothing of the killer's identity."

"Where in hell was Charles?" inquired Preston.

"Bijaipura, south of Jhansi. In the Central Provinces. The region is infested by wild tribes. Our boys will be whipping every native and pariah wretch there until they've found the devil that did this."

Preston stood up and sauntered across to the window of his office overlooking the docks of Diamond Harbour. The news had shaken him and he felt a palpitation that made him short of breath. He had been awaiting Hutchinson's arrival for some days now. He had been away for over six months on the trail of a large cache of Burmese rubies reportedly smuggled in from Goalpara by a fugitive who had accompanied Chandrakant, a young king of Assam, during the Burmese occupation. When Preston last heard from him, Hutchinson was in the Central Province where his inquiries had led him, and where he had set up a base in a dilapidated and abandoned revenue officer's bungalow not far from Jhansi. Privately, several East India Company officials had evinced keen interest in the cache, which had disappeared without trace after the Burmese campaign a few years ago. About a year ago news of attempts to sell the rubies trickled out of the province and had reached Preston's ears through a Muslim trader named Moin-ud-din Nasser who visited the docks every month and who claimed he had seen the cache with his own eyes. After much deliberation Hutchinson had left in the hope of masquerading as an East India Company official sent to lay the company's claim on a "war acquisition." Even if this meant browbeating and intimidation.

"When is Nasser due here again?" Trenton inquired suddenly, as though they shared the same thoughts.

"Within the week. You see some manner of his involvement in this, do you Hugh? But he is a respectable merchant by all accounts. Has his books in order. He did not accompany Charles or show any interest in our quest. Too expensive an enterprise to undertake at his age, he had said. And yet something bothers me about this Hugh." Preston continued to stare out of the window. He wondered if they had foolishly believed the old trader's story. He wondered if Hutchinson should have followed this lead at all. But Nasser, for all he knew of the Mussalman, was an upright and extremely religious man. One whose stature among the trading communities of Cossipore and Bang bazaar was impeccable. Preston's head throbbed. Poor Charles! His expedition had been necessitated by the lean circumstances they had faced these three years. Somehow since their arrival in India, that assurance of a large and regular supplementary income was uncertain. How he hated this country! And the inscrutable language of the natives, this gobbledygook, which only Charles had bothered to learn to some measure.

His thoughts were interrupted by a commotion in the yard. A group of coolies were haggling with a native dockhand, a trusted, strong and energetic Rajput named Bhim Singh, over a consignment of Chinese tea-boxes that had arrived that morning. Bhim was fairly proficient in spoken English, and was an able translator whenever Preston wanted to communicate in Bengali, Urdu or Hindi. The area of the wharf around the vessel assigned to carry this cargo was wet and dangerously slippery. Preston watched the noisy coolies, their loincloth clad and weathered bodies in disgust. He thought of Hutchinson. Strangled to death by a native! He felt incensed enough to want to draw his pistol and shoot one of the coolies through the head. He gathered control of himself and turned away from the window.

Trenton who still occupied the chair in his office broke the silence. "There's one more bit of news I have for you, George. I don't know if it is relevant."

"Couldn't be anything worse, could it Hugh?" Preston eyed the sailor with a deep sigh.

"Have you ever heard the expression 'thugee'?" Trenton asked.

"What in heavens is that?"

"I couldn't be sure, but I have heard many a tradesman speak of it. An ancient cult. Worshippers of the goddess Kali. A hereditary art of strangulation practised with great skill. These men wander in groups earning the trust and friendship of their fellow travellers and intended victims. They are known to lure merchants to predetermined points on the roads before murdering them and robbing them of their possessions. They sacrifice their victims to Kali."

"Has old Nasser been spinning these absurd yarns for you, Hugh? Are you suggesting a gang of these bandits killed poor Charles?"

"No, not at all, but it comes to mind all the same," replied Trenton. "The thugs, or *phansigars*, as they are sometimes called, often waylay the native traveller or pilgrim whom it is easy to befriend. Poor Charles neither fits that bill nor was he travelling. But what we need to know is whether Charles had already acquired the treasure. Only then can we perhaps assign a motive for this murder. This province has been particularly active in the recent months. Only last week a trader at Bang Bazaar was bemoaning the loss of his brother to a group of thugs."

George Preston frowned. Could Charles have finally found what they had been seeking? The infrequent communication he had received from the man however had been disappointing.

"Not that there have been many cases of attacks on Englishmen," Trenton continued, "But then not all deaths of Englishmen under doubtful circumstances have been easily traced to the thugs. Why, my dear George, should I have not recalled this earlier? There is a magistrate stationed somewhere in Saugor or Narsinghpur, in the Central Provinces I think; one Sleeman. Yes William Sleeman, who is sometimes written about in the *Oriental Observer* and *Bengal Hurkaru*. He has been tracking these killers for a few years now and has even apprehended a number of them."

The rubies, thought Preston. The rubies! He had been dreaming of them for a long while now. Could they have disappeared again? Forever this time? He needed to speak to Nasser again, and though daunting as it seemed, felt the need to make a sojourn into the Central Province region before the cache slipped away altogether. He only hoped poor Charles had not been divested of it already.

Preston walked back to the window. Down at the wharf the haggling grew louder as Bhim, his favourite dockhand indignantly wagged a large index finger at the swarming coolies. He knew his thoughts wouldn't leave Charles and the rubies till he had put some sort of a plan together soon.

Thugs! *Phansigars*! What was Hugh rambling about? What exactly had the haggard Nasser detailed to Charles? The squabbling on the wharf was irritating him now.

"What bothers me, George," Trenton continued unabated, "is that Thugs are known to be both of Hindu and Mohammedan faiths. This veneration of Goddess Kali, or Bhawani, as she is also called is common, I believe, to all Hindus. No Mussalman will allow his faith to be tarnished by a naked and monstrous idol. But strangely, thugs of the Mohammedan faith are an exception to the rule. This has been reported by Sleeman and I have heard it spoken too. The *mussalman* thugs revere Kali in much the same way as their Hindu counterparts do. The ways of *thugee* transcends both religion and caste, and they speak a secret language, known only to the *thugee* sect, called Ramasee."

"Damn it, Hugh! What is the point you are trying to make!" Preston inquired impatiently.

"The point, George, is that our old man Nasser contributes generously to the Hindu temple at Kalighat. Should that not bother us, my dear sir?"

Preston blinked. The confusion on the wharf and his own state of mind now angered him. The din of the native language, ever so loud and verbose, seemed to snap his nerves. Picking up a cane that stood in the corner of the room he stomped past a wide-eyed, open-mouthed Trenton. On descending upon the wharf he pounced on the unsuspecting men gathered around the dockyard. Raining blow after blow mercilessly at every panic stricken coolie he could reach, he surveyed with immense satisfaction the mass of brown humanity dissipate from the wharf. Trenton watched the spectacle from the office window overhead, trying to suppress an uncontrollable laughter that was rolling up from his belly. He watched the hilarity of the stampede that followed on the wet wharf as the coolies slipped and fell over one another in their bid to escape the crazed white man towering over them. In three minutes there was silence. The wharf was devoid of any form of life save a gratified George Preston. Only Bhim, in whose aid Preston had descended, stood there mute and guilty at the commotion he had caused.

As he returned to climb the stairs to his office Preston was sure his mind was made up with regard to two things. He was going to incarcerate the old Nasser the next time he stepped into the neighbourhood, and interrogate him till he was sure the man was not some patron of the infernal cult Trenton was raving about. Then he would even resign his post if that was necessary, to trace the precious cache of rubies if they were still in the Central Provinces.

* * *

Kunal rode through the streets of Jhansi just as the sun was setting and the horizon glowed deep amber. The red brick walls of the houses turned ochre, while the people on the streets were awash in orangey light.

He calculated that if he could ride out into the forest while some daylight remained, he would be right on time to retrieve a fine stone from among the remaining thirty before the darkness of dusk made the trip fearful. The spot where he had hidden the slowly depleting cache of rubies was not very deep in the woods, but deep enough to make forage in the night quite daunting.

Besides, it was a night of an early moon. A feature that made entering Sitara Devi's *haveli* later that night a little risky. How he wished he could have ridden openly on his horse to her gate and rightfully claimed her hand in marriage. But that was not possible in this lifetime. His father was a fairly rich merchant, but not noble enough to claim Sitara Devi for a daughter-in-law. The more insurmountable obstacle that stood in his path, however, was his age. He was only nineteen. Fate had brought him to this earth more than a decade later than he wished.

But fate had dealt him another hand in compensation. He had learnt that Sitara Devi craved wealth. He had accompanied his father to deliver various wares at the *haveli*, and she had haughtily looked into his eyes many times in a manner that deeply aroused him. His boyish instincts somehow told him she would give up anything in return for wealth.

On a fateful night, eavesdropping on his father and some guests as they dined, he had overheard them making casual conversation – as merchants were wont to do – about these priceless rubies believed to be in a certain location in Jhansi, presumably brought here for a secret sale. His father was always privy to such news, being among the foremost traders in these parts. It was all merchant-talk, something he had not paid much heed to in the past, but chance revelation of the location of this cache suddenly interested him and gave him a glimmer of hope. Though at that point he wondered if the great lady would present him any favours in return. However, he decided to try and procure the rubies first before attempting to ensnare the desirable woman.

Like a common thief, sweating and trembling in fear, he had diligently dug through the rear wall of the house, at the address he had overheard, and where he believed the treasure was kept. He was surprised at the ease with which he was able to lay his hands on them. There were no guards, only sleeping merchants who did not appear to anticipate such misfortune. All he knew for certain was that two profoundly drunken traders would wake up in the morning to curse and rant and regret for the rest of their lives.

He soon found an opportunity, and offered to go alone to the *haveli* and deliver the noble lady some fine silks she had ordered. Good fortune still shone on him for he found himself alone that day awaiting her arrival on the lawn. Nervous, but displaying all his boyish charm, he had managed to make her smile and even laugh out loud in the course of that short meeting to deliver the silks. And apart from the various other boyish banter he had prepared for her that day, he dropped a piece of information about the rubies.

Sitara Devi's societal smile had suddenly vanished, to be replaced, as he always recalled, by a luscious and charming one, promptly inviting him into the *haveli* to examine the silk cloth other traders had delivered.

"That is a Kanchipuram silk. Did you say you have seen these rubies with your own eyes?"

He had nodded.

"And these cream-coloured silks are the rare *mooga* from Assam. You say you know how to procure it cheaply? I mean the stones?"

He looked up at her a little boldly now, casting his eyes for a brief moment over her feline torso.

"Come now, don't be shy," she laughed, tousling his hair. "I know what you want. And Sitara has what many men would give their lives for."

She forced him to sit beside her.

"Now tell me more about the Manar rubies."

Now as he rode out of the city, he cursed the moon. It was riding up from beneath the clouds towards some inconvenient rendezvous. Kunal crossed the small bridge that marked the end of the city and galloped across the familiar route that led to the forest. In less than ten minutes he was on the edge, and he slowed the horse into a trot to locate the gnarled banyan tree that marked his entry point. When he had found it, he dismounted and walked the horse to tether it to a low branch he had used many times before. While the horse grazed in the deepening shadow, he gingerly tip-toed over a damp and soggy carpet of rotting vegetation, that squelched under his feet. It was a short walk into the pungent undergrowth that brought him to a small boulder he had been using as a marker. He moved the stone easily, rummaged in the thick decomposing soil, and picked up a dirty cloth pouch. With the ease of recent practice, he removed a glittering stone, and after securing the pouch he silently dragged the boulder back into place.

He paused to look at the gem in the failing light. Such pleasure each of them gave him! He wiped the stone vigorously against his crotch before putting it into his mouth.

He would have departed as quickly as he had arrived had he not been startled by a movement many yards away, deep in a clearing in the forest. It caused him to squat immediately and remain motionless. The dusk had just yielded to the dark night. But the outline of a man became visible as the moon sent a stream of light through the trees.

It took Kunal some time to comprehend what the man was doing alone in the forest. He appeared to be moving about, a scarf or cummerbund in hand, swinging the cloth violently in an arc in the air as if at some opponent. But nobody else was there. The man swung the cloth, making an action like he had seen washer men do when striking a washboard or slab, but in this case occasionally looping the cloth around branches and tree trunks. Like some nimble and sure-footed dancer the man swayed, spun and twisted about at an incredible speed, always throwing and looping the cloth around tree trunks and low branches in some kind of bizarre rhythmic frolic.

He dared not move as long as the madman performed this strange frolic lest his departure was noticed. Now the moon rose higher in the night sky showing a clearer profile of the man. He was tall and bearded. Surely a madman, thought Kunal, and affected by the full moon too.

The man suddenly looped his cloth around a thin tree, an adult sapling. As the cloth cruised around the tree trunk, he plucked its flying end out of the air with the other hand and squeezed his wrists together. The tree snapped effortlessly like a garroted neck, the top half of the trunk falling away.

Kunal froze in terror, as the realization dawned on him. A *phansigar* in practice. A thug honing his skills. It was the first time he had ever seen a thug in his life. He had believed the *thugee* was only a myth, stories told by merchants like his father to inculcate a sense of vigilance in their children.

The tall man finally stopped cavorting, pausing to tie a loose end of his dark turban into place.

Kunal crawled out of the forest on his knees till he reached his horse. He was relieved when he was finally able to mount the animal and ride to Jhansi, entering the town as the streets grew empty. Only a couple of wandering minstrels in saffron robes sat singing in a street corner.

Oh you, that chooses to shut your eyes
Are truly blind to life's mission
For those who have truly lost their eyes
Are lucky to still have vision

Late that night, he drained whatever energy remained in his youthful body before dropping a bright red stone into the hungry mouth of Sitara Devi.

* * *

When the nightmares first began, Jack Dawson was in deep slumber in his cabin on an East Indiaman bound for Madras.

It would begin with the smiling face of Robert Pendarrow framed against a dark tapestry in his mind, a night sky speckled with little stars. The smile would then contort in pain, to be replaced by a hurt and accusing expression. For a fleeting moment, Dawson would be aware that he was dreaming. For a few seconds he would be aware of being asleep. But not for long. Bob would then roll his eyes and turn his head upwards as if to look at the tapestry of stars for himself. And this would expose his neck; to reveal a noose, the knot of which Dawson would see slithering and tightening relentlessly. He would hear a painful guttural moan that would rise to a crescendo, a hysterical laughter. Bob's face, his eye-balls still rolled up, would then fade from the night sky and there would follow a high-pitched squeal. Though this would mercifully wake Dawson up, he also woke up to find himself shrieking and laughing uncontrollably through tears and perspiration.

On many nights thereafter Dawson had been haunted by this spectre. Recurring persistently till he was not sure he could keep his sanity.

Leaving London had been a relief. He had found a devout missionary to take care of his dilapidated school in St. Giles. And a friend to replace him at Olcotts. But his journeys in Hindustan had been disappointing on one aspect. There was no trace of the gentleman Mr.John Penmarric. Many times he enquired both at Madras and Calcutta and always ran into a blank wall. It was as though Mr.Penmarric had never set foot in Hindustan.

He took up work at Saugor because it paid him well. His physical fitness regime designed to compliment the children's regular school curriculum drew the admiration of the authorities. It was not a concept fully accepted in high-schools even in England as readily as it found acceptance with the English army stationed at Saugor. But his love for books and his knowledge of theatre and music secured his position in the school's faculty.

But the chilling dreams that returned every night continued unabated like a rebuke to find justice for Robert Pendarrow. The nightmares menaced him so insistently that he sometimes feared the prospect of falling asleep. His mind would often recall the mocked up jury in London that sealed Bob's fate, and the anger it caused him often made him lightheaded and reckless.

In those tormented hours before he fell asleep he would see the despicable sight of their self-righteous faces. Bribed and noshed to their eyebrows, seated in contented composure in the jury box. Preston and Hutchinson believed they had played their cards to perfection. A scapegoat jailed for life was a scapegoat alive, a threat that could rear its head at some opportune moment. To have hanged him now absolved them and their coterie from any damning evidence that might have ever arisen in the future.

Some time ago, news of Hutchinson's death in the hands of some native reached Saugor, and was the topic of great trepidation and apprehension for the English residents. Almost as a consequence, great numbers of natives bound and shackled began to arrive at the penal colony. Often as he watched the cart-loads arriving at the penitentiary Dawson wished he had the power to know who among these scores of miserable prisoners had killed Hutchinson. He would have liked to throw his arms around the blessed thug in gratitude and kiss his feet. And if he could, he would also have dispatched every ingenious *phansigar* in the province into the cozy homes of those scrounging members of the jury. To London, Sheffield, Liverpool, Kensington, Hammersmith and Ealing to exterminate those vermin of English justice.

But for now, while the nightmares reigned in his head, he longed for a vacation far away from every Englishman; some way by which he could forget and be rid of his nightly woes.

He wondered where the other villain George Preston was hiding.

But more than ever he wondered what had happened to that enigmatic gentleman Mr. John Penmarric.

* * *

On at least two occasions during the week that passed Salmi thought she would drop the baby. The child had sapped all the lustre from her light brown eyes these five months in the wilderness. She had heard from the women that the child was not due for another month, but she wasn't sure they were right. Despite her youth and fawn-like countenance the strain of the long journey seemed to wilt her lithe frame. Now seated under a gigantic peepul tree, she watched the men building a camp with a growing sense of anxiety.

The men perspired under the tropical sun, their brown bodies glistening in the fading light beneath the canopy of the forest. Naked, slim waisted, kamarbands soaked in their pungent body salts, they grunted and heaved. Bent backs, bare thighs and buttocks rippled in the golden sunlight. Salmi who could count in multiples of twenty calculated that there were at least forty men at work. Every one of them wore dull hued turbans under which lay bound their long hair, twisted and plaited into place. Wearily her eyes gazed over their wives and children huddled snugly around her under the peepul tree. They kept a perceptible distance from her, but she had ceased to worry much about it. After all she did not belong to their tribe. Her eyes finally rested on a *dhol* slung on a low bamboo clump, and she instantly felt a strange affinity to the instrument. Months ago, it had reverberated in her head the whole night while she lay awake in her house in Bijaipura. It had drawn her out to the forest and to this band of nomads.

They numbered over a hundred men, women and children. A silent breed of emaciated people born to toil, they had long lived on the periphery of a human society that abhorred them. Blessed by an inherent ability to survive disease, starvation and abuse through generations, some natural law kept their numbers from dwindling. Like some sun-baked species of sub-human, browned and fatigued, they had suddenly arrived on this autumn afternoon upon a path in the forest long used by elephant herds.

They were always fugitives of the political changes around them. The faces of the men wore signs of urgency. Children clung to their mothers; the terror of their journey lay imprinted in the eyes of the adolescents and in the strange post trauma slumber of infants. Their possessions were few, but a sparse assortment of primitive weapons was ready at hand.

Now as the men worked to set up crude shelters the women crouched about the base of the mammoth peepul. Salmi sat uneasily in a hollow among its large gnarly roots. Gazing at a patch of dusky sky visible among the trees, she noticed that the night would be upon them shortly. Above their heads protruded the shaft of an iron trident, the prongs of which stood deeply embedded in the tree trunk. On their arrival that afternoon the Ojha of their tribe, the diviner and medicine man, had chosen this site for their camp and had struck the peepul with his three pronged weapon to drive away undesirable spirits. Salmi did not understand his incantations but was awe-struck when a current of cool air, like a deep sigh, emanated from the tree when the spear pierced the bark. She watched with a thrill and a pounding heart when the dry autumn leaves suddenly swirled around the base of the tree.

She also heard a painful guttural moan far in the forest; it rose to a crescendo and suddenly fell silent. It disturbed her that no one seemed to take notice of it. It died away in a hysterical laughter.

Then the Ojha, hands held high had indicated that it was safe to shelter the women and children under the tree. As Salmi crawled under its canopy along with the women she had felt the baby move in her belly, and fear had gripped her again. Was she going to deliver her baby?

Deft hands worked in unison to create what grew into a curiously comfortable cluster of thatched hutments. Broad leaves, branches and twigs were freely used to the best advantage. The small clearing in the forest was now strewn with precariously propped up clumps of vegetation to serve as shelters for the night. As their work drew to completion the Ojha threw a handful of ash into each of them, in quick succession, murmuring all the while, to cast a spell of protection into the night's shelter. The women began to leave the safety of the charmed peepul, children in tow. Night was setting over their heads and the children were fast tiring. Small whimpers of protest, of hunger and of unknown fears could be heard. Fires were lit and the precious food collected in their journey was rationed out. The children fed first followed by the men. The women ate whatever remained.

Salmi ate two dry chapatis handed to her by the Ojha's wife. The Ojha's family had been kind to her despite that fact that she was unwed. He had pledged his protection and the tribe respected it. It might have been because of the higher caste she belonged to. No questions were asked. And all through this unexpected exodus they helped her along as best as they could. She could not have asked for more. For the sake of the unborn she had to live. Following the Ojha's decision nobody had dared to question the antecedents of the child she held. She remembered her guruji at Bijaipura used to say - "the poorest person on earth is one who feels lonely and unwanted." Salmi felt neither, and it raised her hopes for the baby.

The darkness of the night crept over the forest quickly. Except the glowing embers of dying fires and the din of insects, nothing of the forest could be perceived. The men lay down on the bare ground, their torsos slumped on the earth, and oblivious of the insects attracted by the fire crawling about them. The natural and spontaneous nesting habits of the women had ensured that the children were quickly tucked away to sleep in crude beds of leaves. Infants found soft breasts to suckle whenever the darkness confused them.

Now as the moon rose in the sky, silence descended upon the camp.

Only Salmi lay awake. With a feeling of numbness she thought of Shambu and the white saheb she had left behind her. She had ceased to shed tears a long time ago. She hoped again, as she had done every night that her brother would find peace in the village. She hoped he had been able to explain her disappearance to the village elders. It was the only thing she could have done to avoid violence and shame.

But there were rumours. She shivered. Rumours the tribe had heard from other groups in the forest. A white saheb had been assaulted somewhere in the district. Perhaps killed. The Ojha, knowing the retribution that would follow had moved his people out at short notice. For soldiers were combing the area, and it was often the homeless and the nomadic that fell foul of the authorities. It was perhaps her destiny to seek shelter among these wanderers

As Salmi fell into a deep sleep the Ojha stirred. The hair on the nape of his neck bristled. Through long years of wandering, steering and preserving his people, he knew the portent of this familiar aberration that he felt.

He crawled out of his shelter and crouched in its shadow. His ears and nostrils twitched in anticipation. And though he neither heard nor smelt anything, he felt a presence. Of someone of immense power in their midst. Or perhaps something approaching their camp.

He closed his eyes. It always helped him gauge the distance and the direction of an inauspicious intrusion.

He stood up and walked slowly to the edge of the camping ground some distance away from his people to wait and listen. Lanky, loose limbed and of advanced age, his dark eyes narrowed to peer into the darkness. In the moon light the deep furrows on his forehead gave him a hooded appearance. With heavy lidded eyes, like those of an opium addict, he saw the forest as clearly as the nocturnal creatures that moved about in it. His nostrils wrinkled ever so often as he picked up the scent of dung and animal droppings. An ancient incantation played silently in his mind to dispel his fear as he stood on the edge of the woods.

He had kept the spirits away before. He had been aware on more than one occasion that they were always most active while the strange and pregnant girl fell into a deep sleep.

After a moment of meditation, he felt relieved. The strange intrusion he had sensed tonight was not the spirits at work again. It was very human.

It was late at high moon when the object of his vigil made its appearance. The mist was descending, and in a fleeting moment, amidst its wreaths, he noticed horsemen. One, two, three, four...as many as nine. They were headed for the camp.

To take flight or move the camp now was impossible. To alert the men might lead to panic and premeditation that could end in violence. A defensive posture would not be necessary or wise. Deciding to make himself visible and co-operative, he walked slowly to the centre of the camp where the moonlight shone on his thin tall figure. He let his hands hang free to show the horsemen that he was unarmed.

Standing there he could hear them spread out to encircle the camp. They did not dismount nor appear to make an effort to ride quietly. Meanwhile a few of his own men in the camp stirred. The Ojha called out to them in a low calm voice.

"Do not touch your weapons. Stay still. It is nothing to worry about."

As the riders trotted slowly into the camping site he recognised them to be *sepoys*, soldiers of the English Company that ruled the province.

A curt order was addressed to him by a *sepoy*. "Line up the men in your tribe. The saheb wants to identify them. Make no bid to run or escape or you will be fired upon. If the person we are searching is not among you, we will go our way."

The camp was suddenly waking up. Tired bodies sat up one by one while the Ojha tried to calm them. "It's okay. Don't worry. Men and boys, show yourselves. They will not harm you."

When the bedraggled men had lined up, a *sepoy* thrust a lantern in each of their faces, while an English officer, a blue eyed and keen man, looked over each of the men. When he had satisfied himself, another *sepoy* spoke up. "Is there anyone among you who has met or seen a young man in the recent past who calls himself Shambu? A man who belongs to Bijaipura village?

Salmi shrank into the shadow of the hovel. She had been peering out of it in apprehension. But now she was gripped in terror.

The keen blue eyes caught the movement. The Englishman turned and sauntered up to the shanty made of clumps of leaves. He had to kneel to peer inside the crude hutment.

Salmi felt a wave of panic as the Englishman's face suddenly appeared before her in the moonlight.

But the officer only smiled. "You are due to deliver a child. Are you?" He enquired in a gentle voice in Hindustani.

Salmi managed a nod.

"Eat well, then," the man advised, again in a gentle voice.

When Salmi didn't respond, the officer stood up and walked back to the men, still lined up in the centre of the camp.

He spoke again in Hindustani. "You people have no reason to fear. I am searching for three evil men. They are thugs. Phansigars. They are wanted for several murders in the district. If you have any information about them, we need your co-operation to capture them. You will not be troubled in any way. But anyone found giving them shelter or collaborating with them will be arrested and treated as a thug." He paused. "Their names as we know them are, Feringee, a tall individual, who often operates alone, the other an old man named Aleem, and the third," he paused and frowned at the hovel of leaves under which he had just seen the pregnant woman. "The third is one called Shambu of Bijaipura village."

This time Salmi sat still and frozen.

"These men," continued the officer, "may quite well be moving about under various names. But any gossip, any information you gather while you visit the bazaars of these men must be reported to the company *thana* of the area. Do you understand me?"

The men in the line-up nodded.

He mounted his horse and the *sepoys* followed suit. As they turned their horses about the English officer turned his head to look at Salmi's hovel one last time.

"That face, it shines like the moon itself," he remarked to the *sepoy* riding beside him.

The Ojha watched them ride into the woods till they disappeared in the mist. When they had gone he turned to Salmi's shelter. Squatting on the forest ground he looked at the girl with sadness in his eyes. The others slowly gathered around him.

"There is something you have not told us," he said to the girl. "We are simple people, and we do not wish to know anything that does not concern us." He looked about him, and at the faces that gathered there. "Did we not all see the interest the English officer showed in this girl? He is a clever man and he doubts her presence here."

The voices of men acknowledged him in confused agreement.

The Ojha spoke to Salmi. "I am sorry, child. You do not look like the rest of us. The officer must have noted that. You do not look like the rest of the women here. I know how delicate your condition is, right now. But you must leave us in the morning and find shelter elsewhere."

There were loud protests from a few women in the camp who were listening to the Ojha speak, but it subsided when he raised a hand. He spoke again. "We have a difficult life. There are old people and children among us. We do not wish to draw undue attention to this community. We have not committed a crime of any kind. Such things happen only in the towns and villages."

Salmi felt tears well up in her eyes, but she pursed her lips.

"Go back to where you came from, child. Start by dawn. You only need to walk back the way we came. In two hours you will arrive at a village across the riverbed. The village is called Lakshmanghat. They will provide you with some food for the journey. Don't stay here till nightfall. You will find yourself alone. And don't go by the ravine. It is an evil place. Get to this village quickly. God will send someone to help you deliver the baby. Who can foretell the destiny of your child?"

In the morning the Ojha performed their ritual of departure. The shelters the men had built the evening before were torn down, and the leaves and branches thrown back into the woods.

Save one, under which Salmi sat frightened and uncertain.

As the tribe trailed out of the clearing, the Ojha's wife stopped at Salmi's hovel. She pressed a bundle of *chapatis* rolled in a large leaf into Salmi's hand, and placed a gourd of water beside her.

The Ojha set out to march his people deeper into the forest. He felt strangely relieved. The woman they had just abandoned appeared to harbour troubled spirits. Grievously hurt and avenging spirits that roamed about the forest and hovered about their camp these five months since her arrival. It had taken all his knowledge of the occult to keep them at bay. He hoped her child would survive.

* * *

Sitara Devi stepped down from her caparisoned elephant on to the disembarking platform. She had returned from her morning ride an hour earlier today. Her beautiful palanquin awaited her below. Her copious black hair was groomed to perfection, cascading over her slender shoulders. Her oval face was a shade paler this morning, but the beautiful complexion and the slender neck still attracted attention. And she took pleasure discomforting men of position and office.

However, her present object of attention was the lecherous and lusting young man waiting in her bed-chamber for her to finish her morning ride through her estates. From the candid and childlike creature she had actually grown fond of, the boy had grown into a voracious and insatiable animal in a matter of weeks. He was not just brazen and bold, he was demanding and experimental. He teased and tortured her shamelessly, cavorting naked in her bed-chamber, sometimes taking her with a violence that she found both painful and devilishly satisfying.

However the Manar rubies were dropping with uninterrupted regularity into her mouth like sand from an hour glass. In the beginning she was not sure what she enjoyed more; the blatant, wild and unrestrained sex with a virile and hungry boy, or the prize of a full-blooded, unflawed Burmese ruby. On the receipt of the fifth piece she was sure she prized the rubies more than anything else. They were going to be her stepping stones to greater and real wealth. But despite a heavy toll on her time, and the risk of discovery, the thought of the naked Kunal waiting in her room made her legs weak.

But she still managed to gracefully extend a long and sensuous leg to slip onto the *palki*, before being carried away over the lawns of her *haveli* watched admiringly by a small gathering of visitors. It was still early. The usual crowd that thronged her lawn had not gathered yet.

There were only three more rubies to go. And she was determined to have the last one. Kunal had been growing almost sadistic as the precious stones came near to running out. He now treated her like a slave, severe and demanding, to a point when she wondered how a boy so young could have so much vigor. He dragged her often by the hair, did the unimaginable and the perverse, and often left her unsure whether she was satiated or abused. He had stopped making love *to* her. He seemed to make love *at* her. But she had long known there was no real love involved here. No pretence of romance either. Now it was only a matter of time before she showed the boy the door.

The *palki* bearers gone, she entered the *haveli*. It was too early to expect Panna and Paro to arrive.

She decided to fetch herself a glass of sherbet, if she could find some.

She walked through the hall, into another inner hall and then stepped into a corridor that led to the *bawarchee khana*. She might have missed the sounds if she had not stopped for a moment to look at a pigeon roosting high up against a ventilator designed to throw light into the corridor. It came from a large store-room near the kitchen. And its all too familiar rhythmic human resonance and timbre made her head swim for a while. Knowing exactly what to expect, she gently opened the door of the store-room, just a crack, to make sure her suspicions were correct.

They were. Kunal's bare back and naked buttocks flashed at her. Paro's fleshy legs encircled his waist and her upturned skirt completely covered her face. They were totally oblivious of her presence, absorbed in the excitement of their furtive act. The rice-sacks they reclined against had burst, spilling gushes of grain all over the floor.

Sitara Devi silently retraced her steps back to the hall. She decided to do without the sherbet. Instead she stepped out onto the lawns to speak to the gathering that awaited her audience.

She impatiently dealt with the tax collector's complaints, and chided the officers of the local army for their inability to stem the rising incidence of dacoits and robbery in the neighbourhood much in the style of her dead husbands, now a distant memory! She calmed down just sufficiently to bless a young bride, ordered another carpet, and scornfully rejected a silk cloth that showed a minor error in its weave.

About an hour later she left the lawns to enter the *haveli* again.

Three more to go, and no more, she steeled herself. Three more and no more.

Kunal waited for her, back in the bed-chamber, in his now usual style of reception she was growing used to. Naked and flaunting his manhood. Almost waving it at her like a threat. She closed her eyes when he grabbed her fiercely. *Three more and no more*, she repeated to herself before surrendering completely to his latest designs and perversions. Where the devil did the boy find all this energy from? She could imagine a limp and tired Paro flopped somewhere in the *haveli*. Yet he behaved as if he hadn't been milked for a week!

It was over two hours before he was done with her, having exhibited every savagery he could muster. He behaved like a monarch with a lowly and beautiful slave.

Two more and no more, she thought, lying on the floor, drenched in his pungent perspiration.

Somewhere in the back of her mind she wondered what she ought to do with Paro for her disloyalty. But she was too exhausted to think.

* * *

Every time he ventured out of the forest to forage for food and *mohwa,* Shambu remained overtly cautious not to raise the suspicion of anyone who saw him. He had been successfully living like this for some months, somehow feeding off the land and trying not to look emaciated. He bathed and washed in the stream deep in the woods so that he appeared sufficiently clean to find occasional work. Much of the time he carried firewood to the nearest village, and with the money earned he bought himself food. He had managed to dodge the *sepoys* twice, but he dare not return to Bijaipura. He hoped the murderer of the English saheb would one day be caught and absolve him of the crime. But for Salmi's sin he could find no solution. How would she ever return, and how should she continue to live in Bijaipura with a white man's baby? He often recalled that fateful day following the saheb's murder.

Shambu did not know the manner in which the English saheb had died, but the commotion in the village that day had frightened him. It was late in the morning and the *mohwa* he had consumed the night before had worn away. He had searched desperately for Salmi in the throng outside the saheb's bungalow following the uproar when the body was discovered.

A troubled and agonized sarpanch, their village chief, had tried to take a grasp of the situation. He urged everyone to stay clear of the premises, pointing out that there were strange footprints inside which the authorities would need to examine.

The cook who had entered the bungalow in the morning had prepared breakfast, unaware of the master's fate. Hutchinson had been dead for some hours. His body lay in a grotesque angle on the floor of his sleeping quarters, his face contorted in a tortured grin, arms and legs flailed in the final throes of death. The room reeked sourly of liquor and vomit. But the most notable feature of the corpse was a deep indentation around the neck that had turned blue with blood-clots. The tell-tale mark of a strangled body. In his desperate search for Salmi, this important detail had not registered in Shambu's mind that morning.

When he could not trace Salmi, Shambu rushed back into their hut. He discovered that her clothes were missing, and the realization that she might have left the village suddenly dawned on him. How long had she been gone? His worry for her now replaced the trepidation he felt at the saheb's death. He sat on the floor shaking uncontrollably, listening to the commotion at the far end of the village where the bungalow was located.

"They have found a cudgel!" a voice shouted, coming from the direction of the bungalow. Shambu stood up fearing the worst. Could they guess it was his? Would they wonder where Salmi, who worked as a maid in the bungalow, had disappeared? What relief could he expect even if they found her? The news of her pregnancy and his plans to use the cudgel on the sahib would surely spill out.

Bewildered, and in the grip of a dread he could not contain any longer, he pushed open the door of the hut and raced across the paddy fields. He needed to get away and hide somewhere. Running like he had never done before, he reached the base of the foothills that skirted the village, knowing he would now have to keep away from all familiar pathways. He would need to find a way through the forest. Panting heavily and filled with fear and worry, he cut across the well spring and raced towards the forest.

Now that he had vanished suddenly from the village, he knew he was suspect. If the authorities caught up with him he was unsure what fate awaited him. What if Salmi returned? Surely they would not believe a little girl could be capable of so violent an act, especially against an English sahib.

Shambu had only heard that the sahib had been murdered. He had not waited long enough to discover how. The sarpanch had not allowed anyone to go near the body. Shambu only hoped and prayed that the man had not been killed with his cudgel.

He had entered the forest, moving deep into the darkest undergrowth where he hoped no man would follow him. He had run without a destination in mind, only an imperative need to keep a good distance from Bijaipura.

He had managed to dodge the magistrate's *sepoys* twice. And if they continued to fail, and gave up the search for him, he had hope yet of finding Salmi, his sister and the only one he had in this world.

Somehow he knew the *mohwa* he drank would have her materialize again.

* * *

It was over two weeks since she had seen Kunal. Today as she climbed down from her caparisoned elephant, Sitara Devi had every reason to feel cheerful. *One to go, and no more.*

But, it was not to be as simple as that.

For she had an important appointment with an elderly visitor who awaited her on the lawns of her *haveli.* A kind old man whom she trusted to extricate her from her present predicament.

She staggered a little as she climbed down from the disembarking platform, and wasted no time exhibiting her charms to the gathering that awaited her. Climbing hurriedly into her *palki,* she squeezed a slice of lime and sniffed at the refreshing odour. As the *palki* bearers carried her across to the house, she could barely resist the urge to pop her head out through the curtains and vomit on to the lawn. With colossal effort she held the bile down.

Before the *palki* could come to a stop she clambered out inelegantly, much to the shock of her smartly attired bearers. She raced into the hallway of the *haveli*, and then through a maze of rooms before she could find a bathroom. She threw up violently upon reaching it, retching again and again till there was no more to expel. She felt herself slowly sinking onto the cold floor.

When she came to, she realized she must have been down for at least an hour. But her head was clear and the nausea she felt was gone. She decided to spend another half hour washing, cleaning and perfuming herself, before she went to her rendezvous with the crazed beast in her bed-chamber.

One to go, and no more, she reminded herself, as she assumed a cheerful air and pushed her bedroom door open to be greeted by his naked form.

Kunal tossed her down on the bed and ravished her. She moaned and yielded and squirmed as convincingly as she could. She did not enjoy this routine any longer. He worked upon her like a frenzied and demented creature, gasping, grunting and belittling her with verbal abuse, his latest perversion. When he was done, he dropped the last of the fabled rubies into her dry mouth.

The shy and guileless look returned upon his face after many months as Kunal knelt down beside her bed. "It's over isn't it, now that you've got all the pieces?" he whimpered.

She looked at him coldly from where she lay, feeling an urge to slap him across his mouth. But she refrained from doing it. There was too much at stake.

Instead she got up and held his head on her lap for a while, soothing him. "Wait here for me," she told him, gently ruffling his hair. "We shall talk when I return. There are visitors on the lawn I need to speak to. I will be back within the hour."

She arrived outside on the lawns a little later, refreshed and glowing. Her most important visitor that day stood apart from the gathering, indicating to her she had best finish with the crowd before she spoke to him. He was an elderly man with grey hair and a flowing beard, and bowed respectfully when she cast her eyes at him.

Today she spoke with great magnanimity and charm to everyone at the gathering. She was benevolent and understanding. She found no fault with the silks this time, even admired the fabric and the weave. The societal smile had returned. The grace, the arrogance and even the sensual voice was there for all to hear.

When everyone had left, the elderly visitor approached her and respectfully greeted her again. She returned his greeting.

"Namaskar, Aleem Saheb."

"How many weeks is it now?" he enquired in a low voice.

"Four, maybe five," she answered. "The sickness in the morning is unbearable."

The man nodded thoughtfully, looking up at the sprawling *haveli*. "And where is the young stallion?"

"In my bed-chamber," she answered calmly. "He is there this very moment as we speak."

* * *

"*Touba! Touba*!" exclaimed the man, laughing aloud as he watched the little boy's efforts. "You have been at it for an hour now, but you have not managed to make it spin."

"I will be able to do it if you stopped laughing at me," the twelve-year old complained. "The rope is too long."

The two of them were seated under a banyan tree outside the village of Morena, near its little mosque. Behind them the village bustled. Preparations for a wedding were underway, and nobody took much notice of the duo. The man's horse grazed behind them.

"To spin a top, your rope should neither be too long or too short. Here, let me show you again how it's done." He snatched the reluctant piece of bulbous wood from the boy's hand. "Give me the rope and watch me do it."

The boy playfully threw the rope vertically up so as to force the tall man to stand up and pluck it out of the air over his head. "The rope is too long. Too long! Let us seek another rope."

"*Khamosh*!" the man exclaimed still laughing. "Be quiet and watch how I wind the rope." He tucked a loose end of his black turban back into place. "You hold the top in your left palm and restrain one end of the rope upon it with your thumb. Now you wind the rope neatly with your right hand from the prong up, till you have only this knotted loop in your palm. Here, observe carefully how I have kept a little knot at my knuckles to prevent the rope from slipping out of my hand."

From a hut behind the mosque, a motherly voice shouted, "Ismail, where are you? Whom are you talking to?"

"To the same man, ammijan," the boy shouted in reply. "The one who ties his turban with a new twist. The one who brought abbu his new saddles."

The enquirer from the hut appeared satisfied. The boy smiled at the man seated under the banyan tree. "Ammijan is always worried."

"That is her job," laughed the man. "To worry about your next act of mischief."

The boy ignored the taunt. "Alright, show me how you do it. I still think that rope is too long."

"Observe!"

The man raised his hand and in one sharp sweep unfurled the rope, sending the top spinning over the hard ground beneath the tree. It struck the dust, throwing up a small cloud and furrowing a groove wherever it moved. The man's horse tethered behind the tree stomped a startled foot.

The amazed boy danced about shrieking in rapture. "*Hai kamaal*! *Kaise Ajaib*! Who taught you this, Bhai Saheb?"

"A Bhil"

"What is that?"

"A Bhil. That is the name of a tribe of people. They live in the forests."

"Why do they spin tops?"

"They probably use it as a weapon," the man explained. "They have very large tops, some as big as a man's head. They could crack open a skull with a skilfully aimed top."

The boy stared at the little object of his own exertions in awe. "Oh! This could be used as a weapon, could it? Wait till I show it to Syed and Irfaan."

"*Touba! Touba*!" the man exclaimed laughing aloud. "Don't you go hurting anyone with that thing. Now you know why ammijan has to worry about your next *shaitani* act. It might be better if I taught you to fly a kite instead."

"Abbu promised to buy me a kite from the mela when he returns," the boy said, picking up the top and wiping the dust off with his hands. "Can you teach me to fly it?"

"And when is your abbu expected home?" enquired the man, ignoring the boy's question.

"In two days. I heard ammijan tell Aleem chacha so"

"Aleem?" the man asked nonchalantly.

"Aleem chacha, the *hakim* and friend of my father, has returned from Bengal," the boy replied, winding the rope gingerly around the top again. "Passed by this way with his caravan of merchants this morning, headed for Narsinghpur. Tell me, can a Bhil kill Firengee with his top?"

The man's face turned solemn. It clouded over. He looked about him and the mirth seemed to have vanished from his countenance for a moment.

"Why would anyone want to kill Firengee?" he enquired.

"Because he is the most dangerous *phansigar* and thug in all Hindustan. Abbu and Aleem chacha curse him so very often."

"And do you believe this too?"

The boy wasn't listening to him any longer, for the top had finally begun to spin.

"I've done it! I've done it!" he pranced about again, seized by an unblemished joy only children were capable of. "Wait till I show abbu this."

"There! Was that so difficult?" remarked the man, now standing up, preparing to depart. He tucked the end of his turban in placed once again. "Now you owe me a favour in return."

"*Kubool*. Name it," the boy beamed at him.

"I want you to deliver a letter to the dak-runner who will pass by this village later today." He produced a paper and an envelope from the folds of his long robe and walked around the tree to his horse. From the saddle-bag he pulled out a little jar of ink and a bamboo stylus. Placing his foot on the stirrup, he gingerly spread the paper on his thigh and began to write.

The boy watched him eagerly.

"Aleem chacha has a son my age," Ismail said, watching the man write. "But he is blind. Blind from birth. He cannot spin a top or play the games I do. So Aleem chacha tells him stories. Interesting stories of Allah-ud-din and Sindbad and Ali Baba." He frowned at the paper on the tall man's lap. "Why do you draw birds in your letter, Saleem chacha?"

"Just so that the letter looks pretty," the man replied.

When he had finished, he sealed the letter with a chunk of glue that he moistened with his tongue. He handed the envelope to the boy.

"You will do this faithfully, won't you?"

"*Khuda ki kasam*," the boy promised.

"I will come by again," the man said, ruffling the boy's hair. "And the next time, I will teach you not only to make a kite but to fly it too."

He knew, as he mounted his horse, that if the boy delivered the letter as promised, it would mean the immediate arrest of his *abbu* when he returned to the village. Unknown to the boy or his family, his *abbu* was a thug of considerable notoriety. It was ironic that the boy should carry and deliver the instrument of his own father's demise. It was even more ironic that there was no other child that he could find in the whole village who was as guileless, sincere and reliable to entrust the letter with as this thug Gafoor's own offspring.

As he turned to take the road to Narsinghpur, he honestly wished he would find an opportunity one day to teach Ismail to fly a kite.

As he rode, he looked forward to seeing Aleem again after nearly six months.

* * *

Mohammed Mir Aleem, or simply Aleem, was fifty years of age but looked older - and perhaps more dignified - due to the long grey hair and luxurious beard covering his gaunt fair face. He was of medium height, but the long robes he donned concealed a strong and energetic constitution.

He had an honoured and creditable position among the country healers and mendicants of central India. His patients ranged from the noble families of Meerut, Delhi and Agra in the north to Gwalior and Jhansi, down to Bhopal, Indore and Amaravati in the south. They also included the *zamindars*, the *banias* and a great number of soldiers. He was learned in the *Unani* system of medicine, spoke Urdu, Arabic and Persian, apart from Hindustani. He also spoke a smattering of broken English. Aleem could handle a horse with ease and often disappeared into the hills and forests to collect *jadi-booti*, roots and herbs, to prepare his ointments and potions. He relied upon the many wild tribes in the area to gather his requirements. They replenished his stock of raw material from the more inaccessible parts of the forest. For he believed he practised an exact science and would never wish to use an inferior herb or root that did not possess the required potency, and which could harm a sick man, woman or child.

He also believed he practised an exact religion. He prayed five times a day to Allah, the all merciful. And in the night or when the opportunity presented itself, he cast a ruhmal around an unsuspecting human neck, garrotting him for the appeasement of goddess Bhawani.

His sense of generosity and benefaction in the tribute to his medical practice was only matched by the extreme grit, cunning and ruthlessness he exhibited when strangling rich merchants on the highways of Central India.

Mohammed Mir Aleem was a "thug", a word derived from the Hindustani word *thugna* or *thuglana*, to deceive. He was born into a family of traditional thugs, whose style of dual existence kept them from being discovered. Even among the natives, and especially among the ruling East India Co. the existence of such a secret society was considered a myth for many years. There were well-founded rumours, of course: the inexplicable disappearance of thousands of travellers throughout India. Whispers among the travelling merchants and pilgrims, of *phansigars* befriending travelers in Northern India and surreptitiously eliminating them, of the *Ari Tulucars* of the Madras

Presidency and the *Tanti Calleru* who use wire or cat-gut to sever the necks of victims in the kingdom of Mysore.

Aleem's charity and compassion as a healer was not just a guise, for he was without doubt a good Unani practitioner. He would never harm a patient and would go to great lengths and perseverance to relieve his charge of pain and suffering. He derived the same satisfaction from seeing his medication work and effect a cure as he would from stalking a rich merchant, pitting his cunning against the man, seeing suspicion change to friendship and trust, until that ecstatic moment when a life is ended by the unfailing *ruhmal*.

He had comfortable plied his trade for many years. Curing and killing, both activities being immensely enriching, had led him to every town and village of Central India. His wife and three children would know him only as a merchant and a healer. The rest of society also respected him as a distinguished healer and a dignified and wealthy gentleman.

But above all he enjoyed the secret respect of other thugs of Central India whose company he had to cultivate discreetly in order to carry out some of the more dramatic killings. They rarely acknowledged him as an acquaintance openly, and when they did, they spoke only in Ramasee, the thug-dialect. And it was always to deceive travellers who trusted him. Posing as fellow travelling merchants they would aid him in strangulating the unsuspecting victim. Motivated by the immense potential for enrichment, they targeted their *bunij*, caravans of merchants transporting gold, silver and jewels from one commercial centre to another, barely encountering any resistance or pursuit.

Until now.

Aleem's concern was not the appointment of a new magistrate in Narsinghpur district, the resolute blue-eyed white man named William Henry Sleeman from Cornwall, England, who was in the process of systematically eliminating this ancient society. Aleem was well aware of how Sleeman, accompanied by a dozen *thanadars*, had been riding from town to town in their campaign to ferret out information through arrests and intimidation of the *phansigars*.

Twice they had been at his heels, following a vague suspicion with regard to his name. They were uncertain of his full name, and on the second occasion, when he was surrounded and challenged by the company *sepoys* for bearing the name Aleem, the people of the town who had gathered around them had both ridiculed and protested against their harassment of the well-known healer.

Aleem had immediately ceased to worry about the English officer. "Why him?" an elderly Hindu lady of great wealth, sitting on a *palki*, had queried, and Sleeman had looked abashed. "Why the *hakim*? You can hardly expect this old man who has nursed women and children back to health all these years and refused little remuneration for the same, to be a thug! Have you all lost your mind?" and her loud squeals and peals of laughter could be heard down the street till her *palki* had disappeared around the corner of the bazaar.

"Saheb," Aleem had then addressed the English officer politely, "we are all very grateful for the concern you show in wishing to put an end to this scourge of our highways. But is it the sin of my parents that I should also have been named Aleem? The name of some thug you so detest?"

The English officer had since ignored him.

And no victim of Aleem had ever lived to identify him. If he had any minor reason to worry at all, it was the confessions of the thugs arrested in the district. But they knew him by various names, much to Sleeman's confusion.

Aleem's chief worry was, therefore, not the company's authority manifested in William Sleeman and the dozen *sepoys* that rode with him. His chief cause of trepidation and anxiety was the existence in the same region of another *phansigar*, known only as Feringee, and who, through masterly deception had been identifying and luring rich thugs into his trap. A predator who preyed on the thugs themselves. A grand swindler and bandit who dispossessed the plunderers of their pillage, Feringee, by all reports, operated on his own. He was often referred to as the Prince of Phansigars. Aleem had had a close encounter with the man once and experienced genuine terror for the first time in his life.

About six months ago, Aleem was informed of a small caravan of traditional jewellers setting out from Jhansi for Gwalior to participate and sell their wares at a grand *mela* patronised by the Maharaja. A young thug of his acquaintance had visited the *hakim* in his *dawakhana* in the guise of a patient to give him the news. The details, such as the size of the travelling party, the exact number of able-bodied men in the caravan and the intended time of departure were discussed. It was, by all calculation, an auspicious time, and it was decided that no less than six thugs would be required to accomplish the task. Of particular interest to Aleem was a rumour in the bazaar that a collection of exceptionally rare rubies was changing hands. The rumour was that Sitara Devi, a lesser noble lady of Jhansi's royal family wished to trade the rubies with the Maharaja of Gwalior for some undisclosed sum or favour. Aleem had often heard the intriguing history of this treasure that had found its way into the Central Indian kingdom all the way from Burma, and had been constantly making efforts to trace it. It startled him to know that Sitara Devi was in possession of it. It made no difference, however. For it was going to be on the road, and his plans for its acquirement had been forged.

A puja to goddess Bhawani was performed in the night and a detailed plan was devised to ensnare the *bunij*.

On the appointed day and unknown to the party, four thugs rode on the road to Gwalior, keeping ahead of the travellers by a few hours. This group had a dual purpose. One was, to see if the road was being patrolled by the English magistrate or any of the *lashkars* of the Maharaja or local chieftains. They would then proceed to a predetermined spot off the road, conveniently close to a ravine or a dried up riverbed where bodies could be quickly disposed off. There they would wait.

Meanwhile Aleem befriended the travellers on the road at the commencement of their journey along with another thug in the guise of his assistant. This was accomplished with ease, for apart from being a well known *hakim* he was able to drop names of members of distinguished families of Jhansi whom he had cured of their ailments. His assistant Abdul, who had two harnessed horses in tow, carried a load of boxes and bottles, and Aleem cheerfully informed his fellow travellers that the annual *mela* they were attending was the breeding ground for most of the diseases that Gwalior's citizens suffered from.

"People from all over the province gather in this one place, partake of the food and water there and end up crying for me, their hakim-baba!" he smiled beatifically. They listened to him, laughed at his conservative old ways, admired the kindness he showed his assistant, and in a few hours loved him quite like a father.

But as was the custom of the rich and the cautious, they would not admit to him they were carrying any expensive merchandise.

"We are off to Gwalior to witness the *mela*," they lied. "Perhaps even sell them some of the sweets and pickles we carry here."

Aleem rode along smiling beatifically again. "That is very unkind of you," he teased them. "Our sweets and pickles from Jhansi will not make them ill. On the contrary, they will be fat and cheerful. How do you expect a poor *hakim* to ply his trade there?" He paused to hear them laugh. "However, you and I are better off than the rich *seths* and *nawabs* who travel this road" he added.

"Why so?" they queried.

"Don't you know? A gang of Pindaris, remnants of the Ameer Ali band the English could not vanquish, have recently regrouped on this road along with a gang of dacoits, and have been stalking and robbing rich merchants."

Aleem revelled in the silence that followed; his plan was working. There was now a general consternation among the members of the party as they rode.

"How recently did these incidents occur?" asked one of the men, riding up beside him. "And how many of them were there?"

Aleem made a quick calculation. He worked out that since the party he rode with had only about a dozen men capable of fighting, an announcement of a figure of twenty should be sufficiently devastating.

"At least twenty," he said, still smiling with rapture. "But we need not worry. They only kill if we resist them. And indeed, why should we? Surely they would not be craving for your pickles and my medicines."

Another silence followed. This time longer, while some of the men exchanged whispers. It amused Aleem to watch them steadily blunder before ending up in his snare.

Finally the man riding beside him asked, "Hakim baba, since you travel on this route so often you might best advise us as to what we should do to avoid these Pindaris."

"Don't worry," Aleem replied complacently. "They won't touch a hair of your head when they see what you are carrying." He surveyed what looked like small chests and boxes tied in coarse cloth slung from the saddles of the entire caravan. Silence followed again while the party rode uneasily along.

Then Aleem spoke. "Unless you simply want to avoid them altogether."

"Oh yes," came earnest voices from the group.

"There is one way we can avoid them," Aleem advised. "We can organise a decoy. It has worked before, and I have been able to save a number of women and children from their rapacity."

"And how is that done?" they wished to know.

"I will tell you how. But surely, you should not worry too much, considering you do not carry much of value. If the situation arises, I will guide you. So, stop worrying yourselves about it." As always, he decided not to disclose any kind of plan to them, for it always gave travellers time to think about it, analyse it, even find faults with it. He would have them act spontaneously when he required them to.

All went well till they reached a desolate road some hours before the village of Dabra.

It was the middle of the day and the sun shone mercilessly on the little group on the dusty road. A few vultures circled the far sky.

Suddenly the youth who rode as Aleem's assistant raised his hand to slow their march, and pointed in the direction of the road ahead of them. He had detected an unusual movement.

"Something is lying on the side of the road, baba," he spoke loudly to Aleem.

The party halted.

"Don't just sit there Abdul, you frightened nitwit!" Aleem said reproachfully. "Go, ride ahead and see what it is. At your age I would have…"

Abdul immediately handed over the reins of the horses he held in tow and was off in a gallop, throwing up a cloud of dust behind him.

The party watched as he approached the object of curiosity far down the road. He dismounted and appeared to be bending over something. After a moment he straightened, and seemed then to be assisting someone, laboriously helping a stranger to mount his horse.

"The boy is mad!" Aleem remarked. "What in God's name is he doing?"

The others in the group nodded hesitantly.

They watched the horse slowly return with the two riders.

"What has happened? Who is this?" Aleem inquired sternly.

"His horse has been killed. He is injured." The young man replied. "Baba, we can't leave him here. He is still alive, look!"

The man appeared delirious. Bent over, his face buried in the mane of the young thug's horse he seemed to be muttering and blabbering insensibly.

Aleem immediately dismounted and helped the apparently injured man down from the horse. They carried him to the side of the road and placed him under a tree. They then poured some water into his mouth.

"Pindaris!" the man gasped aloud. "Pindaris! They have taken my wife and daughter. They have taken my money!" he winced, holding his side, where, through a tear in his garment, blood oozed out between the fingers of his hand.

"How many are they?" Aleem inquired aloud, urgency in his voice.

"I don't know. Maybe twenty-five, perhaps thirty!" Aleem hoped the man would not exaggerate. So far the performance had been well acted out. Now all he needed to do was to apply a balm and tie a bandage over the hole in the man's garment so that the unmarked skin under the man's resolute fingers would not be noticed.

The party of travellers now stood a distance away on the road, stricken with fear and looking over their shoulders. As expected, nobody came to the aid of the injured man.

The wounded man groaned loudly as the bandage was applied. He even gagged and retched till Aleem had to ask him to shut up in low voice, speaking only in Ramasee.

"It's convincing enough, Imran-Bhai. Don't overdo your *nautanki*."

Having accomplished this much Aleem returned to the middle of the road leaving his assistant to tend the wounded stranger. He was gratified to see a timid and cowering group, looking at him wide eyed for his counsel and guidance.

"The plan, baba! The decoy! Tell us what we should do?"

Aleem waved his hand in an act to dispel their fears. "That fool chose to travel with his money and two women! Even a sage would be tempted to rob him. Come, we must now prepare ourselves to ride past the Pindaris without antagonising them. We don't have women travelling among us. And they can taste your *mitahee* and pickles, and even my medicines if they wish."

"We wish to avoid them if we can, baba!" one of them requested fervently.

Aleem looked over the group like a patriarch. In an act of confusion, he stroked his silver beard.

"What a fool I have been," he remarked sadly. "You people must be carrying articles of some value. Otherwise you would not be so afraid." He turned to his assistant Abdul, who was still under the tree. He spoke loudly. "Look son, I am sorry I have to put your life in such danger. Your mother will not forgive me for this. Let us go our way. We endanger our lives by travelling with this lot."

The group looked alarmed. Some sheepish, others even angry. Before anyone could speak, the old *hakim* raised both hands and said, "It is alright. I do not wish to know what you possess or what it is that you carry in your saddles. I only wish you had been a little more honest at the start of our journey. Your foolishness could jeopardise valuable human lives. Anyhow, if you wish to live and arrive at Gwalior without incident or loss, you must listen to me and do exactly as I say."

They calmed down and nodded in unison. Aleem finally felt a sense of complete control over the group. An important milestone in his ploy had been achieved. He could now speak with the authority of a leader.

"The able bodied among you will remain on the road and ride on to Dabra, then on to Gwalior. The older men may join me on a circuitous route. I know this district well and there are many villagers and tribesmen who will give us shelter and come to our aid if we so require. The Pindaris don't expect travellers to take the forest paths. They will be lying in wait on the highway," he paused to study their reaction. "If you possess anything of value, you may transfer them onto our horses."

"A few of our armed men could ride along with you, baba," a young man interlocuted.

"And draw the Pindaris to us!" Aleem shot back. "I cannot agree to that. Let us be very clear as to what we intend to do. I require the able bodied among you to ride on in a large and visible group, for I am certain the Pindaris already have advance information of our caravan's arrival in these parts. If they suspect that a number of us are missing, or have broken away to travel through lesser-trodden paths, they will be on the hunt for us. We will be caught and murdered. And so will you. On the other hand, if you would be kind enough to distribute these boxes and bottles of medicine I carry amongst you while you ride on the highway, you can safely surrender yourselves to their scrutiny. That way both my medicines and your wares, whatever they are, will have reached Dabra by nightfall, and nobody need engage the Pindaris at all."

They fell for it. He was convincing enough. After all, they believed the old *hakim* had done this many times before.

The goods were separated and exchanged. Aleem's innumerable bottles of ointments, balms and tonics were loaded onto the saddles of the men in the party. The travellers parted with their wares, which were hitched onto the horses accompanying the *hakim*. The precious cargo was somehow accommodated onto the saddles of five horses. Five men, the oldest of the lot separated from the party on the highway to join the *hakim* and his assistant.

A convenient meeting point was quickly discussed. It was decided to reunite at a point near a *dargah* between Dabra and Gwalior.

"It's a five hour march from here. You might have to wait awhile," Aleem informed them. "The path we take could delay us by over two hours. We have a wounded man with us too. However, take good care. And God be with you."

They waited as a group of wandering minstrels passed them by singing soulfully, playing on the *dhol* and *do-tara.*

Oh Mother, the wind and the birds spoke to me
Of your hunger, and what they bring to thee
Be patient with your sons, for they have the wanderer's lust
Feast on their food, Mother, if the offering is just.

Then they were on their way. While the party of merchants rode, the vultures circled overhead and flew closer to survey the dead horse on the side of the road.

Aleem and his party of seven left the highway to take a narrow path through the forest. They watched a lone wolf appear ahead of them to their left, and slink across the road to inspect the carcass.

Aleem cursed silently. A lone wolf moving from the left to the right. It had been so many years since he had heard any thug beset with that omen. And at that time he had heard it said that a great thug leader had lost his entire family to Bhawani's wrath. Aleem often wondered what had become of that great man.

They rode for an hour through the jungle before Aleem and his team of horsemen arrived near a deep ravine. Below them a dried river bed wound its serpentine way occasionally flashing reflected sunlight, indicating that a small stream of clear water still trickled in the sand.

"There is a narrow path down this ravine," indicated Aleem. "We could water the horses and refresh ourselves. We are indeed making good time. Our road now lies on the other side of the Sind-mori."

They nudged their horses down the inclination till they reached the soft sandy surface of the rivulet.

The party stopped on the sands to remove the water-skins from their saddles. It was time to deliver the *jhirnee*, the secret cue, the signal only the members of his gang understood.

At this point, Aleem sneezed violently, and dismounted. The others dismounted to lead the horses to the shallow rivulet of water.

Aleem sneezed again. Then clapped his hands to call Abdul. "Bring me the balm from the saddle bag, Abdul!" He called out aloud.

The cue was heard. From around the steep wall of the ravine where the river meandered, a few yards from where they stood, there suddenly appeared four horsemen riding purposefully towards them. A length of cloth extending from their turbans covered their faces. Fear and confusion ensued. Within seconds the first two victims were struck on their heads from behind with rocks as the men rode up to them so that they fell unconscious. Aleem required that they survive to absolve him from the crime. The three remaining men were strangled and dragged to the water screaming and gagging. Only one of them attempted to fight hard but was subdued by a violent kick in the genitals. Then his face was pressed into the running water of the rivulet until he stopped breathing.

While the slaughter was in progress, Aleem made no action. Even as one of the thugs, a brutish Rajput who limped miserably on a deformed leg struggled to secure the ruhmal around a fat jeweller's throat, he just stood his ground watching the melee. In this operation, as had been planned, his part of the task had been accomplished the moment he had sneezed. Only Abdul and Imran, the thug who feigned injury, joined the others in the carnage, throttling and asphyxiating their victims with relish.

When it was over, Aleem knelt down to examine the two men who had been struck on the head. He felt about their necks. They were alive. One of them had an ugly gash above his temple. The other moaned but appeared quite knocked out.

"I hope these two survive to tell the others at Dabra and Gwalior of our misfortunes," he remarked in Ramasee, the language only his men understood.

They removed the precious cargo off the saddles and placed them on the riverbed. But before dividing the spoils they would carry out a sacrificial rite making an offering of jaggery or "the *goor* of the *tupounee*," as it was called, to the goddess Kali to bless their sacred

Kussee, or pick-axe. Following this there were three dead bodies to bury in the sand.

All had gone well. Aleem had quite forgotten the omen of the lone wolf.

It was at this moment that their stratagem received a catastrophic blow.

From around the same steep wall of the ravine where the river meandered, rode towards them a solitary rider in a black turban, his face masked in similar fashion, his body covered in a dark robe. Even before he had arrived near them, a loud report from a fire-arm was heard, and one of the thugs fell dead at Aleem's feet as the shot found its mark on his face. Everyone froze, for none of them possessed a firearm.

Abdul, the young thug who accompanied Aleem suddenly broke away from the group, his sword drawn, to engage the oncoming rider. Another shot rang and echoed in the ravine even as the rider's horse trampled upon the lifeless body of the youth.

The stranger did not appear to want to slow down as he galloped towards them. Before they could react the rider was upon them. They recoiled and leapt to evade the onslaught but not before another thug was yanked off the ground, a *ruhmal* skilfully thrown around his neck by the dark rider. He made a jerking motion as he rode past them and released one end of his *ruhmal* despatching the thug with ease on the sand with a broken neck.

Three of his men were dead even before Aleem could comprehend what had befallen them. The rider swivelled his horse around without a second's respite. Seeing him prepare to charge again, two of the thugs scrambled in panic towards the path along the slope from which they had descended by the side of the ravine. The crippled Rajput had to climb on all fours as his leg failed him. Aleem, now frozen, dropped to his knee in horror as Imran, the only member of the gang who still stood beside him was similarly yanked off his feet by a *ruhmal* thrown skilfully around his neck. The galloping horse brushed past Aleem's face nearly knocking him out. He saw the rider make a heaving and twisting action at the throat of the helpless thug who dangled beside him as he rode. Then with an ease that exhibited great physical prowess, he hurled the lifeless body onto the sand and swivelled his horse around again.

Aleem, now alone, remained on his knees. Helpless, in a game of subterfuge he thought he had mastered, he now for the first time prepared himself for death. This was the most awesome display of horsemanship and thug prowess Aleem had ever witnessed in his life. He closed his eyes, praying, hoping that death for him would not be a prolonged or painful one.

However the rider did not charge this time. He rode up to Aleem and stopped. Then he silently dismounted looking at the bearded man through his hooded face.

"Spread your turban on the ground and empty the contents of every box you have here," he commanded in Hindustani.

With trembling hands Aleem obeyed. He also noted that the man's accent, though vaguely familiar, was not from these parts, nor was the style in which his strangely twisted turban lay bound on his head. But in his trepidation, he could not deliberate further upon it.

The boxes the caravan carried were opened one by one. Exquisitely crafted jewellery of gold and silver studded with all colours of precious stones and ivory tumbled out of the boxes in a heap upon the cloth. Aleem's eyes nearly fell out of their sockets when the last box was opened. It contained at least forty rubies of exceptional size and lustre. Like red pigeon eggs they seemed to bleed upon the cloth on which they lay. He recognised them instantly.

"So, these are the fabled Manar Manik," the stranger appeared to have recognised them too. "And you must be Aleem."

Aleem was mystified. This sinister creature seemed to know all.

"Tie them up securely," he ordered Aleem, and when it was done, he hitched it casually on to his saddle. Aleem felt unnerved at the extremely ease and nonchalance with which the man went about his task. He appeared in no state of hurry or anxiety.

He stood there regarding Aleem for sometime. Then he leaned his tall frame against the horse and spoke slowly, almost as if he was speaking to himself.

"You know, I have recently derived more satisfaction from seeing a *bunij* die in my hands than taking his wealth. He was a *pardesi*. He was, like you, a vile and depraved individual. What amazes me, by Bhawani, is how your kind discover and fall in with one another, even across continents."

Though his face was still masked, from the wrinkles in the corner of his eyes, Aleem was sure the man was smiling, perhaps jeering. His accent bothered Aleem again.

"And who should I believe is responsible for my fate today?" Aleem hazarded in a quivering voice, speaking in Ramasee. "You are one of us, a thug, aren't you?"

The man mounted his horse, still looking down at him. His deliberating slow movements and his state of indecisiveness frightened Aleem. It appeared to him as if the stranger was wondering whether to leave him dead or alive. He even began regretting he had asked the question.

The stranger tucked in a loose end of his turban and glanced once again in the direction in which Aleem's two companions had fled.

"Ever heard of the name Feringee?" the man then enquired as if in reply, "Go home. Your little boy needs you more desperately than the wolves of these ravines." And without awaiting a response from Aleem, turned his horse and rode away in the direction from where he had appeared.

This was about six months ago, and Aleem had offered many sacrifices to Bhawani since to invigorate his shattered nerves should he cross paths with this man again.

He continued to practice healing as a *hakim* in the central Indian districts whenever he visited his family. For his covert thugee operations he now preferred the north. Agra, Lucknow and even Punjab, where the death of the rajah, Ranjit Singh had thrown the kingdom into confusion. Shifting loyalties and migrating populations were fertile ground to ply his trade. He had been informed by some of his associates to stay away from the eastern provinces, for some Englishmen of the docks were seen making enquiries about him there. He could not afford to have his name tarnished in Bengal.

In Bengal, in the markets of Cossipore and Bangbazaar, he had always been seen walking with a slow and dignified gait or hiring a *palki* or *cranchee*. He would never be seen riding a horse. For there, among the commercial and trading community of the city of Calcutta, he was an ageing and patriarchal figure. A benefactor and a pious man, known only by the name of Moin-ud-din Nasser.

* * *

Salmi had no intention of endangering her baby. If it was destined to survive, she would find the village. She trudged along the path in the forest, stopping only when the movement of the baby in her belly became quite intolerable.

She could not remember having lingered in her hovel for very long. Her memory was hazy. After the Ojha and his tribe had left, she remembered rinsing her mouth. But she had no recollection of when she had devoured the dry *chapatis*.

She believed she had waited only long enough to bundle her clothes. They barely fitted her anymore but she had secured them in a shawl and slung it over her shoulder. Every time her back tired she would sit on the bare ground and lean on the soft bundle.

She now ambled through the forest knowing it would take much longer than the Ojha would have her believe. And when it was noon, she still could not see any sign of the village or the dry riverbed.

It was another wearisome hour before she realised she had lost her way. She waddled along a path above what looked like a deep ravine.

She sat down on a flat rock overlooking the river wondering if she had unknowingly walked too far upstream. She wiped her flushed face, breathing heavily, and feeling an overwhelming sense of deprivation.

The baby in her womb had stopped moving and she felt about her abdomen with concern. Her back ached and her legs were exceedingly heavy. She shut her eyes and prayed. Her guruji's voice reminded her - "Let us not pray for lighter loads but for stronger shoulders." But it sounded out of context and did not give her much comfort. She was not sure her prayers helped her in any way.

Slowly she slid off the rock onto the dry grass. It felt soft and extremely comfortable. She decided to lie down for awhile tucking the bundle of clothes under her head. She could hear the incessant drone and the buzzing of insects all around her. In a minute she was fast asleep, like a child under deep sedation.

She must have been dreaming, for she suddenly heard a demonic laughter pierce the air. A long drawn high-pitched squeal. Not of mirth, but of suffering and pain. Carried by the wind, it grew louder and seemed to be trying to reach her. A voice seemed to ring in her ears.

"Hai Bhawani, what have you done to me? I must see the end to this!"

It rent the air with a shrill that silenced the buzz of the insects. Then the squeal turned into laughter and seemed to fade away in the distance. Salmi moaned helplessly trying to wake up. The satanic laughter abruptly ceased in a staccato of soft chuckles.

Salmi now awoke with a start and sat up. She looked about her, but all was quiet. Judging from the length of the shadows, she must have slept for a long time. She surely must have been dreaming. She felt possessed by something not quite her own self. The insects still buzzed in the air but they were fewer. She suddenly felt afraid, and stood up. Her legs felt heavy but the ache in her back was gone for now.

She decided to retrace her way down the path she had come in the hope of locating the village somewhere along the river downstream.

She plodded along the path for an hour. It was approaching dusk, and the fear and uncertainty she felt almost made her burst into tears. Her anguish was further heightened by the numbness she felt around her abdomen. The baby had not moved in a long while now.

It was another half an hour before she saw the dim lights of human habitation. Her footsteps quickened in anticipation. A sense of relief swept over her. Now every time the path deviated a little she decided she would not lose sight of the lights. The village was still far in the distance, but at least it was there. "After all both rain and sunshine are needed to make a rainbow," her guruji had said. She was prepared to walk, walk without faltering…

A twig snapped somewhere close by among the trees. It startled her. Dusk was upon her and she nervously peered ever so often over her shoulders and tried to walk as fast as she could.

Another twig snapped, now some distance in front of her. She halted, breathing heavily. With anxious, tormented eyes she stared hard in the direction of the sound. There was a creaking, then a loud crack of a breaking branch. A loud thumping followed, and there broke onto her path some yards away in the forest, a gigantic tusker, an elephant of enormous proportions. Its head and forelegs were clearly visible as it stood menacingly surveying the path she would take.

Salmi recoiled and froze, transfixed in horror. It appeared to be preparing itself for a wild charge. Then it trumpeted as if in panic, long and loud, trying to back into the undergrowth it had emerged from.

Struck by an inexplicable fear, she began to scream.

A human voice suddenly spoke in her ear. A gentle voice that said, "Don't worry, just step back slowly. And stop screaming."

Startled again, she turned her head, fear still writ large on her face. But she stopped screaming. The man who stood behind her held her by the shoulder. He gently nudged her away from the path.

"It can smell you, but it hasn't spotted you yet. Just keep moving slowly. You seem to frighten the animal."

They slowly side stepped through the forest and scrambled some yards through the shrubs. A horse was tethered to a tree, laden with a leather bag securely strapped under the belly of the animal.

"You are in no shape to ride," the man exclaimed softly. "What are you doing in the forest alone at this time?"

When Salmi did not answer, the man said, "It's okay. I don't want to know. But let me get us out of here before that rogue finds us. I wonder what stopped its charge." Without warning he lifted her easily and gingerly placed her on the horse. Salmi, a little abashed was shaking uncontrollably and held fast to the saddle horn.

"Don't worry, I will walk the horse. There is another path we can take." The man said. "It is getting dark. Let us pray that we don't meet up with an entire herd of elephants."

Salmi held tight to her only chance of deliverance.

He walked beside the horse holding its reins, while Salmi swayed uncomfortably as they descended into a dry riverbed. She tried to discern what the man looked like, but in the darkness she could only see his black turban and beard. He was tall and lean.

"The animal was downwind. Why didn't it charge?" The stranger looked at her in confusion.

They walked for nearly half a mile before the lights of the village became visible once again.

Salmi felt at ease again. "I didn't think the village was this far when I saw the lights from the forest." She remarked.

"Never judge the distance of a light at night or a mountain in the day," the man replied laughing. "Do you wish to dismount and walk now?"

"I don't belong to this village," Salmi said in reply.

"I know," the man sounded indifferent. "Neither do I. But you need to find shelter and rest. Your condition is very delicate."

"I don't have a husband, or a home," Salmi added meekly.

"That is obvious," he again sounded unconcerned. "You cannot expect much kindness from people in your state of destitution. That is the way of the world."

She nodded in agreement. "I will try and walk," she said, wondering why the stranger had bothered to take this much trouble. "I am grateful to you for saving my life and for the pains you take."

He helped her dismount. "My pains are far from over," the man laughed again. "Come on. Let us see how the village receives you. You may require my help, yet. I have seen women in your state driven out of villages to die by the road. It is far better to remain in the company of a man. At least you will be treated like a human being."

Salmi felt a sudden sense of uneasiness. She stumbled, and then stopped.

The man brought his horse to a halt. The lights of the village were clearly visible now. A lantern shone from the window of a house nearby. Salmi could smell jasmine and incense.

"What is it now?" the man asked, turning around.

Salmi spoke hesitatingly, looking at the heavy leather bag, "Are you some official in this province? You...sometimes you sound different.

You don't speak like a native. Sometimes you speak like a pardesi, an Englishman, a firengee who has learnt to speak Hindustani. Are you?" She could see his face vaguely in the light of the lantern. He was swarthy and sunburnt and the hair on his face was black. She noticed that his turban was tied in a strange unruly fashion.

He stood there beside his horse twisting a loose end of his turban into place and regarding her for a long moment. It was a long time since anyone had scented his antecedents. Only this time it amused him hearing it from a young, guileless girl. "Let us just presume that I am. Does that bother you?"

Salmi shook her head.

"For the sake of your child let us not worry too much about who I am," he continued. "I did not concern myself with who you were before I helped you out of the forest. All I can assure you now is that I mean you no harm. It is up to you to trust me."

"I am sorry," Salmi apologised quickly. "I did not mean to offend you."

He pointed to the village. "Come, let us knock on a door or two at Laxmanghat. And remember, we are only pilgrims on our way to Varanasi. There is dignity in such an announcement, and village folk will never refuse food and shelter to a couple in our condition."

Salmi flushed slightly and continued walking demurely behind the tall stranger.

* * *

"For, the life that you now lead," wrote Lucy Polgarth, holding John's letter in one hand and writing to him with the other, "I fear, will take you further down the chasm. Down to such depths, John, that I fear I will never reach you in that abyss. It is by God's grace that I still continue to hear from you, however infrequently all these years."

A tear rolled down from her eye.

"After all that you confessed to me the night before you set sail for Hindustan, I prayed like I have never done before. I asked our Lord to give you strength and peace and most of all I prayed that He keep you safe. My prayers have not been in vain, John. For your letters have kept coming these three years. And I continue to mail mine to the address of that Hindu priest in Calcutta. God bless him, for he is my only conduit to you.

"You asked me if I was happy. Yes, I am happy, yet not wholly so. For I remain perplexed and worried about your well being. During my short residence in that country I have always been bewildered by its climate and its complexities. Life is so uncertain, disease and death so rapid, that unless you are insulated from it all by living in a society that is conscientious, you will perish. I don't wish to frighten you dear, but the differences of religion and the habits of life, not to speak of the innumerable languages and dialects, are so incomprehensible to us that we would, I believe, be best preserved by remaining aloof. So I beseech you, John, do not live in total exclusion of our society there. I pray you understand that I do not wish to delve into what you do there. It must be sufficiently lucrative or satisfying for you to stay this long with it. It only alarms me often that you have gone so native as to remain unseen and unheard of by the society to which you belong. If it is by choice, I do understand. But the remorse you felt in London must one day heal if you are to go on living.

"I am aware I make a confession here. But I do no longer wish to hide the fact that my happiness is now fastened to a letter that arrives here from around the world every six months. For John, since you left, I have not looked to anyone else for comfort. And I will wait as long as it takes for you to return to civilisation again."

* * *

John Penmarric stirred at dawn, as was his habit from his Cornish upbringing. And in that opiate moment between sleep and awakening he unfailingly saw the seagulls flying in great arches over his village on the sea front. Their screeching grew louder, until he awoke with a start and sat up rubbing his eyes.

He looked out of the window. Parakeets and mynahs were chattering discordantly in a mango grove through which a hint of the first rays of the sun could be seen. He could smell jasmine and incense in the air.

He removed his feet from the charpoy and placed them on the cool floor. He regarded the sleeping figure on another charpoy at the far end of the room.

"What is your name?" he asked her when he saw her move.

"Salmi," she answered softly, propping herself up on an elbow.

"Did you sleep well?"

She nodded, though it was untrue. Wrapped in a sheet of coarse cotton, she had tried hard to fall asleep. But the events of the day and the prospect of sleeping in the same room as the stranger had troubled her for a long while. If sleep came, it was only the torpor of extreme fatigue.

The stranger had been correct in his assessment of the situation the evening before. They had called out aloud to the people on entering the village, and in response had been immediately accosted by a gathering of armed men brandishing sticks and swords. Her tall stranger had calmly greeted them with a "namaskar", holding both hands in front of him, and had politely addressed them in Hindustani.

"Brothers, I am a *munshi* from Bardoli village of Surat. My wife is pregnant, as you can see, and we are on our way to Varanasi on a pilgrimage. We have come a long way from Surat and only wish to rest for the night. It is extremely unsafe out in the open. We noticed elephant dung on the road and narrowly avoided a rogue."

An elder of the village made a cursory inspection of their possessions and the saddle. Once satisfied that they carried no weapons, he became more cordial. "We did not intend to frighten your wife in her condition. But you understand, don't you, that the approach of strangers is always met with curiosity and caution. It is the way of every village. So it is with Laxmanghat."

Soon the irrepressible women folk were pouring out of the huts. The rare traveller who stopped here was always a spectacle, they told her. A pregnant woman was indeed a novelty. And they teased her about her tall and handsome husband.

Having, in some incomprehensible and unspoken way, determined that their caste was sufficiently unblemished, they were allowed to use the well to draw water and bathe.

The two magic words, pilgrim and pregnant, had the desired effect. For wholesome food arrived, and a room beside a granary was immediately prepared for them to sleep in.

"You might wish to stay a few days," they had suggested, "especially since your wife looks very weary. But then, who are we to decide that for you..."

This morning, as she lay on the charpoy she wondered how she would ever repay the kindness of this strange young man. She could not even muster enough courage to ask him his name. Now, as he stared out of the window she noted his handsome features and his young beard. Salmi thought he looked extremely strong, but his eyes appeared to be sad and distant.

"I have to wash, and also to graze the horse," he said suddenly and left the room. Salmi stood up and walked slowly to the window. The sun was rising as the man walked towards the well to perform his ablutions. He held his unravelled black turban in one hand and his long black hair bounced about his shoulders. He appeared more comfortable without the turban that he wore in such a strange fashion.

As if they had been waiting for a cue, the morning stillness was broken by the clanging of pots and vessels. The women of the village appeared to suddenly need water from the well. They streamed out from all directions and unabashedly headed for the well. Salmi turned away from the window, wondering why the voices of the women suddenly irritated her.

Then for a fleeting moment she was once again beset with the feeling that she was not herself. She felt the warm presence of someone else inside her. Not her womb, but in her heart and in her mind.

She would have given the feeling more thought had it not been for a strange pulsating in her lower abdomen.

She had begun to labour.

* * *

"Alright, let us for a moment agree that you are telling the truth. A standing vertical leap of over three yards, perhaps four. And achieved by special means that only the champions of your village know. Tell me Nandu, would that not render many minor forts in this region ineffective against your village folk? This should have been the subject of some serious consternation in every kingdom in Hindustan."

It was late in the evening. The duo walked outside the sprawling cantonment of Saugor, Jack Dawson trailing a fine Rajputana mare he had borrowed from the club's stables. He was trying to come to terms with the incredulous claims of the *kathputli* guru one last time. To Dawson it was not important even if this claim was somehow true. Giving allowance to some native exaggeration, even a small mud-fort or a musketeers' lair might be scaled by an athletic man with some acrobatic skills. But to Dawson it was now more imperative to ensure that his next and carefully choreographed puppet theatre, to be performed on Christmas Eve at the club, not involve the antics of the mythological Hanuman or some superman from the Hindu pantheon.

But Nandakumar was unrelenting. "Masterji, in this land of frivolous jugglers, snake-charmers and magicians, there are also some who can perform true feats of skill, strength and endurance that require abnormal mental faculties and arduous training. Don't judge human capability by the average bazaar trickster. They belong to the lowest rung of achievers."

"Nandu, if I were to take you any more seriously, I should be riding out of Saugor this very moment to see for myself these champions you speak of. I was an acrobat and a trapeze artist myself." Dawson was determined to resolve the issue. "But I implore you, does the entertainment of a few ladies and children under a *pandal* require so much dispute?"

"Ah ha!" exclaimed Nandakumar in his characteristic style. "Masterji, the dispute is not over the entertainment of ladies and children. I could not care less if Tipu and the Mysore rocketeers were dead, or if Firengee was captured and hung. It is over the existence of my village champions, as much as over the odds of achieving such special feats that you choose to argue with me!"

Jack Dawson now thought he saw a chance. "Let us agree for a moment that it is possible. Giant leaps over fort-walls and coconut trees. Beyond doubt, by some specially gifted men of your village. Can we now please come to an agreement not to allow these antics in our next performance? It's the Christmas day performance and I cannot have Joseph leap over the manger!"

"I am a Nair by caste," Nandakumar interrupted. "Warriors, in a land that broke the Mysoreean resolve to conquer, hold and subjugate. As with my family and clan, I share every bit of abhorrence against Tipu for his invasion of my homeland and my village. But to watch every brown puppet laughed at and scorned in an evening of entertainment at a clubhouse does not contribute to the morale of my troupe."

"Dear Nandu, there will be no such thing," assured the school master. "It will be just like your baby-Krishna story: A raja called Herod orders that all new-born babies in the kingdom be killed. The parents try to save the baby. There is a flight for life. A divine birth. Some miracles. And for Christ's sake, this time let there be no scope for impressive leaps over fort-walls. If you had understood English a little better than I speak this Hindustani, I would have you understand how important Christmas is to us"

They now stopped at the gates. Nandakumar stared silently at the setting sun, while Dawson waited for a word of cooperation from the master puppeteer.

"That will not be necessary. But this shall be my last performance for the English this season," he declared. "Masterji, you have my assistance and my cooperation. There will be no clowning around or antics. We shall play by your choreography. But when that is over, consider what I have to offer you. You are a teacher of gymnastics. Join me on a tour to that beautiful land of my ancestors, Malabar. See for yourself the wonderful acrobatics and martial traditions of my village. Perhaps I could request a guru to teach you to do those leaps which you find so hard to comprehend."

Dawson considered the offer for a few minutes, removing his hat and scratching his silver hair. "Well, it does beguile the mind," he whispered under his breath. But the sincerity with which Nandakumar made the offer was unmistakable. "What do I stand to lose? A couple of months to any place away from Saugor is a vacation. Alright Nandu, I promise to travel with you to Malabar after Christmas."

That Christmas Eve, to the delight of the chief guest Henry Sleeman, the magistrate of Narsinghpur, *The Nativity* was performed in peace and tranquility under the *shamiana* of the English club at Saugor.

Part III

Lord William Cavendish Bentinck, son of the third duke of Portland, once Governor General of Bengal, now Governor General of India peered at the one time soldier who stood stiffly before him. The handsome, self possessed and tenacious man who had transferred from the army to the civil services as a junior assistant magistrate in the Northern Territories of Saugor and Maratha was now magistrate of Narsinghpur.

The Governor General had been reading a report the young man had written, the contents of which made up several pages, together with attachments of maps and statistical figures. The contents of the report also made some of his morning's breakfast and some bile rise to his throat.

"This is grisly Sleeman, a hellish piece of document if ever there was one that made its way into our offices. It reads like the apocalypse, my dear fellow!"

The magistrate nodded in acknowledgement but stood in silence.

"These natives, this sect you speak of, do they have a leader of some sort? Perhaps a patron, a chieftain or a raja that encourages these deeds?"

"I believe they have a loose confederacy, your Excellency. Each band is aware of the existence of another band or brotherhood and often compliment each other to accomplish their task. In fact it is this link that I hope to exploit. I have no information as yet of any single leader or spiritual head guiding their activities. But I suspect there are people in power sympathetic to thug activity. Men of rank and wealth in territories not under British jurisdiction. Much of my findings I owe to an informer, a person who put me first on this trail."

"Your report also indicates these criminal bands exist throughout the length and breadth of Hindustan. So many ethnic groups, classes, castes and religions, not to speak of languages. How do you hope to identify and rout them out?"

"Your Excellency, in all that complexity lies an inherent pattern and some common features. There appears to be two reasons why the thugs commit these atrocities. One, in the exercise of a religion that sanctions this act, and upholds it as a virtue to dispossess a stranger of his life as an offering to Kali, or Bhawani, their goddess. The other is purely the lure of easy wealth. This apart, the method employed in killing is unique to the sect. Strangulation. When a suspect is arrested they stand absolved as no conventional weapon is found on their person. They speak a common tongue called Ramasee, which appears to be a language designed out of an entire astute vocabulary required for their chicanery, duplicity, deception and stealth. It has little grammar, and more nuances and subtleties than any language I've known. Emboldened by long immunity and devilish cunning in the enticement of travellers, they have over time perfected a method of murder and disposal, leaving little trace or evidence of their deed."

"And you still harbour the will to pursue them?"

"I admit, your Excellency, that we have here a very engaging task. I would have been less inclined to bother you with this but for the magnitude of this abominable practice. It behoves us not to remain aloof any longer. I can quite understand why my reports earlier were met with disbelief and indifference. I found it hard to believe some of the stories myself, till the bodies were exhumed as stark evidence. The frequency of this crime in the provinces I have mentioned far outweigh the self immolation of widows, or sati, as they call it. While we have outlawed Sati, Thugee remains relatively unknown due to lack of evidence. Until now. Relatives of victims maintain a frightened silence. More often other bandits such as the Pindaris are blamed, despite our own intelligence sources indicating that no such band of robbers were ever seen in the district for months."

The Governor General placed an inkpot on the sheaf of papers that lay before him. He leaned back in his high chair and closed his eyes.

"I quite appreciate your concern for our subjects in the provinces, my good man," he said, his eyes still closed. "But are you sure these rumours are not as extravagant as they seem. You mentioned you had a native informer. Who is he? Can I for one be assured that much of this is not hearsay?"

Sleeman smiled for the first time. He had verified every lead his informer had given him. He had made arrests without losing time. And fresh bodies had always confirmed his informer's credibility. He had also taken great pains to compile his report. Was that all the Governor General wanted? To be personally assured? For this, Sleeman had arrived at Calcutta prepared. This was better than the official indifference and outright opposition he had faced earlier, before Lord Bentinck had held this office.

"Your Excellency, my report will bear me out. In Narsinghpur alone I have apprehended eighty-four men, thirty-two of whom have turned approvers. Knowing that a death sentence was a likely alternative, more than a few leaders of Thug gangs were willing to turn informer on their partners in crime. They have divulged their methods to us. As my report has indicated, graves of intended victims are often dug in advance of the killing. We have come across bodies that bear deep gashes to hasten their decomposition, thereby reducing the likelihood of scavengers and carrion eaters uncovering any evidence. The confessions of these thugs led to our disinterring more than four hundred graves. Another ninety-six bodies, or at least the traces of so many gruesome deaths, have been discovered in ravines, in dried up riverbeds, bheels and well shafts. Many are women and children. Of all this carnage, nearly two hundred have been committed by a single thug over a period of three years. This man, by his own account, is an average thug."

The Governor General's eyes were wide open now. "You ask for extraordinary powers to pursue and apprehend these thugs, far from your district, province and your magisterial jurisdiction. You have, I note, also requested for men and resources."

"And, if I may be permitted to add, your Excellency," Sleeman used the opportunity, "I would like no opposition from my British brethren. That is how I intend to rout this evil. I need complete co-operation."

After a long silence, Lord Bentinck spoke. "The exegesis of your report was necessary only for me. Perhaps I needed justification to act on something like this. You may have what you need. It is a worthy cause, and perhaps one that will further emphasise our intolerance to this wanton waste of human life, be it sati or thugee."

"I am grateful, your Excellency. You will not see me waver. Indeed I only feel stronger, for it has been a lonely crusade for some time now."

The Governor General smiled for the first time. "Well said my boy. But I have a word of caution for you. And I take the liberty of being rather personal here." He stood up and walked towards the stiff figure of Henry Sleeman. "I am informed that your young wife accompanies you to the camps in the forests and ravines where you hunt these monsters."

Sleeman reddened. How the devil did this information reach here? He remained silent.

"Only a word of caution, my boy. I leave this entirely to you. I am only concerned about the welfare of the courageous young lady. Would she not be safer at the garrison or one of our stations in the province?"

Sleeman nodded only because he felt he was expected to.

The Governor General returned to his high chair. "And may I ask again, who is this native informer who first revealed to you of this band of robbers?"

Sleeman hesitated. He stammered in embarrassment. "I have not seen him yet, sir. He sends information in messages through the dak-runners where such a service exists. His information sometimes arrives through strangers, even native children, who have so far not been able to give us a good description of the man." Sleeman wondered whether he sounded silly.

"And you trust this information?"

"Yes your Excellency. His information has always led to our apprehending of thugs. His messages are sometimes mysterious, almost cryptic. My *sepoys* have been tipped off by specially coloured kites flown by this informer right under the noses of thug groups to point at their location. I admit we have been on a strange and unconventional trail for many months."

He was not sure if the Governor General might begin to doubt his sanity, but Sleeman could not think of anything more insane than the truth of what he had been uncovering in the districts of the Central Provinces.

"We have even identified some of the powerful patrons of the thugs among native rulers. Just as there was a band of them sheltered at Srirangapatna many years ago when Tipu fell in the Mysore war. We could use some of the evidence as leverage against them," added Sleeman. "But some difficulty presents itself when many reside outside British jurisdiction."

"A native who will not venture forth to identify himself," the Governor General chuckled. "My good man, would it not be necessary at some point to check his antecedents? He must have a dubious existence himself to have access to this kind of information. What is your assessment of this native?"

"Your Excellency," Sleeman shuddered at the thought of having to mention it. "A month ago we were required to present ourselves in an area where our informer had lured three notorious thugs. The exact location where these men congregated was indicated to us by a red kite fluttering in the sky. We also found the men overpowered and bound." He paused now feeling a little abashed. "The letters and messages we receive are written in Hindi, and can be instantly identified among the mail by strange birds encrypted upon them, looks to me like the seagulls back home, drawn on the top of the paper. Sir, in answer to your question, I would say our man is an uncommonly strong and resourceful individual, who, though shy, is also perhaps as insidious, evasive and dangerous as the ancient cult he has made it his mission to destroy."

* * *

It was midday. The scent of jasmine lingered in the warm air. Salmi lay on her charpoy dreamy-eyed and weary, a gentle smile on her face. Her baby boy was born, alive and healthy, and lay beside her wrapped in a soft muslin cloth. She appeared to be sleeping.

John sat on his charpoy, leaning against the wall, his knees up, arms rested on them, his eyes closed. He appeared to be meditating. He was keenly listening to the muffled conversation of the women gathered outside beyond the granary.

The debate had been going on for an hour now. In the peculiar accent and dialect of the region. A hoarse voice was continually stating to the others that the child was a white child, white as those of the British and the Europeans. Not wheaty white as a fair Hindustani should look! But white like *chuna* with a tinge of *sindoor*. A shrill voice could be heard reminding them that the child was only just born. You could not judge a child who was only just born. You cannot judge a child who has come from God's lap! But who is judging the child, another intervened. We're judging the mother. Who are we to judge the mother? They are only pilgrims. They will be gone tomorrow. Oh no! They will not. The sin will be on our heads if we turn a new-born out before the completion of forty days. But they are the sinners, not us. Has the father looked at the child, one more intervened. Has the father looked at child's head? Can't he tell it is not his? Is he a fool? Don't you dare. He is of a high caste. Didn't we hear the *sarpanch* say so? But the child. God Forbid! The child looks like a mussalman, or a British. Have you informed the *sarpanch* of this yet? What are you waiting for girl? And let the curse of an innocent child fall upon my head? No, I shall say nothing of the kind. But the *panchayat* must know. The village elders will blame us for not informing them in time. The child's hair is yellow!

John decided it was time to act. He placed his feet on the floor and stood up as silently as he could. Salmi still appeared to be in the kind of trance only a new mother could be. Nothing appeared to be of any significance outside the invisible bubble that surrounded herself and child. He tiptoed out of the room and found his leather sandals outside. He strapped them on and casually walked around the granary.

On sighting him the huddle of women suddenly fell silent.

"I need some flowers to offer at the village temple," he told them. "Marigold flowers, because I have been blessed with a son. The baby is most certainly the reincarnation of my father. You see, he had yellow hair too."

The gathering recoiled slightly, trying to look unabashed.

The hoarse women found her voice. "Of course then you also need the priest," she suggested guiltily.

"That will not be necessary," John lied again. "I am a priest." He slipped his hand into his shirt and exposed a cotton string on the left shoulder. Then turning around, with the air of a happy father, he returned to the quarters where Salmi slept.

The shrill voice now took a higher pitch. "That's what you all deserve! To be cursed by a Brahmin and the reincarnation of his father! I told you not to judge the child! Yellow hair, green hair, what does it matter? They are pilgrims. And we of Laxmanghat are blessed that a Brahmin needs our help! For God's sake, find the marigold. The sarpanch will whip us for gossiping maliciously and throwing aspersions at the guests of this village."

Back on his charpoy, his eyes closed, John listened with a smile as the women arrived at a consensus.

A noble father. A beautiful child. Definitely an incarnation! A courageous wife to travel in this condition! Reminds me of Ram and Sita! Such a beautiful woman too!

Their voices faded away in search of the marigold flowers.

"Why are you smiling pardesi?" Salmi awoke and looked curiously at John. "Is everything alright?"

"Yes, everything is alright. I lied blatantly again," he laughed.

"But why are you laughing so strangely since you came in?"

"Oh, I am not laughing at you." He told her about the little encounter he had with the women outside. "You see, great children are born under great controversy."

"Is that so?" She looked over the tiny sleeping figure by her side then turned to John again. Her face was troubled. "I am sorry you need to lie to protect me."

"And the child," John reminded her. "The baby has brought us luck. You cannot be asked to leave the village for forty days. "We will be staying here for a while."

"*You* have brought us luck Pardesi," Salmi emphasised. Her eyes were filling with tears. "Whoever you are, you arrived on time as if on divine instruction." She began to cry. "For the dignity you bestow upon an innocent and helpless child, you will one day go to heaven."

It was a long time since anyone suggested he go in that direction. John shifted uncomfortably on the charpoy. In the folds of his robe, his hand touched a large silver coin slipped into the hem of a tenacious silk cloth. A girl's dupatta he had acquired many months ago. He could close his eyes, and still hear the girl sobbing. The silk felt cold. Cold like the death it administered when the cloth was cast and the coin landed cleverly on the Adam's apple of his victims.

* * *

The two men traveled mostly by horse and ferry arriving at Bhopal to begin an arduous journey over the Vindhya Range, an endeavor wrought with danger. Qodsiyya Begum, the regent of this kingdom now a British protectorate, had long given up policing the highways and ravines of this wild region and had welcomed the British efforts to quell the rise of dacoity and murders in the province. The school master was not easily daunted and the *kathputli* master admired his horsemanship.

"There are some perils one had best not know of," Nandakumar philosophized, as they took to the hills upon leaving the city. "There are innumerable hazards in these parts that one is better off not comprehending. If any one of them should befall us there is no escape anyway. It is best to remain oblivious and enjoy the view of the countryside, the mountains and the road before you. Otherwise the beauty and nicety of your journey is unnecessarily obliterated by fear. The stress and the gloom of an impending danger that one may never encounter, would far outweigh your need for a vacation."

They were now climbing along a winding section of the range that was deeply forested. The Englishman listened to the puppeteer with interest.

Nandakumar laughed and continued to talk. "You know masterji, I was enjoying a quiet swim in our ancestral home in my village in Malabar before I was carried away and locked in a dungeon in

Srirangapatna in the kingdom of Mysore by Tipu's men. I lay there on the floor of that crowded cell quite sure that I would be executed before the invading English forces reached the dungeons. To relieve myself from the terrible anxiety of a condemned prisoner, I played a game in my head. In my mind's eye I saw my executioner, but always as a puppet. And I imagined myself holding the strings. Every time he made an attempt to severe my head I would make him dance and hop about in the bumpiest fashion, that it quite reduced my anxiety."

It was the school master's turn to laugh. "You have not matured much since then I can see," he quipped, bringing back memories of their contentious puppet shows.

"Imagine my predicament," Nandakumar continued. "There I was, with a choice that was extremely difficult. To have my head severed for being a Nair or have my penis circumcised and become a Muslim. Tipu needed fresh soldiers, preferably those who embraced Islam." He laughed again. "Today I travel freely into more lands than Tipu could have ever done, dangling a puppet that bears his name and making him dance to my tune. I have my penis intact while Tipu has to entertain all and sundry without legs."

If they had not found and accompanied a well armed caravan bound for Godhra up in the precipitous slopes of the mountain range, the journey might have sprung a hazard or two of the kind Nandakumar had earlier philosophized. Further west was Baroda, a town swarming with the fiercest warriors they had encountered so far. "Another regent, another British protectorate," remarked Nandakumar. With long, well-groomed black hair under peaked helmets, tall, gaunt and extremely lithe, they were an alert and watchful militia. Only the sight of the *kathputli* master brought a few smiles of recognition. "Sayaji Rao Gaekwad, the regent and the English resident James Williams have both seen my performances", he declared proudly.

Jack Dawson made a few friends. One of the soldiers, noting his curiosity, offered him a peaked helmet which he gladly accepted.

"Now what on earth would you want a helmet for?" laughed Nandakumar. It however eased their march to Broach, as a number of very dependable soldiers rode in the same direction. They reached the old port city of Surat, the scene of the landing of the first Englishmen more than two hundred years ago to take a vessel bound south along the picturesque western coast of the peninsula.

While they travelled the many weeks over land, the regular frequency of those dreadful dreams that Dawson experienced at Saugor had ceased to some extent. The rigors of the journey exhausted him sufficiently each night and helped him sleep. But as they boarded the quaint Mughal merchant vessel in the harbour at Surat he began to dread the voyage by sea.

His apprehensions were well founded for on the very first night on the ship, the nightmares returned to haunt him. For much of the journey in those weeks at sea, the crew would know of this troubled *Angrez* who screamed and laughed in his sleep. Nandakumar was alarmed. If the crew believed he was possessed by some malevolent spirit they would perform a ritual killing to allay the demon, and respectfully throw the English school master's body overboard. It took great ingenuity and some unmentionable story telling by the master of *kathputli* to convince the superstitious sailors that all was well. And to keep the crew in good humor they even performed a kind of burlesque on a few occasions when the sea was calm, using coconuts wrapped in turbans as puppets.

The vessel kept a wide berth, steering many miles far out into sea as they passed the Portuguese port of Goa. The seas about here were often the lair of pirates, operating for and against the Portuguese – it was hard to tell who was friend or foe.

"People in Malabar know Goa only as the place where a great man named Kunjali Marakkar from my province and many others were treacherously killed by the Portuguese more than two hundred years ago. A fine place that little city," remarked Nandakumar. "Idyllic beaches like my home. I have seen Goa many years ago. A calm and soothing sea and a happy population nestled within an undulating land of plenty. Devilish food, expressive music and a fine place for a vacation if the Portuguese were to allow it."

Further south, they sailed into choppy seas. The crew looked vexed as the rafters of the vessel creeked, and the sails flapped violently.

"An early monsoon, by the look of it," remarked Nandakumar. It was only the middle of May. The South West monsoons that swept the sub-continent every year were normally expected by the end of the month. This was a time when the fishermen dare not venture into the sea for the storms that accompanied the first onslaught of the monsoons were legendary on this coast. "They call this the Arabian sea after the first and perhaps the most frequent traders in these waters. You know Masterji, we are now sailing by what was once the kingdom of Mysore, where Tipu thought he had me for ever. And this is my third visit home since the battle of Srirangapatna." Dawson noted that his voice was joyous. "In two days we will be on the shores of Malabar. We can make it yet ere the monsoon reaches the Mappila Bay. That is our destination."

* * *

George Preston hated travel in this strange land. But his careful enquiries at Cossipore and Bangbazaar had convinced him he was on the trail of a man who was deliberately keeping away from Bengal. Hugh Trenton had picked up several leads and addresses that could be followed up in search of the elusive Nasser. He would then have to unravel what exactly had happened to Hutchinson and to the cache of rubies. Exercising extreme discretion he found access to the East India Company records that contained mention of the Manar rubies. Its history, and the mysterious circumstances under which it might have changed hands and disappeared. The report was however inconclusive as he had expected. But both Trenton and he were now sure that such a treasure existed. Nasser had been right.

But Trenton had been reluctant to relinquish his position at the docks with the East India Company. So Preston was left with only the dockhand Bhim and his son to accompany him in his pursuits. Which was fortunate. The language and the style of speech of the natives seemed to vary so drastically with each district that he was only content to keep the father and son on a short leash. However, to appear benevolent he had advanced Bhim a generous purse to resign his post and join him. For he knew he could anyway rely on the Rajput, and the man's natural loyalty to authority would only be strengthened by such an act of generosity.

Their trail by boat and horseback led them from Dumdum, where Nasser was well known to Serampore, a Danish settlement where Nasser was last seen. From there the trail led them up the Ganges to Berhampore among the silk manufactory where Nasser had repeatedly traded. Further it led them to Peer Point where Nasser appeared to have been healing people and buying herbs. From Monghyr to Revelganj, from Meerganj to Hatimpore, the story was always the same. He traded and treated people. Everywhere they were told he was a respected man, a hakim, a generous soul. Preston now wondered about Trenton's insinuations about the old man. It just might be unfounded. Just a coincidence perhaps. What stops a generous hearted *mussalmaan* from making contributions to a Hindu temple? Even a Kali temple? After all in 1802 as a thanksgiving for the conclusion of the Treaty of Amiens between Britain and France an official government party had gone in procession with a military band to Kalighat and paid a substantial sum at the shrine. And on many occasions Preston had known of Christians and Mussalmans visiting the shrine out of curiosity and departing after making a contribution.

It was therefore with mixed feelings and an extremely short temper that Preston arrived at Gorakhpore.

Reade, the Collector of Gorakhpore was of some help. Some of his staff appeared to recognise the old trader after Bhim's detailed description of him in the local language, but they however appeared confused by his name.

This was when George Preston, for the first time, heard the name of Mohammed Mir Aleem, and his doubts about the old man were once again reinstated.

Their trail now lay on the long road to Narsinghpur.

* * *

"What are you writing Pardesi?" Salmi enquired.

It was their second week in the room beside the granary.

Salmi was attempting to suckle the infant in the manner the shrill woman had shown her. It involved so much of rapt focus and alignment to steer her pinched nipple into the small mouth that she wondered how she would manage the manoeuvre again when she needed to change hands to conduct him to the other breast. For all her effort, the baby would hardly suckle for a minute before falling asleep.

John was sure he could not be of any help. It staggered him to see how fortuitous and accidental, how wrought with peril the creation and nourishment of life was. Why was the taking of life so easy?

He sat on the charpoy, trying not to look at her, resting a sheet of paper on the bottom of a flat vessel. A bottle of ink stood precariously balanced on the wooden frame of the charpoy. He held his improvised bamboo stylus between his fingers. A smoky oil lamp hung between them, the acrid smell of which assailed his nostrils.

"I am writing a letter," John replied.

"To your mother?" She enquired, still focussed on her child.

John let his eyes wander fleetingly over her naked breasts. "She is dead."

"Oh, your father then,"

"He is gone too."

Salmi looked up at him. "My mother and father are gone too. I only have a…" she paused, looking troubled. "A brother, I have a brother somewhere."

"Somewhere?"

"It is a long story," Salmi's attention shifted to the baby again.

John resumed writing. And when he did, it transported him out of this inert world of jasmine and incense to a well-lit dining hall, where the only fumes that reached his nostrils were those of Lucy's French perfume. He wrote for half an hour in silence, during which time he presumed Salmi and the baby were asleep.

"Is she beautiful, pardesi?"

John was startled. He looked up from his writing.

"She must be," Salmi answered her own question. "You are not offended that I ask questions, are you?"

John shook his head.

"When somebody smiles through his troubles, I believe he must be in love. You smile so much."

John couldn't help another smile escape his lips. But this time it was more out of the endearing remarks of this hapless girl trying to feed her child.

"Look, my baby smiles too," she exclaimed. As she caressed the infant's forehead, she seemed to forget she was talking to John. She appeared to lose herself in her thoughts as she gazed upon the child's face.

"The baby loves you," John said. "Only you."

Salmi sighed. "If I had not made the mistakes I did, this child's life would have been easy and secure."

John remained silent.

"You don't ask me anything about myself. You don't want to know, do you?" She asked.

"Only that which you wish to tell me," John replied.

After a long pause she said, "My child's father is a British saheb. I thought he was kind to me, but now I understand he has deceived me. He ensnared me because I was innocent. The saheb had come to our village on some work. We did not know what. I worked at his bungalow. He loved the food I cooked. My brother Shambu was very angry when I told him I was pregnant with his child."

She stopped and looked keenly at John. "I can trust you can't I?"

"I cannot ask you to," John replied.

Salmi hesitated for a moment, then continued to speak. "I am greatly indebted to you. I cannot keep secrets from you even if they are inconsequential to you. But don't allow yourself to be burdened by them. It is just that I need to talk to someone."

John smiled and nodded to encourage her for whatever it was worth to him.

"My brother is a good man. After my parents died he worked hard to look after me. We had a house and some paddy fields. We owned cows too. My brother was kind. He allowed me to study. He always boasted that I could read and write better than our village sarpanch. Even my guruji often told me I was an exceptional child. Have you met a woman in these villages who can read and write? Not many will you see. Well, I can read and write. My brother was very troubled and was always scheming as to how he should punish this saheb for what he had done to me. So I ran away to save his honour, and lived among the wandering Ghonds. They were kind to me."

John stifled a yawn.

"But we heard a rumour that my saheb had been killed. I was never able to confirm this. But I feared greatly for my brother. There were soldiers searching for Shambu everywhere. Their leader, one British magistrate named Sulaiman even spoke to me."

"Sleeman," corrected John.

"Oh, do you know him?" Salmi looked apprehensive. John shook his head in denial and yawned again. "You know I still do sometimes feel you are an Englishman of some sort. Though you speak Hindustani very well and have black hair, you sometimes sound just like my saheb." Salmi looked at him keenly again. "But then how could you have become so dark?"

"And what did Sleeman say?" John asked, trying not to show his discomfort.

"He asked me to eat well for the baby's sake," Salmi replied.

John laughed. "Didn't he ask you about Shambu?"

"I am not sure if he made the connection between me and Shambu. I should think not. It was late in the night that he visited the Ghond tribe's camp in the forest with his *sepoys*. Shambu was absconding. Sleeman had already checked Bijaipura, my village."

John felt an uneasiness creep all over him.

"Bijaipura village? Is that where you belong, where you come from? What was the name of this British saheb, the father of your child?"

John was suddenly wide-awake, and Salmi looked at him curiously.

"The name of the child's father!" John repeated, a rising anxiety in his voice, but suddenly remembering that by the Hindu custom, a woman would not utter her husband's name. "You can tell me his name since you were never married to him. I want to know his name."

Salmi wondered why John was suddenly taking so much interest in her narrative. Bewildered, she replied "I think it was Achin or Hachin-Saheb, we called him," she struggled to pronounce the name.

"Hutchinson?" John asked.

"Yes," Salmi's eyes lit up momentarily. "Char-les Hutchinson."

John knocked the inkpot over. It did not shatter but left a dark blotch on the floor.

Salmi looked distraught. "I am sorry. Was he your friend? Did you know him? Please believe me when I say that Shambu did not kill him. He did mean to, but couldn't. I feel sure of that. My brother is innocent." She began to cry.

John tried to keep his composure. "Your brother is indeed innocent. I am sure of that too. So stop crying. All will be well. Try and sleep."

He folded the letter he had been writing to Lucy and slipped it into an envelope. His hands trembled. Salmi lay back on her charpoy, looking exhausted and confused.

And all the while John could not take his eyes off the little baby with the golden hair.

"Was there something in my story that bothered you?" Salmi asked, covering the baby and herself with a sheet.

"No," lied John, as he lowered the wick of the oil lamp in preparation to sleep. "Someday, perhaps, I'll tell you mine."

* * *

"I have spoken at any length to only three Malabarees in your village, but have already received seven opinions," exclaimed Dawson in an exasperated voice. "Besides, I have four posers, two wagers, outright disrespect from one, and another who swears my point of view is gospel truth. Nandu, doesn't a soul speak Hindustani here?"

"Malayalees, not Malabarees, Masterji," corrected Nandakumar, who was everything a translator, an interpreter and an arbitrator could be to the interested English school master as equally as he was to an extremely engrossed group of Nairs. "Meaning, a community of people who speak the language Malayalam. By nature people here are fond of tossing an issue or a problem about in their heads to arrive at various options and opinions. You will even find many who answer your question by countering yours with another question. There is an entire range of mutual Malayali communication possible by the mere shaking of the head."

On his impromptu vacation at Nandakumar's village, the English school master found the language and the mannerism of the people incomprehensible. It bore no resemblance to the languages of the north which he had begun to become accustomed to at Saugor.

They were standing outside Nandakumar's *tharavad*, or ancestral home, a rambling baroque structure of red laterite bricks with innumerable exquisitely finished teak-wood pillars all around. In the centre of this sprawling structure was a courtyard the corridors of which were adorned with heavy bronze and brass lamps. Some of the lethal weapons that the Nairs carried lined the walls of the inner walkways.

Nandakumar's father who was once incarcerated at Srirangapatna was now a frail old man, who did not speak much. Both his uncles had died over the years. Nandakumar knew he would now have to take charge of the family and the *tharavad.* In the crisis wrought by Hyder and Tipu's invasion of a few decades ago, very few female members of his family had survived. A tolerant English administration was now in loose control of the region, and he knew the future would be a period to rebuild and consolidate the Nair community once again.

Dawson noted that they were a well-built and energetic people high up in the feudal hierarchy of the land. They were meticulous in their physical fitness regime, personal hygiene and religious rituals. They favoured loose white cotton cloth for garments in the humid climate of the province and the men carried their weapons with dignity.

Today, three days since their arrival at Cannanore, Nandakumar took it upon himself to conduct the necessary introductions. Many family members as well as other Nairs were arriving to greet their hero of Srirangapatna; and Nandakumar took pains to explain to them the English school master's gymnastic abilities, his expertise in music and theatre, as well as his need for a vacation.

It was on the fifth day of their stay at the *tharavad,* and after much anticipation, that there arrived two men, younger cousins of Nandakumar. They rode ponies, carried weapons and sported thick moustaches. "Kannan and Unni, my brothers," introduced Nandakumar. "They are from the Kadattanad region and champions of many *angams*, duels or challenges you might call it."

As the two men were introduced to the English school master, a faint smile materialized on Kannan's face. "Happy to have you as our guest, sir," he uttered in the English language. A hand was extended in English style, holding Dawson's in a firm handshake.

Dawson recoiled in shock. He had been managing in meager Hindustani with the *kathputli* master for over a year and a half, and in a land that spoke the most complicated and bizarre language, the sound of King George's language, albeit with a strange accent, was like music to the ears. Even Nandakumar looked a little taken aback.

"I am a friend of the English stationed at Thalassery Fort at Thiruvallapad, and also of the officers at St. Angelos Fort and the new cantonment at Cannanore," Kannan declared. "I have taken to the language with as much dedication as I favour my *kalari.*"

"And what is that?" queried Dawson quickly embracing the immediacy and advantage of language that Kannan offered.

"*Kalari payyatu*, sir. Our art of fighting. I gather from my brother that you are quite a gymnast yourself."

"But not in the style suited for combat," answered the school teacher.

Nandakumar discussed at length with the two warriors in Malayalam. When he was satisfied he turned to Dawson and spoke in a solemn tone. "At sunrise you will accompany my brothers to the *kalari*. This is not a regular *kalari* that most traditional Nairs would go to for martial training. It is a strange place. The *kalari* of a rebel among us. But a revered man. I am glad you have somebody who speaks to you in your language. Go in there with reverence and respect, and follow meticulously the traditions and techniques of the elders. Learn to keep vows and secrets, for it is a rare request that has been conceded to today. No foreigner has to date stepped into a Nair *kalari*. And this particular *kalari* is to a Nair what Mecca is to a Mappilla. But I have made the necessary arrangements. Choose for yourself how long you wish to stay in Malabar." He broke into a smile. "When you are done, show me a leap or two that you will learn there. Then the antics I employ in my puppetry would have been justified."

"I have in my possession a helmet I acquired at Baroda in case I land on my head," Dawson countered, grateful to his friend, the guru of *kathputli*, for having kept his word.

* * *

Cornwall to Calcutta. The memories of a different identity, that of the Englishman John Penmarric, lingered behind a kind of gossamer web in his mind. And behind this thin curtain he knew, lay ignominy and shame. Of having departed from honourable and virtuous friends at the Sailor's Bell. Of having allowed himself to be drawn by the gaudy vulgarity of London. The memories of the treachery of his employers at the yard. The bribery, the questionable trial following Bob Pendarrow's arrest. John had become bitter with the society he lived in and perambulated about. A race he wished he did not belong to.

And finally, Bob's execution had put him in an abyss of gloom. For a while all hope had fled, and despair had seized and benumbed him. His brain reeled under the confusion of what was right and wrong. Myriad thoughts crowded into his mind. He could not find a premise to start his life again. Not even with Lucy, who was at this time his only solace. At least not until he had repaid Bob in some way. Vainly striving to collect his wandering senses and indulging in vain regrets, he discovered that only anger now sustained him. An anger at his own inability to have saved Bob's life in some way. A kind of burning fever had possessed him for sometime as he took leave of a deeply troubled Lucy to sail for Hindustan.

On the vessel, every faculty of his mind was crying out for revenge. The memory of Bob's mockery of a trial, the planted jury, and the hasty sentence sickened him. It took months of the incarceration out at sea to calm him down. He found every man and woman on the ship repugnant and avoided their crass attempts at humour and social niceties. If they despised him for it he didn't care or take notice. His resolution of revenge now gave him the desire to live for it. He was here for Hutchinson and Preston. And one day, if he could, to expose the jury that sentenced Bob. He existed, but no more.

Calcutta had bewildered him as much as London on his arrival there. A nettle of masts and sails. An overwhelming aroma of spices and sweating natives, a mass of frantic brown bodies in turbans and sagging white cloth clumsily bundled about their loins scurrying among heaps of sacks, bales and boxes of all descriptions. There were native soldiers in uniform and English officers shouting out orders. Beyond was the city where women in saris and gold jewellery, holy men in saffron, and muslim traders in long robes and turbans swarmed. From the frying pan into the fire, thought John.

His thoughts were confirmed only too suddenly when, having barely set foot on land, he spotted at the end of the pier four men, two of whom he recognised instantly. Hutchinson and Preston stood talking animatedly with two natives. One, bearded and dignified, appeared to be an elderly merchant, if John's imagination of a Hindustani trader served him well. The other had his back turned towards him. It also surprised him that the crisis of his fate had dispelled all his dread of the duo. For he felt none of those debilitating sensations associated with fear. It only required opportunity. A calculated hunt, before he saw the demise of the two men. For a moment, he wished he had some divine ability to rush into them and toss them into the bay. If he had been carrying a firearm he would most certainly have shot them down like animals ere he went a step further into this strange land.

He had more surprises in store for him. The white man in Calcutta he realised dwelt apart from the natives in clearly demarcated wards of the city. Unlike London, Englishmen here greeted one another even if he was a stranger. He shook hands or waved, and bowed or doffed his hat at the sight of ladies. It became clear to John. In Calcutta, an Englishman noticed another Englishman, and a newcomer was somehow always recognised as such. John stayed at a working class hotel under an assumed name, but found his fellow lodgers too intrusive. In the dining room questions were often asked as to how he happened to come by these shores and who his employers were.

Soon he realised that Calcutta did not offer a secure hiding place to plot the destruction of the enemy. Unwittingly, he was living a life not very different from the London fugitive that he had been since his misfortunes commenced. Once again he found himself stepping out of his rooms only after dusk, hiding from the society he thought he had left behind. How he wished he could lose himself among the natives who were so varied and numerous. Not to speak of the Chinese, the Armenians and the Africans that coloured the streets of Calcutta. Only, he felt his problems would be compounded by his total incomprehension of the Hindustani culture and the language of the natives.

It was therefore with an extreme sense of discomfort and caution that he roamed the bazaars that lay outside the English wards and cantonments. But native faces always stared at him. It was unusual to see a well-dressed Englishman walk. Especially a civilian. They would watch in horror or amusement as he tried to negotiate his way around puddles and heaps of dung and slush. He was not sure if all this was causing him to become something of a spectacle, something he did not wish for. On at least two occasions *sepoys* from the cantonment had ridden up to him and offered him their horse. But he had declined and trudged on. On another occasion an English officer on seeing him had inquired, "Pardon my inquisitiveness, but are you lost, sir?"

John shook his head and tried to look nonchalant.

"It isn't the time of day for us to be seen on foot and without our retainers in these bazaars sir." The officer continued, "We would like to avoid an incident involving an Englishman if we can. I hope you get my meaning? Would you like an escort?"

John shook his head again, "Thank you, my good man. My servants will shortly join me and we will be on our way. I am grateful for your concern."

"I speak only for your security," the officer remarked as he rode away. But John sensed an annoyance in the officer's voice for it also appeared to John that the soldier was upset by the indignity of having to see a white man hob-nobbing in a native bazaar on foot bereft of guards and escorts, or at least a few servants in tow.

He perceived an element of truth in what the officer had advised, for often among the native faces that stared at him in puzzlement, a few looked extremely hostile for reasons he could not comprehend. He now decided to take a coach or a *cranchee* and be seen in a different part of Calcutta each evening while he idled here. He would sometimes take a boat up and down the Hoogly River, relieved to be afloat and away from the prying eyes of his countrymen. He found strange relief in the haunting strains of the melodious minstrels, clothed in saffron cloth, whose music played on a single-stringed instrument, could be heard across the waters of the Hoogly. But his mind could not fix upon a plan, and every night he reached his rooms he would eat alone, sitting by an open window overlooking this curious city. He tried contemplating his next move. A solution to his fate however eluded him for over two weeks.

One evening he found himself in the crowded and noisy concourse of Kalighat, the ancient pathway to Bengal's most famous Kali temple. There were no Englishmen about, but for a few company *sepoys* occasionally patrolling the area. About him pilgrims headed for the temple thronged the streets. He was caught up in an unceasing din of emaciated sadhus in saffron chanting, beggars of all description pleading and deformed children wailing for alms. Bells adorning elephants, bulls and goats chimed along with the jingling of bangles and jewellery. Drums reverberated constantly as people prayed, chanted, shouted and sang fervently in an unending stream leading to the temple. He was jostled forward by the blind and the hurrying, and the air grew thick with the sweet scent of incense and flowers.

And as he stumbled forward, he thought he heard the word "Halleluiah" rise above the din. Perplexed, he looked about him, but all around swarmed a sea of native humanity.

"Halleluiah! Halleluiah!" the voice rose again.

Peering about him in the light of numerous lamps being carried by the pilgrims he spotted the figure of a lone Christian missionary, Bible in hand, reading aloud and headed for the temple.

Curiosity and amusement compelled John to jostle his way through the moving crowd to try and reach the only other white man he saw. Though he could scarcely believe it, there he was, a bearded missionary, habit, rosary, crucifix and all, his Bible held open, marching resolutely to the temple of Goddess Kali.

He would have reached by Father Sebastian's side that evening if he had continued to push his way through the crowd except perhaps because the time was now ripe for John Penmarric to meet his destiny.

For the rest of his life John never ceased to wonder at the power that predetermines the course of events in one's life.

There was a commotion, which caused the crowd to heave and rush towards him as if they were trying to avoid something. John nearly fell backwards, and for a moment lost sight of the priest. When he located the man again, he was aghast to see at least five natives, staves in hand, threatening the missionary. The priest looked resolute, continuing to read aloud from his Bible, ignoring his tormentors and still trying to make his way forward towards the temple. The men were pleading for him to stop but the self-possessed missionary kept going. Then one of them appeared to have struck him, for John saw the preacher pitch forward, stumble and fall.

"The fool," thought John Penmarric, "that utmost, profound fool! He's going to be stampeded to death!"

John tried to push through the crowd to reach the priest just as three mounted *sepoys* of the East India Company broke into the mass of pilgrims. He felt relieved to hear the priest's loud voice again as the *sepoys* reached out to rescue him. "Heathens! Give up this pagan banshee! Our father in heaven is forgiving. Halleluiah! Halleluiah!"

At the sight of the *sepoys*, the men waving sticks and staves instantly melted into the crowd. The noisy procession of the pilgrims to the temple continued as if nothing had occurred.

Then there was a cry of, "*Aar ekta belaiti*!" (Another foreigner!) from a man who suddenly materialized from the multitude. A man, who for some reason, looked very familiar to him. He had a hideous bearded face, long hair, a black turban and a bright red tunic. John had little time to think for the men with sticks in their hands suddenly reappeared, their heads and necks craning in the crowd, trying to locate the foreigner.

"*Eidikay! eidikay!* (This way!) *firengee eidikay gelo*!" (The foreigner went this way!) the pilgrims shouted as John watched the men jostling the throng to try and reach him.

Once again, the state of his own mind surprised John. He felt no fear. It appeared to him for a moment that he was waiting for them to come upon him so that he could bludgeon them with their own clubs. He clenched his fists and marched on, expecting them to reach him somewhere down the concourse.

"That would be suicidal!"

A gentle voice beside him spoke in English. John turned to see an elderly native with a red smear anointed on his forehead, walking beside him. "Come my son, I am a priest of this temple." He held John's arm firmly. "We will live to fight another day. You are not safe here now."

For a moment, John hesitated. Then he relented as the old man quickly led him to the edge of the crowd. They passed through a doorway on the side of the street, which the man locked behind him.

The old man wore a shawl over his bare body, which hung about him like a Roman toga. Below his waist he was wrapped in a white *dhoti*, and stood in the centre of a sparsely furnished room in his bare feet, smiling beatifically at John. In one corner of the room, on a pedestal, stood a small black statue of a naked female form, with ferocious painted eyes and a long red tongue. He understood Father Sebastian's revulsion. It was a spectre of all that was diabolic and ghoulish. The eyes seemed to beckon him, the hungry mouth seemed to laugh. John blinked, suddenly remembering that this was the old priest's Goddess. As a mark of respect, John quickly relinquished his shoes at the opposite corner of the room.

"You speak English well" John remarked, opening a conversation awkwardly.

"Perhaps not as well as those whose mother tongue it is," the man replied. "But son, you were very brave tonight! And extremely foolish!"

"Not as foolish as that Catholic priest," John pointed out, and they both laughed.

"Oh, that was Father Sebastian of St. John's Church," the Hindu priest explained. "A very pious, but extremely zealous man. I have often tried to dissuade him but he comes back here again and again."

"You sound quite tolerant about the whole issue!" John remarked.

"I only fear for his safety," the priest replied. "There are fanatics among us too. If he starts a riot, I am unable to predict what the mob might do. The Calcutta mob is a kind of diabolic phenomenon you will never come by in this whole wide world. But come now, do be seated. We will wait the hour till the crowds have reached the temple, and then perhaps you may safely return whence you came from." He peered at John closely in the light of the oil-lamp. "Son, you have the lines, the countenance of an angry man. A very angry man. Are you in pain or some kind of trouble?"

"I have not rested in a long time," John sighed, finding the words lucidly slipping forth before this strange priest as if they had been waiting to be unburdened. "I am committed to a mission that I cannot rest till I see completed. I have neither the resources, nor a safe place to launch my crusade. Yet so consuming has been my need to see justice done, that I will hazard anything to accomplish what I have undertaken."

John blinked in disbelief at his own revelation. He realised how long it had been since he had spoken to a friendly human being.

"Kali Ma would not put a wish in your heart without also giving you the power to accomplish it," the priest said. "You are perhaps not prepared to play the role yet. And that is what is causing your torment. A fish must wait to be reincarnated before his wish to fly like a bird is fulfilled."

"I want to be a Hindu," John interrupted suddenly, almost unthinkingly.

The priest turned to look at him, amused and smiling. "We are all Hindus, my son, just as we are born, knowing only life. This cosmos, this universe, nature, the animals, you, me. Everything is Hindu. You can't help but be it."

John looked at the old man in confusion.

"Hinduism is not a religion," the priest continued. "It is a way of life. Its teaching, in its essence, only requires you to live in harmony with your environment. What to eat, when to fast, how to live, whom to respect. Its essence is often lost in the ritual and the lifestyle of its adherents. If you shed all the idols and dogma that has attached itself to it, you will see a naked and pure human entity. Like Adam. I have often tried to impress upon these youths that you saw today, those young men with sticks who threatened the priest, that they ought to be tolerant about Father Sebastian. They are, if you understand my meaning, essentially assaulting another Hindu every time they strike him."

John shifted about impatiently. "My meaning was that I want to be like an Indian. Dress like a native, and live among the natives."

There was a loud thumping at the door. The old man looked at John. "They have seen you enter this doorway. They think you are one of Father Sebastian's flock. I can see that God favours you more than he does Father Sebastian."

John again looked confused. The old priest smiled. "You see, your wishes are fulfilled by the very force of your circumstances. Come, they will not dare to break down my door, but will continue to make a nuisance of themselves by knocking and thumping for a long time now. In the meanwhile you will undress and let me look for some of our native clothes to put on you. That way you can slip out of the back door unnoticed and be gone. Hai Kali Ma, you must have heard this young Englishman's strange wish, that you grant it so instantly!"

The old priest opened a wooden chest and delved into it for sometime. After some hesitation, he produced a cloth bundle containing a set of neatly folded and well preserved clothes. "My name is Veeru. Veeru Mahasaya they called me many years ago. These belonged to me before I changed my vocation and became a priest," he told John.

John undid the knots and pulled out what looked like a long night-shirt or robe dyed in bright colours, and a pair of loose trousers.

"Tell me if I do not wear it right," he requested of the priest.

While he undressed, the thumping on the door continued, but it became less insistent.

"They have enough respect for me to keep my door intact," the old man reassured him. "Only, I will have to think up some convincing explanation for your visit here."

John undressed and pulled on the baggy trousers. Next he slipped on the exotic shirt, marvelling at the intricately woven black and grey in it. He then pulled out an extremely long piece of black cloth.

"That is a turban," the priest explained, smiling. "Come, let me show you how it is tied."

This was a difficult task, as the thumping at the door constantly distracted him.

The priest withdrew another length of cloth. "This is a cummerbund," he told John as he helped the young man wind the piece around his waist.

"And how might I wear this?" John enquired, picking up a length of silk, with a large knot tied tightly to the end of it.

"This will not be of use to you yet," the old man replied, momentarily distracted. He stopped smiling. "I should have thrown this into the Hoogly a long time ago. In the hands of one as troubled and angry as you, I cannot imagine its portent!"

"But what is it?" John asked in curiosity, holding it aloft.

The thumping on the door continued unabatedly. The old man appeared not to hear it as he looked over John with curiosity and awe. "How you have transformed," he exclaimed, almost in a whisper, as one who was speaking to himself. He stepped back to allow the light of the lamp to fall on the Englishman. He frowned, and looked pained as he whispered, "It was all so long ago, but I now see for myself the final spectre each of the dying beheld!"

"Who? What?" John frowned at the old man in confusion.

"Son, what you hold in your hand is a *ruhmal*. It is, by translation, only a handkerchief or a scarf. Sadly, even its description, which is so simplistic, is deceptive. Some day, I will tell you all. God knows I have waited long enough to unburden its tale. But for now, leave it aside, and be gone. As for your mission, whatever it might be, whose undertaking is causing you so much heartache, give yourself some time. Go out into this great country. Go on a pilgrimage. Give yourself some more time and listen to your heart. Weigh the right and the wrong. Give ear, for an inner voice will speak to you when you are ready to comprehend. In time you will find yourself sufficiently equipped to play the role your life was intended to, and you will cease to feel daunted. For now, divert your anger to a just cause."

John nodded. "For I am the fish who cannot wait to become that bird you speak of. And then I will fly. Fly in triumphant arches, like a seagull."

The priest looked at John thoughtfully for a long while.

"It is some strange destiny that has brought you here," he finally said. He held his hand over his heart. "Give this old man a little time to get to know you, son. He is not yet fully wise to the will and the ways of Kali Ma, in whose name there has been a grave miscarriage of justice for more than a thousand years. Perhaps the time has finally come for which I have prayed all these years. The time for retribution. The time to undo a great wrong. Perhaps I will be able to direct your passion for justice to a greater and more fulfilling end than you have ever imagined."

John left the Hindu priest's rooms by the back door, elated. He did not notice the priest immediately bowing and prostrating before the idol of his goddess, and whispering, "Ma, has the time finally arrived? If it is your will, then I am ready."

John retraced his steps out of the temple complex determined to visit the old man often enough to learn how to begin his intercourse with the native life of this strange sub-continent.

And it would be a long time before he saw Father Sebastian again.

* * *

What little John learnt and believed to be Hindustani, his first words in the native language were essentially Bengali, the language of the region around Calcutta, called Bengal. It was only when he joined a caravan travelling into the heart of the country that he found himself among the people who spoke the commonly understood lingua franca of the land, a kind of colloquial Hindi enriched by local words picked off the prevalent languages of the various provinces. He realised that the best way to learn a language was to be left with no choice but to learn it. He was a quick learner and understood how culture, customs and beliefs changed the nuance of the language. Within the year, he was able to joke, curse and even quote a few proverbs and meaningful verses. He grew accustomed to the food and the curious practices of the various religions. On those rare occasions when his foreign character was recognized, he never denied the fact that he was an Englishman even though it aroused curiosity, and sometimes suspicion. But mostly the revelation was met with a great deal of respect. He stuck for a year to a simple explanation when asked what he was doing. He was nobody. He had nobody. He was unemployed. He was on an expedition as he wished to see this great country of Hindustan. The truth was the easiest thing to say.

John had a sizeable purse on his arrival at Calcutta, and it sustained him through the first year. He grew swarthy and let his beard grow in the fashion of many a native. And with his natural black hair, he felt an empathy with the soil he walked on. Only a few who knew his antecedents continued to call him *Firengee*, meaning a foreigner.

In the years that followed he made no long term friend or enemy. Just acquaintances and fellow travellers. At most times he found himself completely alone. Sometimes accompanying a caravan of laden horses and camels, he kept abreast with the trade, the merchandise and the goings-on in the various provinces he travelled through.

The heart of Hindustan, where the priest of Kalighat required him to go was in a state of indescribable confusion. A plateau the size of Germany, France and Portugal, a land of mighty rivers, hot rocky flats, thick steamy forests and ravines, the region was once ruled by the Mughal governors of the Deccan. With the diminishing power of the Muslim rulers, the warrior clans of Rajputana, of Samurai-like valour, known as the Rajputs, had conquered the region. Over time the Rajput chiefs were overrun by another powerful Hindu confederacy from the west, the Marathas, who though not very united amongst themselves, lay claim piecemeal to much of the areas of Central India.

A history of merciless savagery that nearly depopulated the land now became the ideal breeding ground that spawned a new scourge, Pindaris.

The Pindaris were loose bands of mercenaries owing no allegiance either to a ruler or a religion. They were Pathan and Hindustani men of arms who served those who paid them best. They sometimes served a predatory Maratha chief, or on their own, lived solely dependent on plunder. Every year as the rains came to an end, groups of marauders wrought unimaginable chaos and lawlessness. Their instances of murder, pillage and rape soon brought them into conflict with the English East India Company's forces.

The East India Company's forces routed the Pindaris with the same ferocity the mercenaries had subjected the populace to for over a decade. Beheading them on the highways, and leaving their heads on a spike to serve as a warning, handing a captured and sometimes injured gang member over to the community or village whom he had pillaged and raped, or simply blowing them from guns without a trial, were just some of the methods employed. The last, though painless to the criminal, was terrible to the beholder, and soon the scourge began to ebb.

In a land where one did not dare venture for water to the village well alone, where one tilled the land with armed guards and never took a highway for fear of having one's clothes torn off or even killed for two dry *rotis* in one's possession, the excesses committed by the English forces were welcome. It was well directed and effective, and peace was soon established. Peasants reappeared in thousands like ants come out of the earth, to claim and till a soil that had been fallow for two decades. Commerce increased as a natural consequence. John roved and travelled through much of this human drama enacted in the Central Provinces, aware of both the luxury and the risk of being unattached and without moorings in a savage and beautiful land. A mute witness to the throes of a society caught up in rapid change.

But despite the apparent peace that settled upon the country, a lurking fear, and a mystery that predated the worst wars, still haunted the heart of the native traveller for his path was beset with a sinister and indescribable peril that neither he nor the English fully understood. However fearsome, it was possible to comprehend a known enemy. In the days of the Pindari, many a village watched gaunt, hard-looking men come riding across the fields on camels and horses, swords drawn, with their matchlocks and water-skins slung beside them. Despite their ferocity, it was possible to comprehend the visible enemy. But the mysterious disappearances of neighbours, friends, relatives and associates coupled with extravagant rumours of a terrible secret society of ritual murderers left the populace extremely confused.

It was about now that John began slowly penetrating the heartland of this sinister society. With detailed instructions from his native mentor at Kalighat, the years spent in acquainting himself with the various bands that operated on the plateau were not wasted. He understood their alternative methods of communication apart from their secret jargon and slang. He learnt to mimic their subtle greetings to one another and imitated their covert signs of caution, signals for help, and their curious direction indications on paths and trails. As he entered fresh territories, the symbolic language varied minutely, but he was amazed at the rich content of their semiotics that must have been honed over generations of murder and deception. Some gangs were even adept at using drum-beats and messages of knotted strings to communicate over distance their sinister notes of warning and requests for help.

He fell foul of many bands whom he befriended but whose expeditions he refused to be party to, despite a normally acceptable explanation: He had vowed to Bhawani not to seek *bunij* until he had completed a forty day period of prayers following his last killing. This was a ritual observed by the older *phansigars* for generations, but scoffed by the young thugs of today. Something even the priest of Kalighat had not prepared him for.

"This is your only means of deliverance," Veeru Mahasaya had warned. "Or you will find yourself party to the very evil you have set your heart to destroy."

Yet there it was. A rebellious generation gap even among the most depraved murderers that walked the earth.

One day, about four years since his sojourn into Hindustan, he stood watching a stream of refugees escaping the English army who had forayed into their region in pursuit of a few mutineers in their native ranks. A deluge of villagers, tradesmen and their families, the old and the injured swarmed into the town of Sheopur. Some of them spoke to him in the local language of the province, which he scarcely understood. Others spoke in Hindustani, relating the devastation the East India Company's army had caused in the district. Even as he spoke to them at great length, he was plainly able to see that they had not realised he was of the same race as the enemy. The transformation must have been complete a long time before he realised it, but the Englishman, John Penmarric, had finally faded away into a temporary oblivion.

That same human migration also saw the arrival of three men who would soon affect another great change in John's life. Three men, who, amongst themselves spoke a cryptic language that, every time he heard it, raised his hackles. Ramasee.

Refugees converged into the town setting up shelters wherever they could find a patch of bare land to pitch a tent or construct a hovel. Their tales of woe, both truth and exaggeration, could be heard throughout the town, sending a wave of panic and consternation among the local residents. That evening John was seated on a circular brick platform built under a tree, disinterestedly listening to a group tell the story of how a cannon shot had landed in their village causing them to pack and leave in haste. There was a ludicrous discrepancy as to where exactly the cannon ball actually landed, as each man or woman related the story. John let his eyes wander to three men who had just arrived and seated themselves on the platform behind the tree. They spoke Hindustani with a smattering of Urdu thrown in, from which he gathered they were perhaps all Muslims. But occasionally they would address each other in Ramasee. They were in the guise of some small-time tradesmen, and John might not have cared for their conversation, had it not been for a single word articulated that caught his attention.

"Hutchinson."

Had it been uttered louder, he might have been sure. So he turned away and closed his eyes to allow his ears to follow the conversation again in the cryptic tongue. One of the men uttered the name again, and again he was unsure. In his disbelief, he tried to think of words, in the dialects he had learnt, that might be mistaken for what he had just heard.

When it was spoken one last time, "Hutchinson sahib", he was sure he had heard right. But were they speaking of the same pier master? The name was not uncommon among the English. And yet it set him wondering. Hoping.

For the next two days he would keep the three men within his range of vision, trying not to look directly at them. If they wandered about, he wandered too. Mingling in the confusion that the refugees caused about the town, he watched them from dawn to dusk, always wary, trying to detect any indications that might suggest that they were about to depart. On the evening of the second day, the eldest of the three suddenly walked through the crowd up to John and enquired in Hindustani, "Would you be kind enough to give me the direction to Bijaipura village? I have some medicines to deliver there."

If he was startled John did not show it. But with this man up close to him, his doubts were more or less confirmed. A vivid memory jogged his mind. This elderly trader with the grey beard was perhaps the same man he had seen on the pier along with Hutchinson, Preston and another native within the hour of setting foot in Calcutta. He politely gave directions as best as he could to the old medicine vendor. But as he mounted his horse the following morning, John saw them in the company of three more traders, their horses and camels heavily laden with merchandise. He followed the six men out of the town, keeping a safe distance, often losing total sight of them, but secure in the knowledge that his extreme discretion would not cause them to ever disappear completely.

Their intended destination appeared most certainly to be the village of Bijaipura for they took the road as John had directed the old man.

They rode leisurely for some hours until the sun rose high in the sky. At noon they skirted a forest where the sound of a *dhol* constantly reverberated through the trees in the still hot air. John had seen such nomadic tribes before and knew they kept wild animals away by the constant beating of their drums. In the queer social structure of the land it also served as a kind of warning to the higher caste natives who avoided them as untouchables.

In the afternoon, the party stopped outside the village of Bijaipura. It was a quiet place with paddy fields all around and a number of cattle lazily grazing beneath a few barren hills. Only the grey-bearded elderly medicine vendor appeared to have an errand in the village. The others waited outside on the road. The medicine vendor rode on the path that separated the rows of small houses and thatched dwellings with dung cakes drying on its walls. There were a few people about. He approached a large house set apart from the village and dismounted. John sat on his horse at the edge of the forest and watched.

A door opened, and John saw a man step out to greet the old man. The trader was bowing respectfully while the man of the house spoke to him, with some gesticulation of his hands. But he stood well within the dark shadow of the roof, which covered his face and shoulders. John squirmed from his hiding place beside a wellspring at the edge of the forest to try and recognise the man. The shadow appeared to be clothed in the fashion of an Englishman.

For an agonising half an hour the two remained in conversation while John hoped in vain for the resident of the house to show himself. Then the old trader mounted his horse again, riding back through the village to rejoin his party of merchants.

It was only when the riders had left on the road leading further from the village that John spied the Englishman again. This time the man stepped out of the house onto the grounds of a fenced-in compound. The sun was high overhead, and in an instant he saw the unmistakable blond head and protruding jaw.

Hutchinson, at last! And the long suppressed anger, the consuming rage he had felt more than four years ago welled up, sending shudders through his body. He withdrew into the forest leading his horse, determined not to let this opportunity go by…

It was late in the evening when he returned to the forest edge overlooking the village. A strong breeze blew from the paddy fields before him, undoing an end of his defiant turban. Somehow he never seemed to get that one item of native clothing right. He noted that the moon was up early and he could see the light of a few lamps in the huts below.

Then John thought he heard a singular voice in the night air, spoken in a soothing feminine voice that blended so subtly with the wind that he could not discern if it was, after all, only the breeze. While he strained his ears to listen to it he was still unsure of the direction from where it emanated. Yet it caused his horse to rear and kick, as if some spirit in the forest was close at hand.

A dog howled somewhere in the night as if in an attempt to harmonize with the high pitched singing of minstrels he could hear in the distance.

Listen to my tune, I have been singing since you were born
Your lives are all entwined and your fate was cast afore
You think you do as you had wished, waking up each morn
What has to come, what has to pass, was decided long ago

The sound of a couple of startled partridges caused him to withdraw into the shadows again. The night was bright and he detected a movement, not far to his left, where he had seen a spring dribble out of the slope earlier that day. There stood a villager apparently filling water, and flailing the air with some sort of club or cudgel. He might well have been trying to strike at some insects or a night fly. John waited, hoping the man would depart soon. But the man had dropped the club and was now drinking from a small pot. Even at this distance the crisp night air carried the smell of the *mohwa* he was consuming.

The lamps of the village went out one by one as the hour wore on. Only one light flickered in the darkness. Soon the man left the well spring carrying the water vessels towards the village. The night air still reverberated with the sound of the *dhol* coming from the nomad camp in the forest. The dog howled again in the wind.

John now walked his horse out of the forest and tethered it to a tree near the spring. Except for the wail of an infant, the village slept soundly. He sat down on the grass and decided to wait till it was past midnight before he made his move.

As he waited in the darkness he could not fathom why his mind suddenly dwelt on his dear friend Veeru Mahasaya, the priest of Kalighat. He could not keep the old man out of his thoughts for some disturbing moments. John drank some cool refreshing water from the wellspring and filled his water skin.

The moon was well past its zenith when John descended on foot to the path leading into the village. He walked stealthily between the rows of houses till he arrived at the large house Hutchinson occupied.

The sight of the front door lying ajar, through which the light of a lamp streamed out, made him squat instantly behind a thorny stockade. He could hear voices. He peered over the fence at the doorway again. A cloth bundle lay on the verandah. He could now unmistakably hear Hutchinson's voice. He felt the warm surge of adrenaline. It made his palms sweat. He wiped them with the loose end of his turban before securing it into place. The other voice, that of a young woman, was crying. He pushed the small bamboo gate open and stepped warily up to the wall of the house. Keeping to the shadows, he made his way around the bungalow till he reached an overgrown flower-bed below the window through which he had seen the light flickering from the forest.

The mournful howl of a dog pierced the night.

The voices were more discernible now. Hutchinson was verbally abusing the girl in English, using some of London's choicest invectives and slander, followed by jeering laughter. He sounded drunk. The girl, confused by his incomprehensible gibe in a foreign language, continued to cry. John wanted to peek through the open window to see a face, but before he could do that he heard a struggle and the thumping of bare feet.

"Please let go of my *dupatta*! I am leaving the village. I will not come back here again!"

"And whom will you go to, you cringing, cowering nightingale?" Hutchinson's voice rose. "Lift a skirt for me, you servile, grovelling hoyden! Then blame me for putting my seed in you. How dare you pin that child on me?"

Then it all happened in an instant. A length of silken cloth, perhaps that which the girl struggled to repossess, came sailing out of the window onto John's shoulders. Something or somebody knocked hard against the wall and the flickering lamp in the room went out. In the ensuing darkness, he heard the girl sobbing and the sound of her bare feet as she ran out of the house, headed for the front door on the far side.

"I await you in Varanasi," she appeared to scream from the far end of the house.

"You miserable bitch!" Hutchinson shouted behind her.

Under cover of darkness John leapt into the house through the open window, landing as he did straight down on the pier-master's mid-section. The man had been lying on the ground, apparently pushed by the desperate girl, his stout frame unable to raise itself up immediately.

There was a groan as John's feet landed on the soft belly of the man, and it took all the wind out of him. In the moonlight, John quickly recollected his senses, every faculty alert to detect if Hutchinson was reaching for a weapon or a firearm. But before the older man could move, John pinned him down using the girl's silk *dupatta* in a manner as if to garrotte the man. He had scarcely passed the cloth around the pier master's neck when he heard Hutchinson plead.

"Oh my God! Oh my God! Aleem! Why me? We had an agreement. Thugs don't kill Englishmen! You know the consequences, Aleem!"

John wondered who Aleem was. In the darkness Hutchinson obviously could not see his assailant.

John kept the man pinned to the ground firmly. He tightened the noose, just about allowing the man to speak. In the moonlight the lantern jaw trembled. His breath stank of liquor. In his fear, or drunkenness, the man was totally under the illusion of a mistaken identity.

"Aleem! How can you do this to me?" Now Hutchinson spoke in Hindustani. "The Manar Manik is safe. If you kill me you will never possess it."

"Where is it?" John hoarsely responded in Hindustani, without a clue as to what the man was talking about, but beginning to enjoy the state of torment he was subjecting him to. He wondered if Aleem was the name of the old medicine vendor or healer whom he had followed here.

"Aleem, I have protected you, protected every thug who needed to hide. How can you betray your associate, your partner?"

A thug? That explained their speech in Ramasee!

"How indeed!" John hissed at him, memories of London, swirling in his mind.

"Aleem! Spare my life! The Manar Manik has been located, and I am bidding for it. It is safe with a lady in Jhansi. We can take it yet, if you so need it. It will be on the road again a day before the Gwalior *mela*. And I have the money to buy it before it does. I can show you, I have the money here. We can share it two ways, and Preston need not know. Aleem! Aleem!" He was attempting to scream but his voice failed him. A foul odour emanated from his throat as some of the fluids he had consumed bubbled out of the corners of his mouth

Sitting there astride the pier-master, silhouetted against the moonlight, John felt that familiar, near debilitating rage well up inside him again. Hutchinson, he realised, was hatching another betrayal. This time directed against Preston. The insatiable avarice in the man, that had taken Bob's life and nearly ruined his own, was up and rearing its head again. John now lost all self-control.

"Die in darkness and confusion, my dear Hutchinson," John now spoke aloud in the language of King George. "John Penmarric of the West India Dock Company at your service, sir." He tightened his grip and he heard the man gagging. "And I wish you good tidings on behalf of our friend Robert Pendarrow. You remember him don't you, Hutchinson?" He hoped the piece of the girl's clothing he now squeezed in his hand would not rip apart.

But it held.

He let himself out of the front door of the house a few minutes later carrying the largest hoard of gold *mohurs* he had ever laid eyes upon. He wondered how so much gold had come into the dead man's possession. He still shook violently, trying hard to shed the anger he felt.

The dog's howl somewhere in the village now sounded like a high pitched squeal, a hysterical laughter that ebbed away in a bay of intense pain.

He wondered what the Manar Manik was, for the purchase of which a sum as large as this had been amassed by Hutchinson.

He would soon find that out. As soon as he caught up with this man Aleem.

He breathed deeply till some of the anger left him and he felt calmer. Perhaps, another change of identity, of his name, was due. Saleem, a common name among Muslims in the region that rhymed with his new quarry was as good as any.

He stepped silently out of the house. The cloth bundle he had seen on the verandah was gone. So was the girl.

But John kept her *dupatta*. It was tenacious silk. He had use for it.

* * *

On the edge of the forest near the small town of Lalitpur, Henry Sleeman absorbed the warmth of the early morning sun with pleasure. His feet were propped up on a collapsible canvas stool. Against the breakfast table leaned his firearm, sword and cane. A number of large white tents, horses and bullock carts dotted the grassy slope where they sat. They were encamped here for two days now. Amalie, his beautiful young wife had just instructed the servants to clear the table, save the hot tea, which Henry still sipped. Then she stood up, kissed him, and started up the gentle grassy slope towards her tent.

"*Venez aussi vite que possible*," she said. "I have something special for lunch."

"I hope I retain some appetite," he complained. "This task is grisly and terrible. But I'm succeeding, darling."

"She turned and stood there looking concerned. "*Ne forcez pas votre talent*. They are so many in number and scattered all over this land. I really don't know how you will manage."

Sleeman continued sipping the hot tea with relish. "*Succomber sous le nombre*? Never." His blue eyes keenly surveyed a line of prisoners being marched towards him far in the horizon. He also noted that one of them limped visibly. "I have always had a plan of action, my dear Amalie. Now I have the powers and the resources. You know I cannot be cruel. But a firm hand is called for to deal with such murderers. We are dealing with a terrible crime. I have already put my plans into operation. *Tout ce qu'on peut faire, c'est attendre la suite*."

"*Tiens! Voila pour toi*," she exclaimed pointing to the men." *Au revoir, Mon cherie*. I prefer resting in the tent. *Je ne l'aime pas. C'est ennuyeux*."

As she climbed the slope, Sleeman was glad Amalie was getting quite used to the macabre business he was handling. He loved her for her cheerful disposition and the support she extended to him in his grim task.

Amalie de Fontenne was the daughter of a French nobleman whom he had met in Mauritius. From the day he had married her she shared his zeal for eradicating *Thugee* and had insisted on accompanying him in his campaign through a difficult life in the camps. She took the torrential rains, the searing heat and the discomforts of a terrain full of snakes, leeches and mosquitoes in her stride.

As the row of men marched slowly towards him, Sleeman noted with satisfaction that his *sepoys* were taking great care to comply with his instructions. There were seven prisoners all of whom wore heavy ankle shackles. Most had well groomed beards, turbans and wore long robes. Their arms were bound behind them. A heavy iron yoke placed on each neck and linked to a similar yoke on the neck of the prisoner behind him prevented anyone from making an abrupt movement. The *sepoys* armed and wearing bayonets kept a few feet away from the prisoners.

Sleeman had lost two good men a year ago and had learnt that even when restrained and shackled with care, it required only a foot of slack chain or rope for these men to overcome their captors. So fine-honed was their art, so incomprehensible their cult-language, so subtle their signals to one another, that they could convert a lax situation or even a slack piece of cloth to their advantage with deadly consequences.

The men were lined up in a single file before him. One of them, a tall grotesque figure with a grey stubble limped as he marched, and now stood before him crookedly, a painful grin smeared on his scarred features.

"Your names," he enquired sternly. "Your real names. And the town or village you belong to." He picked up his cane and pointed it in the direction of the first man in the row. "Then you will tell me the number and the precise spot where you buried the bodies."

Meanwhile Amalie was content to remain in her tent reading ***Les Liaisons dangereuses*** by the late Pierre Choderlos *de* Laclos, an army officer whose single novel was in a letter form and dealt with moral corruption. It absorbed her despite being interrupted every now and again by the *khitmutgar* and the *bawarchee* from the neighbouring tent where lunch was cooking. Outside in the distance, from the end of the grassy slope she could hear an occasional sing and swish of a cane as the interrogation progressed. This grim pageant had become for her all too familiar in recent months, especially when Henry received a succession of those strange letters, imprinted with curious sketches of birds that kept him awake all night. She had lost count of the number of human skeletons that had been exhumed in the vicinity of various camps like this in the district following an interrogation. She firmly believed Henry was doing a marvellous job, but sometimes her heart yearned for the comfort and the sea breeze of her home in Mauritius. But only sometimes, for her heart was with her beloved Henry, and he had promised that as soon as he was done with this campaign, he would relinquish his services, and they would retire to his home in Stratton, Cornwall.

The men, still securely shackled, were marched a little distance from Sleeman's breakfast table on the edge of the woods where three graves had been dug up by the *sepoys* following the confession of one of the thugs. Human skeletons with a few strips of tattered cloth clinging to otherwise bare bones revealed their horrifying fate.

"The remains of Badrinath Seth, his brother and a fellow tradesman," A *sepoy* announced.

"You will hang for this," Sleeman said quietly to the first man in the row. "But that will be six months hence. Meanwhile, we will break your body slowly, finger by finger, limb by limb. We will skin you alive and have you watch the dogs feed on your body parts. Then we will look for your family. Your parents, your wife, your children…."

Before Sleeman could say another word, the grim faced thug fell to his knees. "Have mercy Sahib, I shall confess to everything I have done. Everything. I will show you the graves of all the people I have killed these last few years since I became a *bhurtote*. But please leave my family out of this. I will surrender whatever loot I possess to the authorities. But please leave my family out of this. They don't even know I'm a thug."

Sleeman stood menacingly over the man who grovelled at his feet. "Not enough, Raghubir. Not enough. Neither you nor your family will live until I have the names, addresses and occupation of every one of your associates, every thug you know in this district and beyond. I shall know where you sell your loot. I shall have the name of every beneficiary of this murderous trade you have been plying all these years. You will sit with my sepoy this very minute and relate to him everything you know. I must have every detail of every act and every person associated with it. Failing this, I shall begin carrying out what I promised and your pleas for mercy will not stop me then. Do you understand me?"

A *sepoy* separated Raghubir from the rest. He unlocked the yoke and led the stooped figure of the cringing and heavily shackled thug to a tree where he was chained firmly again. Then seating himself comfortably on the grass, the *sepoy* opened a notebook.

"Start talking," he ordered Raghubir.

"Next!" commanded Sleeman. The prisoner he indicated was a young well-built man who trembled uncontrollably. He had no beard and a corner of his upper lip and eye were swollen from blows received from his fellow prisoners the night before.

"Your fate is sealed," Sleeman addressed him quietly. "I have evidence of at least one dastardly crime you have committed. Before we hang you, I only wish to know where your earlier victims lie buried."

"I have not killed a single human being in my life, Sahib," the young man sobbed. "I am not a thug. I am not like the rest of them."

"You disappeared from Bijaipur village the day Hutchinson Sahib was killed. Your sister too. Where have you hidden her? Do you want us to hunt her down too? Shambu, talk to me now. You may not get another chance."

"I have told all, Sahib. I am willing to confess and become a thug if it pleases you. I have told all, Sahib. I have been begging these men to tell me the location of some their victims so that I can call them my own. After all, if I were to confess, I need to show you at least one dead body. Instead these men kicked me and attacked me with their shackles last night thinking I had been planted among them by you to extract information."

The tall thug with the limp laughed contemptuously, his grotesque features wrinkling as he sneered at Shambu. Sleeman disregarded him. He addressed the young man again coldly. "Are you also denying that you killed Mr. Hutchinson? Did not your sister work and cook in the bungalow of the saheb? Where is she? Is she in league with the man who did it?"

Shambu sobbed. "I wish I could help you in some way. But I did not kill the saheb and I don't know where my sister has gone. Hang me if it pleases you, Saheb, but don't make me utter false statements."

Henry Sleeman held justice above anything else, and the young man's words made him wince. There were enough *phansigars* in the land without having to force a young man to admit he was one. Yet Sleeman felt sure this young man was in some way linked to the death of Charles Hutchinson. The native insidiousness, the propensity to lie and deceive among the criminals he had dealt with made him doubly cautious.

"You will nevertheless stand trial for the death of Mr Hutchinson," Sleeman told the cowering young man.

Amalie meanwhile wondered why her otherwise intrusive pair, the *kitmutgar* and the *bawarchee*, had not informed her if lunch was ready. Placing *de* Laclos on the pillow beside her, she left the tent to investigate. She paused awhile outside the kitchen tent. The sunlight outside was dazzling and she squirmed. Looking down, far below the slope of grass at the edge of the forest, she could see that the interrogation was still in progress. Henry was pacing about animatedly while the prisoners and the *sepoys* stood listening to him intently. This was his world, she thought; mobilising and congregating men, herding the fallen and amoral towards fidelity, liberating this land of the malfeasant and the ghoulish. Her knight in armour!

The scent of spices emanated from the kitchen as she stepped into its dark interior.

What happened next was instantaneous. So sudden, that she lost her breath and her balance. A shadow, deeper than the darkness she had stepped into fell upon her from behind. A strong arm encircled her immobilising both her limbs. The palm of a large hand clamped her mouth shut disabling her from screaming or even uttering a sound. She struggled in panic, but could barely twitch her supple frame within the vice-like grip. Her voice stuck in her throat. The man, this dark, warm and agile creature that held her from behind, gripped her so firmly that she went limp with despair. She was aware of her own trembling, her strength was fast failing her, and the terror she felt almost made her faint. She felt his head resting on her left shoulder. She could feel his breath on her ear.

"*Tenez-vous tranquille*," a voice hissed in her ear. She was startled now, even in her state of limbo.

"*Restez tranquille*!" it spoke again in French. "I have no intention of harming you. But if you do not co-operate, your husband will have one more dead body to add to his list."

She managed to nod in resignation. As her eyes adjusted to the darkness in the tent she noticed that her two servants lay bound on the ground, apparently unconscious. The curry was still cooking in a slow flame. Wood smoke drifted slowly out of a hole on the top of the tent.

"*Cette viande est bonne*," he whispered. "*C'est tres bonne*! But I do not have the time to taste it."

He led her in his grip out of the tent and into the dazzling sunlight. They stepped forward to the edge of the slope.

He let go of her mouth but instead she felt the barrel of a pistol at her throat. She tried to glance sideways but could only see a black cloth drawn over his face and a black disorderly turban.

"*Ma tete tourne*!" she gasped, but he held her firmly, the muzzle of the pistol still at her throat.

His voice boomed now, in Hindi. "Don't anybody move, or I will put a bullet in this woman's head."

The shock of what was happening registered on the group of men below. Sleeman stood frozen, cane still in hand, his other hand poised to pick up his rifle.

"Don't drop your weapons!" the voice boomed in Hindi, "or you will have a good many thugs on the loose again." The row of shackled men stood agape in terror of something they could not comprehend.

A *sepoy* suddenly crouched, and Sleeman screamed at him. "Don't shoot, you fool. He is too far out of range. Can't you see the man has a pistol to my wife's head?"

Sleeman gazed up the slope. The figure of the man stood silhouetted against the tent. Little Amalie in a white dress stood silhouetted against him. She was evidently alive and unharmed. The Governor General's words of caution swam fleetingly through his mind. Who was this stranger and what did he want? How had he descended on the camp so daringly and unnoticed?

"I want you to release Shambu," the voice boomed in reply to his confusion. Sleeman turned to the young prisoner chained among the file of thugs.

"Who is that man?" Sleeman enquired softly, a pale dread transforming his countenance.

Shambu appeared confused. "I don't know him. I don't know why he wants me." Shambu appeared visibly terrified. "Saheb, don't release me. I don't want to go with him," he pleaded.

"But he has taken a great risk to seek your freedom," Sleeman told him in a quivering voice. "That lady you see in his arms is my wife. I should have shot you the minute I set eyes on you."

Shambu was now sobbing in terror.

"Who exactly are you, Shambu? And who is that man?" Sleeman's eyes blazed as he enquired again. "I will release you only because he holds my wife. The wife of a British magistrate. Do you know what this means?"

"I am a dead man!" sobbed Shambu. "Please Saheb, I would rather you hang me. Don't send me to him. Please Saheb, believe me. I don't know this man or why he is doing this!" Shambu now looked demented. "Why do you want me?" he cried out hoarsely at the man. "Who are you?"

Sleeman signaled to a *sepoy* to unshackle the young prisoner. He prodded the reluctant Shambu with his cane. "You are not dead, yet. But that will happen soon enough. I am a fair man, Shambu, and I intended to give you a fair trial. But that does not appear to be your destiny."

Shambu now stood unshackled; free and uncertain. Sleeman regarded his behaviour curiously, his mind fearful of what might befall Amalie. "Go! Go to him!" he commanded.

Shambu took two steps forward, and halted hesitatingly again. His legs seemed unable to carry his weight.

"You son of a dog," a *sepoy* screamed. "Why don't you move forward? If anything happens to the Memsaheb, I will put a bullet in your head."

The tall black silhouette on the top of the slope stood still holding the lady firm in his grasp. Sleeman felt his heart sink. This could go terribly wrong if this young fool did not move. He regretted he had not left a couple of *sepoys* to guard the tents. In desperation Sleeman tried to keep up a dialogue with the stranger who now held control of his camp and Amalie.

"If you're so keen to rescue him why doesn't he come to you?" He enquired loudly. "You can see for yourself that we have unchained him. Will you let the lady go now?"

"Why do you want me?" Shambu called out again, looking at the stationary figure holding the lady. He stepped forward again in hesitation.

There was a moment of silence. A lull of uncertainty that seemed destined to end in some kind of tragedy.

"The person who reads and writes better than the Sarpanch needs you," the tall stranger suddenly shouted.

Shambu recoiled for a moment, then seemed to suddenly find strength in his feet. He scrambled up the slope towards the tall stranger.

Sleeman spoke aloud again. "So you remembered the magic words. Now let go of the lady or I will hunt you down mercilessly. Are you aware that the man I have just released for you was absconding when an Englishman was found strangled to death in his village?"

The tall masked man made no reply to Sleeman. Only Amalie heard him mutter softly in her ear, "*Les absentes est toujours tort.*"

When Shambu reached the top of the slope the man spoke to him in Hindi through his black mask. "There are horses some yards away. Run along with me and we will reach it. I hope you have not forgotten to ride! Come on! Get ahead of me!" Shambu sprinted off. Still holding Amalie, he now addressed Sleeman aloud in Hindi, "This was necessary Sleeman Saheb, for it was I and not Shambu that strangled Hutchinson."

With that he released the young woman, and raced between the tents swiftly directing Shambu towards the horses.

Amalie, relief sweeping over her immediately ran down the slope towards her husband.

With Amalie now safely by his side, Sleeman signalled to his *sepoys* to pursue the duo. Five men mounted and spurred their horses up the slope disappearing behind the tents and out of sight.

He held Amalie close to him. He could see she was in no condition to speak. He would have her rest as soon as he helped her to their tent.

There were five *sepoys* left to guard the prisoners. He ordered them to secure the prisoners well and continue the interrogation in the afternoon.

As he ascended the slope towards his tent with Amalie, he heard the lame thug laugh again. Sleeman turned around, now visibly angry at the man's insolence.

"That was Firengee!" the deformed man laughed again, squatting on the ground with the others. "You have sent your sepoys to their deaths!" He guffawed uncontrollably and sounded like a crazed animal.

"And how is it that you recognise him so easily?" Sleeman enquired, his curiosity replacing anger.

"That is his style!" the thug exclaimed, "That's his method!" He could not stop laughing.

"How do you know for certain that he was Firengee? Sleeman enquired again. "He was masked and he stood far away from us."

When the man laughed again, Sleeman suddenly noticed that the thug was laughing in an effort to conceal some kind of terror. Laughter was this unfortunate man's mechanism to quell his fears. While he laughed, his eyes still stared at the tents up on the slope in unmitigated horror. He appeared to have become almost hysterical since setting eyes on the man he recognised as Firengee.

"His turban, Saheb! Did you not see the peculiar shape of his turban? No Hindustani ties his turban in such a strange fashion. And he carries a firearm. How many thugs have you known to carry fire-arms?"

"Then you have seen him before?" Sleeman probed.

"Yes! Yes! I have seen him. I have seen him kill. The Sind-mori massacre was carried out by him single-handed. He loots without discrimination. Every human is his bunij. Even a thug is not safe around him. I was lucky to get away with my bad leg. He is in possession of the Manar rubies!"

"You have an interesting tale to tell me, I am sure," Sleeman spoke to the cripple. The Sind-mori massacre, Firengee and rubies! What a story! Think it over well. For soon, I will be taking you apart, and what I need to know had better be rich in truth and detail too."

Sleeman had had enough excitement for the morning. He did not entirely believe Firengee could so easily vanquish his five *sepoys.* They were hardy men who understood the guile of the thugs and would pursue their quarry to the end.

He gathered Amalie and walked up to their tent. Once inside, he held her close to him, kissing her face tenderly. "I should not have allowed this to happen. I could never have lived had something happened to you."

"Henry..." she began, stifling a sob.

"Its okay now, my darling! I am extremely sorry!" He patted her again, consoling her. "You were brave. Very brave."

"Henry, this man. He speaks French."

"What?"

"Henry, this man! This Firengee, he spoke to me in French."

"Amalie, my dear. You are imagining things. You are hallucinating. It happens in moments like these. You need rest, my love."

"Henry, believe me!" She said firmly. "I was frightened, but I was not hearing things. I can repeat to you everything he said!"

"Then he is perhaps from one of the French held territories. I wonder if that is why they call him Firengee. It means foreigner in Hindustani."

Sleeman's thoughts were interrupted by a *sepoy's* voice outside. The *sepoy* had just untied the *Khitmutgar* and the *Bawarchee*. Both men were babbling incoherently in terror and appeared to have no clue as to what had happened to them.

"Calm them down!" Sleeman ordered the *sepoy*, stepping out of the tent. "Calm them down or we will have to go without supper. I will question them later."

As he turned to re-enter his tent, his eyes caught a movement on the horizon, far up the dirt track that led to the road to Lalitpur. He entered the tent and rummaged about till he found an old army telescope that had served him years ago in the Gurkha war. He now often used it when out in the countryside.

Standing before the camp, he trained the instrument in the direction of the movement on the horizon. Three men were riding slowly towards their camp. One was a large white man. The other two were natives. An occasional glint in the eye of the white man appeared to be a monocle.

* * *

It was another night of anxiety for Jack Dawson as he tried to sleep at the *tharavad.* For one who had been visited by the same nightmares so often, he could perceive the familiar throb in his head in the instance it was due. The night was not going to pass quietly. Like a predator creeping around in the shadows, the horrible visions awaited, waited till his body fatigued and drew him into the mire of sleep. He knew they lurked in some dark dimension, watching him. To come for him.

Outside, a ferocious monsoon stormed, flashing and thundering incessantly. The rain beat upon the roof mercilessly and he could hear the torrents gushing through the drains around the house as if he were out at sea. Trees creaked and branches snapped. An occasional crash of dead coconut leaves, as they yielded to the gale, startled him.

When the day dawned he would have to make that momentous visit to a strange *kalari* that Nandakumar had ordained for him. He would meet a mysterious teacher and learn to do with his body what no acrobat in England, nay Europe, had ever dreamt of doing. The anticipation did not help his efforts to sleep, but it was a welcome diversion from the looming shadows of another impending nightmare.

When sleep finally overwhelmed him, he surrendered, feeling tears running down the side of his face. When it came, it began with the smiling face of Robert Pendarrow framed against a stormy sky in his mind, a night that flashed and thundered. The face contorted in pain, replaced by a hurt and accusing expression. For a fleeting moment, Dawson was aware that he was dreaming. For a few seconds he was aware of being asleep. But not for long. Bob's eyes rolled, and he turned his head upwards as if to look at the stormy sky for himself. He exposed his neck, revealing a noose the knot of which Dawson could see slithering and tightening relentlessly. Bob's face, his eye-balls still rolled up, faded from the night sky and there followed a high-pitched squeal and laughter. Only tonight the squeals did not wake Dawson up. He did not wake up as he always did to find himself shrieking and laughing uncontrollably through tears and perspiration.

For a new image had entered his dream, an apparition he had never encountered before. A shadowy specter whose presence soothed him immensely. It stood there, on what appeared to be a regular London cobbled street, dressed in shiny black oil-skin, a mask, a cape, and wearing Dawson's peaked helmet which he had been gifted in the garrison at Baroda. Lying there on a thick and comfortable *chaggari* mattress, Dawson experienced for the first time a feeling of power and control. The dreams vanished, and Dawson relapsed into a deep and restful slumber.

Only Kannan's pony, as it trotted into the rain swept *tharavad* grounds early in the morning, woke him up.

It was dawn, and the sun climbed a cloudless sky.

* * *

The lure of the Manar rubies brought Aleem back to the Central Provinces again. But the road before him appeared hemmed with obstacles.

He felt the burden of age. A masquerade that he often performed, but now felt beleaguered by. He knew he did not possess a potion to cure that malady. He often thought of his family now. A daughter approaching the age of marriage. A son who took care of the cattle. And most precious, his youngest child, blind at birth, a boy of four who would be waiting for him to arrive home and listen to the many stories of which Aleem had no dearth. How the boy sat spellbound while he repeated time and again the tales of Sindbad, Allah-ud-din and Ali Baba! He now only wished for a bountiful *bunij* before he retired from the *thugee*. This child of his could never walk in his footsteps. Allah be praised for this!

The manner of death of Charles Hutchinson perturbed him. The news of the Englishman's murder was all over the region as soldiers and native informers combed the district and the neighbouring provinces for the killer.

He often dwelt upon his indirect role in the death of the man. The kind of avarice he had detected in Hutchinson's manner every time he had visited the docks at Calcutta had spawned the idea in his mind. He had hoped that the Englishman would use his official position in the customs department to influence the magistrate and lay claim over the cache in the name of the East India Company, the moment its whereabouts were detected. Which would not have been an easy task. Aleem was well aware of the difficulties associated with ferreting out information regarding personal wealth in this country.

Aleem however had expected to locate the treasure himself. Besides being a native, he had made remarkable inroads into the affairs of the wealthy families of the region due to his medical practise. With the women in particular, whose dark secrets were forever safe with him. If they had a skeleton in their cupboard, it was, after all, Aleem who helped them secure it there. They trusted their old *hakim*, and often used him as a conduit and an instrument for various less than noble purposes. He could never forget how he had secretly conducted a successful abortion for the unwed Sitara Devi of Jhansi. Or how he had collected a small fortune from her to see the demise of the young scoundrel responsible for her condition. She had even obliged to have the boy neatly buried on the lawns of her *haveli* in the dead of night, meticulously rolling the green grass back into place before the break of dawn.

These women were, in return, also conduits for gathering information. Information he had subtly used in the past for his more surreptitious non-medical profession. Only the whereabouts of the Manar rubies confounded him. If he had only located the treasure he would have side-stepped at a convenient juncture and let the English East India Company authorities, personified by Hutchinson, take over.

Once Hutchinson procured the cache, Aleem had his own dark plans to divest the Englishman of the hoard, but the untimely murder of the man had prompted Aleem to lie low for a very long time.

How ironic it was to also learn later from the jewellers of Jhansi, after their misadventure at the Sind-mori ravine, that the rubies had actually been in Sitara Devi's possession even while he was conducting the discreet abortion, the result of her misadventures with a local lad; and that an Englishman named Hutchinson had at that time been secretly bidding for it. The dog had never revealed to him that he had, after all, traced its location! How, by Allah, had he come by so much money to bid for it? From where had Sitara Devi amassed the fortune to procure it? How, *Khuda*, did she pay for it? Or was all this deliberate misinformation, perpetrated by that shrewd lady especially following Hutchinson's death, to throw local merchant's and the Raja's officers off her trail? Aleem wondered if he would ever know the answers to those questions. No wonder Hutchinson had shown such reluctance in seeking the magistrate's help in searching for the treasure. The swine had always known where it was, and unknown to Aleem, had perhaps already been in touch with other wealthy families of the provinces to quickly dispose the cache at a profit. The wretched cur had however paid with his life for his duplicity! Aleem could not shake off the sensation of having been cheated by the white man despite having had to eventually surrender the cache to Firengee at Sind-mori.

Twice had the treasure eluded him, and now he hungered for it as never before. He firmly believed he would be lucky the third time.

Aleem also learnt that the Englishman had offered Sitara Devi Hindu standard gold bullion, *mohurs*, for the rubies, but no such hoard in gold had surfaced when Hutchinson's body was found in the house in Bijaipura. It was extremely risky to visit the village again, and anyway, if Firengee was somehow ensnared, he would have his hands on the rubies themselves.

Moreover he had to exercise extreme caution, as the community of jewellers had not completely absolved him of involvement in the attack on their caravan a few months ago on the Sind Mori. Most of them were taken-in by his age, reputation and feigned injuries. That despite the murder of Abdul, his young assistant, he had apparently single-handedly and against great odds, rescued two injured jewellers and brought them back to Dabra, and even nursed them back to health. But some of them still questioned his decision and insistence on taking the detour through the forest that fateful day, before the tragedy befell them. For they had not confronted any Pindarees, after all. Aleem knew it was only his close association with some of Sitara Devi's ailing family members that kept the community from active hostility towards him.

But Aleem wondered which gang or *burthote* had dared to kill Hutchinson. Strangling a white man was a rare and extreme step. Socially separated, a thug would rarely find an opportunity to get sufficiently close to one. Moreover to do such a thing was to immediately draw the attention of the authorities, who, backed with their resources, could prove a nuisance and even the gangs undoing. There were enough native travellers and pilgrims on the highways of the subcontinent for them to prey upon. This was a land of bountiful *bunij*.

The manner of Hutchinson's death, coupled with the cloud he was under in the eyes of the jewellers and the troublesome magistrate of Narsingpur had kept him underground and lying low. Now only something of the value of the Manar rubies could give him the impetus to wager his chances in the district of the Central Provinces again. He believed it was worth one last try.

With extreme caution he approached each town. Arriving on the outskirts at dusk he would begin his enquiries. Familiar with the region, it did not take him long to learn that the other Englishman of the docks, Preston, who wore a glass over one eye, was on his trail and indeed had overtaken him in the direction of Narsingpur. He also learnt that two natives, a father and a son from the docks, rode with the enormous Englishman. He had only now to keep in touch with his local contacts to monitor their movements. He decided to risk another journey to Narsingpur.

Besides, if the big Englishman was on this trail, he felt confident that one of these days either Firengee or the Manar rubies would show up.

And this time, he reflected with a growing confidence, Mohammed Mir Aleem alias Moin ud din Nasser would not fail.

* * *

"It gives me great pleasure to meet you in person, sir," Preston smiled warmly as he shook hands with the magistrate. "It certainly is a pleasure."

They were standing outside the tent that served as the magistrate's office. Sleeman smiled and waved towards a seat.

"We have been reading of your exploits with keen interest," the visitor lied. "Your work has evinced great excitement at Calcutta."

Sleeman frowned. "I did not see much excitement on this account while I was there a few weeks ago."

"Oh, God be merciful!" Preston exclaimed heartily. "They would have feted and feasted you had you stepped into Spencer's. My dear sir, the ladies there have nothing else to speak of the whole of their evenings."

"And what is this official business that brings you to these parts?" Sleeman enquired.

"Official or unofficial, history will judge us in good time, I am sure." Preston began a well-rehearsed speech. "It is sufficient to say that this matter relates to the year 1822 and to the fugitive king of Assam named Chandrakant who was resisting the Burmese forces that occupied his land in the north-east provinces. He took refuge that year within the British territory of Goalpara. The Burmese threatened to invade our stations there if we did not hand over the fugitive. From both Dacca and Rangpur our forces rose to the occasion and prepared to engage the Burmese. We have yet to ascertain what exactly took place then. We have it from authoritative sources that a certain cache of rubies, popularly called the Manar rubies changed hands."

Sleeman's eyes narrowed. This was the second time that day that he had heard the name of this treasure uttered. He now doubted if it was only a coincidence that this East India Company official was in his camp today. From where he sat he could see the native duo who had arrived with Preston outside his tent, their eyes riveted curiously in the direction of the prisoners below the slope.

"I hired them at the docks," Preston explained. "They are naturally not privy to the purpose of my mission here."

Sleeman nodded in understanding.

"The Burmese had crossed into our territory, plundering and burning villages," continued Preston. "There was wanton slaughter of the young and old, women and children. We are not sure if this treasure was paid by the Assamese king to our officers as a fee for seeking shelter or as a bribe to our native subordinates. Mr.David Scott, the magistrate of Rangpur had received orders, that should Chandrakant, or any of his party appear in the district, they were to be disarmed and removed to safety while our forces engaged the Burmese. But Chandrakant was never found.

"Another story goes that the rubies were paid as an inducement to the British Officer commanding at Goalpara to permit the king to raise troops in the district. Still another story doing the rounds is that these rubies were paid to one Mr. Robert Bruce, who obtained for the king three hundred muskets and nine maunds of ammunition from Calcutta. Though we know for a fact that Mr Bruce saw no such treasure.

"You see sir, the ownership of the Manar treasure is in dispute. Many believe that it should rightly belong to the Company whose troops and resources were employed in the Burmese campaign. But while we are yet to sit judgement on that issue, I have been assigned the duty of tracing this treasure and restoring it to the Company."

"And under whose orders are you here?" enquired Sleeman.

"That is a very confidential matter, sir. We do not want even the pursuit of this treasure to become known. My errand is a delicate one. Once the jewels are located and seized, the Company will make the matter public. I have no doubt of that. Until then we do not wish to leak any information for fear of the treasure disappearing again as it did for some years now."

"And why do you believe it might be in this district?" asked Sleeman.

"We have been gleaning information from native gossip," lied Preston, wiping a trace of sweat from his forehead and adjusting his monocle. "We have been on its trail for sometime now. We have intercepted native communication and our informers have traced its movement into the Central Provinces. You see sir, the Manar rubies are hard to sell. Even a single ruby, by its sheer size and lustre, would arouse suspicion. Not a bazaar in this land would accept it without raising a commotion. That is why it has remained in the hands of the ruling classes for so long, until now. We believe, sir, that you hold a prisoner who might have some useful information."

"And how do you know that?" Sleeman enquired incredulously.

"My clerk, the older man who accompanies me, made some enquiries with natives at Jhansi. A jeweller we spoke to thought he recognised a thug you arrested a few days ago. This jeweller had been attacked and struck on his head some months ago by a gang on the road while he carried these rubies to Gwalior. But before he fell unconscious he noticed a man with a remarkable limp in his gait, as one among the thugs who dismounted and attacked their party. I believe sir, that you now hold such a man."

* * *

"I can shut my eyes and think that I see you darling," wrote Lucy Polgarth. "I see my London boy in strange Oriental robes riding on the dusty plains of that strange country. Sometimes in the humid forests and sometimes mingling in the bazaars that exude the scent of spice and sandalwood. If I sounded peevish and irritable in my last letter it was, I confess now, on seeing you amidst beautiful Oriental women. Shame on me! But jealousy is so much a part of love. I hope you will forgive me for engaging such vivid imagination.

"At times I fail to see the boy, the polite and innocent Cornish boy who made vain attempts at dressing fashionably just for me. I only see a man, toughened by terrain and circumstances. Your letters have, over time, begun to sound like a man well past your age and experience that I find myself addressing an older man each time I write to you. I console myself that perhaps it is your unusual mission there that is causing these great changes in your personality, and that you will emerge a better man for it. Your mission, avenging and evangelical, that perhaps only I fully understand, darling. You were right. For people who are to be happy together the great point is not so much being free from all peculiarities of manner, as a perfect understanding of one another.

"I do not recollect ever feeling better than for the last few days. Father is once again contemplating an investment, a new venture this time. And being on the search for a trusted partner, he often enquires about you. Your whereabouts. The man loves and trusts you, darling. The times are just perfect for us.

"As I have declared so many times before, John, I will not judge you from the activities you have engaged in since you left for India. I know it was your state of utter despair, anger and guilt, and the severe and consuming need to see justice done that has driven you to that country. I am most happy that you have honestly revealed your pain to me. I now only wait for you to emerge again to hold me in your arms.

"Father has been in conference with a group of gentlemen who wish to form a Tea Committee with the intention of cultivating the crop in some north-eastern region of India. He was excited and hopeful that perhaps this tea grown and manufactured within our own colonies would be capable of competing with the Chinese product. Only posterity will determine if his excitement is justified.

"For my part I could only close my eyes and once again give wings to my imagination. I tried to imagine you as a tea planter in a vast valley riding a horse and ushering labourers to work. And all this, while I kept a beautiful house and a warm fire for you to come home to."

* * *

"Shambu! What have they done to you!" Salmi wanted to cry out loud, but would not have the people of the village rise in curiosity and pry into the cause of her despondency.

She held her brother's face close to hers. "I knew in my heart that I would see you again. Oh Shambu, you have suffered so much because of me!" She touched the bruises on his face and he winced. "But look at my child! Beautiful as he is, he is a white child. Tell me you will not hate him for it Shambu! Tell me!"

Shambu tried to smile through his pain. The *mohwa* he had just drunk helped to numb his soreness. "We do not have anything to return to, Salmi. The authorities or the panchayat would have seized our property."

"But my prayers have been heard, Shambu. You have come back to me, alive. Now I am sure we will find the means to live in peace somewhere."

Shambu was full of questions. "Who is this man? How did you meet him? Why is he so charitable, to even risk his life to rescue me?"

The long ride and the *mohwa* was beginning to do its work, and as Salmi spoke to him, he slowly nodded and fell into a deep slumber.

She smiled tenderly at him. "A little longer, my dear brother," she said passing her hand over his brow. "He did not choose Varanasi by accident. Your trials are almost over."

The subject of Shambu's curiosity was at this moment on the outskirts of the village watching the road to see if they had been followed. The ride from Sleeman's camp had not been easy. They had given the magistrate's *sepoys* the slip twice, only to find those hardy and skilful riders back on their heels, arriving relentlessly through little known paths, bursting upon them through ravines and thickets. Curiously, it was only when they were compelled to ride through the small but very populated town of Lalitpur, through narrow, unsanitary lanes, and take a serpentine course through the crowds at the *haat*, the weekly bazaar on its outskirts, that they realised that by some divine miracle their pursuers had finally given up and vanished. Shambu had exhibited excellent horsemanship, and kept out of musket range. They had no difficulty retracing their way through the myriad dirt roads and mule tracks before reaching the village where Salmi awaited with her baby.

John however was cautious. They had ridden past several travellers and men on horses, and their evident hurry could not have gone unnoticed. On several occasions as they retraced their way to the village, John had been aware of a few *dakwallahs* of the district galloping behind them. While they could not slow down to identify the riders, John could only hope and assume they were what they appeared to be. They had taken the precaution to separate before entering Lakshmanghat and John had awaited an anxious half hour before Shambu arrived from somewhere reeking of *mohwa*.

John had been in a state of hibernation in the village for over two weeks, before deciding upon this daring rescue. It had taken meticulous planning, riding out of the village on some pretext every day in a variety of guises to scour the region and ascertain *sepoy* and troop movements. He had learnt of Shambu's arrest and the location of Sleeman's camp, and had waited all night in the nearby forest to observe their activities before he made his move.

He had also resorted to paying the villagers of Laxmanghat modestly, and in small change, for grains, vegetables and milk that they partook. Despite an initial show of reluctance on their part, the villagers accepted these payments. It made his refuge there legitimate, and to some degree less of a burden on the simple country folk. In any case he had decided to leave after the stipulated forty days that the custom of the land permitted.

Where to then?

He sat on a boulder and stared out into the road that meandered out of the village and disappeared around a bamboo clump by the forest. The dusty Indian dusk was once again gathering upon him. The cattle were returning home to the village, and a brown cloud drifted lazily in their wake. His thoughts took him back momentarily to his first ride to London. The Salisbury toll where the cattle were being driven to Smithfield. It was so long ago, or was it just five years? Since then time had never stood still.

Behind him some distance away in the room beside the granary the siblings would be trying to come to terms with their altered and pitiable circumstances. He wished to leave them alone for some time.

Only the day before, as he set out to attempt to rescue Shambu, he had for the first time carried Salmi's baby in his arms. What an abominable dissembler fate could be, he had wondered, to have him look into the cherubic, guileless eyes of the child whose father he had so mercilessly strangled to death. To Salmi's amazement and curiosity tears rolled down his face and he knew he could perhaps never kill again. Some of the anger and the vengeance he had felt since Bob Pendarrow's death had been surmounted. He knew George Preston was still alive and well somewhere, but the child had vanquished the enemy for now, and all feeling of wrath seemed to have abandoned him. The baby gave a sense of peace within his being and he had become determined to rescue the innocent Shambu from the trauma and torture he would undergo for no fault of his.

Now, for the first time in years, John felt tired of his way of life.

He looked at his hands. His palms had grown rough and grainy. It reminded him of the large hearted Jack Dawson. Dawson of St.Giles. The acrobat with silver hair and strong, calloused hands. Only it had perhaps taken that denizen of St.Giles a lifetime to disfigure his hands. He wondered if that man had found peace in all these years.

Looking behind him he could see the light of the first oil lamps and lanterns of the village; he began to think about Cornwall and the screeching of the sea-gulls; and he began to think of Lucy.

* * *

Descending into a large rectangular hall ten feet below the level of the ground, Dawson followed Kannan into the *kalari.* The training hall was empty. On the outside, the structure and the roof-level matched other buildings in the vicinity, and on casual observance might have been mistaken for any barn or stable. But owing to its depth below ground level it had an unusually high ceiling, a cool atmosphere, and acoustics that did not allow the spoken word or the clash of weapons from permeating out of the arena. Daylight shone and fresh air filtered in from a series of ventilators high along two opposite walls, without allowing a draft or breeze into the training hall. Two-thirds of the hall was smoothly paved with flagstones while a third was a bed of fine dry sand.

"We have arrived very early," Kannan said. "Look around you and familiarize yourself with the place, while I pray and perform my morning rituals."

Kannan bowed with folded hands before the presiding deity, a carved, black granite figure of the goddess Kali, surrounded by other deities, one of whom Dawson recognized was the monkey god Hanuman. Dawson did the same and waited while Kannan lit a lamp and some incense sticks. When the warrior had completed some basic rituals, he prostrated before the deity for a few minutes, eyes closed, lips moving in prayer. When he had finished he sat on the floor, legs folded, to assume a common posture used for meditation.

Dawson paced bare footed upon the smooth floor of the *kalari*, stopping sometimes to look closely at the weapons on the wall. Long shining blades of the finest kind he had ever seen kept proud vigil alongside lances, daggers and round shields of engraved bronze. He saw bamboo sticks and staffs of various lengths as well as bulbous maces of polished wood alongside a series of leather whips at the far end of the training hall. It was many moments later that he became aware of what looked like a coiled serpent hung on the wall at the far end, in the shadows cast by the enormous wooden pillars. It hung there like a resting whip, looped several times to restrain its obvious length. On closer examination, Dawson noted that it was a metal blade, extremely pliable and capable of flexing like a leather belt. So pliant that it was probably worn like a belt around the waist of its owner. He removed it from its hook on the wall, and it noisily uncoiled in his hands. Its length was unusual, perhaps well over five feet. Holding it by its well-worn hilt, it appeared almost alive, quivering, shimmering and impatient to spring forward at some invisible adversary. Dawson shivered as if some cold hand had been placed on the nape of his neck. The weapon in his hand taunted him in some inexplicable way, teased him and even seemed to mock at his incomprehension. He was so engrossed by the object that he did not notice the appearance of a man behind him. And when the stranger who had mysteriously materialized behind him spoke a few words in Malayalam, it startled him. Turning around he found himself face to face with a wiry, gaunt and bearded man. His copper brown torso was bare and he wore a cotton *mundu* tied firmly about his thighs and loins.

"He wishes you to know that what you are holding in your hand is an *urumi,* drawn in battle only for mass combat," Kannan who had also been startled out of his meditation translated. "He also wishes you to immediately return it to its place on the wall."

Kannan rushed forward to touch the man's feet in obeisance, while Dawson beheld the guru of the *kalari* in ignorant hesitation, not quite certain how he should greet or pay his respects to the man. He bowed as respectfully as he could, and the guru returned the bow in mock imitation, a faint smile traversing his face.

Dawson felt relieved. In a land where rigid customs and tenets of courtesy ruled, this man seemed almost to have a sense of humour and informality. He felt a sudden respect for the man he had only just met.

The guru made a sign for them to sit, and sat down himself on the stone floor.

"Today, we shall spend sometime in talk and mutual assurances," the guru declared, and Kannan translated this important introductory message to Dawson as best as he could. "We shall establish the psychological basis and the means of correct communication between us. We will endeavour to maintain a discourse of truth in all our interactions. And with patience we will put you through the training one day at a time. Remember, *kalari* begins within, and belongs to the mind. The body will do only as much as the mind commands."

* * *

As he sorted his mail, the letter he most awaited invariably never caught his eye. It would lie among the many nondescript brown envelopes on his table. Until he tore them open, Sleeman would not see which contained the letter with the remarkable sea gulls. But the letter, when it came, always contained a reliable list of names of thugs and their possible whereabouts, their various identities and some information about missing people. The first of those letters had started arriving at his office as early as 1826 while he served as a civil administrator at Jubbulpore. They were written in poor vernacular. Every few months the elusive informer would replenish him with a new list. Sleeman had to act fast each time as he was aware the list contained a very mobile gang of men and most of them were named against a town or village where they were last seen. While he wondered about the anonymity and ingenuity of the author of these letters, he often wondered if his own Cornish background was responsible for mistaking the little sketches for seagulls when they were actually vultures, or perhaps eagles. He had ceased to bother about the identity of the birds as much as he had failed to discern the identity of his informer.

The style and manner of the Hindi language improved over the years until Sleeman had reasons to doubt if it was the very same informer that wrote the first of the letters. Except, ofcourse, for the omnipresent birds.

However, from markings on the envelope, he was able to know the nearest town from which his informer routed the mail through the *dak* runners. Sleeman had even twice attempted to trace the origin of these letters through his *dak* runners. However, he faced a dead end when on both occasions his trail led him to children, who could not describe the stranger who had rewarded them for carrying the letter to the nearest *dakwallah*. On seeing they were addressed to the magistrate, and assuming them to be of importance, the *dakwallahs* had accepted the letters without question.

Shortly, a letter bearing a single bird, its wings closed, perched on a small rock arrived. It contained a succinct message. "Do you wish to ground me? The children serve us both well, do they not? It is for their tomorrow that we must do what we do today. Surely you have other trails to follow!"

Sleeman did not wish to discourage the informer for the useful service he was rendering, making the administration's task only easier. He made no further attempts to trace his man, but could not help checking the official stamp of origin each time just so as to determine his informer's possible location in and around the district.

Now as he sat at his desk in the tent, he casually asked an impatient George Preston if he knew any of the native languages.

Preston shook his head. "How could I, sir? I hate Hindustan. I detest these people, their clothes and their language. Their only redeemable quality is in their food. I might have set sail from this land a long time ago had that too been as hideous."

Sleeman laughed, tearing open one envelope after another, "There are many fine qualities these people possess if you keep an open mind..." his eye caught a piece of paper with flying birds drawn at the top. He tossed the paper across to Preston. "What manner of bird would you call that?"

Preston adjusted his monocle and peered at the paper. "An eagle, a hawk perhaps?" he ventured.

"A seagull?" Sleeman enquired.

I couldn't tell if it were," Preston replied, but something about the sketches bothered him. He frowned at the magistrate in askance. Sleeman only shrugged.

"Where did they arrive from?" Preston asked.

"Ganeshpur, near the forest. A useful native informer. Only we have never been able to establish contact with him. Perhaps he might even know of the whereabouts of your rubies."

"Why do you believe so, sir?" asked Preston.

"The cripple we arrested believes the Manar rubies are in Ganeshpur. A difficult terrain, and the domain of a notorious thug named Firengee. I doubt if he knows much else. Perhaps in due course we will determine how much more information he has."

"Sir, I wish to ask. What delays our interrogation of that lame prisoner?"

"I have my reasons, Preston. Just wait awhile till I am ready."

Preston closed his eyes to somehow contain his impatience. As he held them closed, he remembered something.

"Odd that I should remember insignificant trifles all so sudden," he remarked. "I once had a young lad in my charge in London who did birds like that all over the port's ledgers and books. A dishonest blighter he was. Never cared to find out what happened to him though."

Kali

Part IV

Bhim Singh Rathore questioned, and tried to find answers to most of the events that had occurred in his life. He had ridden for weeks across the Gangetic valley with his son Arjun accompanying the Englishman he now served. He had brought his son of twenty along with him only because the boy, born in Bengal, had not seen the Northern provinces that was once the range and domicile of the proud Rathores.

Bhim, a Rajput, had fought in the battle of Merta in 1790 when he was a youth of fourteen. The Moghul general Ismail Beg and the Rajput rajas of Jaipur and Jodhpur were in arms against the Marathas led by Madhavrao Scindhia. The Rajput and Moghul cavalary had been destroyed at Patan by the Marathas led by a brilliant French adventurer and general named Benoit de Boigne. At the point of defeat the Rathore women had taunted the wounded and bedraggled Rajput army who assembled outside Merta to make their last stand. The Raja made an appeal to every Rathore capable of bearing arms to volunteer, and swear to restore their honour or die fighting. Young Bhim, who had never seen a battle, playfully volunteered. Indeed, even an hour before the call for battle had been sounded, he had been playing a game of *kabaddi* with the youth in the village. So when dragged away along with the other boys, and clothed in saffron to be marched off to the Rathore camp to consume opium in preparation for battle, he had presumed that they would play a few more rounds of *kabaddi* once the battle was over.

Merta had been a disaster. At that tender age he had seen his fellow clansmen shot down and decapitated by the thousands. He remembered how he had stood on the battlefield outside the little town questioning the whole purpose of his wasted existence if he was to die that day. The saffron clothing they wore meant that they would neither give nor take quarter. It was to be a fight to death for every Rathore. He had barely managed to fight, perhaps just warded off a few Maratha swordsmen, before a charging horse knocked him out. When he regained consciousness and stood up again he found the battle was nearly over. Only about a dozen Rajput soldiers stood scattered among the heaps of the dead and dying. They were vainly attempting to fight the swarms of enemy soldiers sadistically tormenting them in an unequal battle, till a sword or the point of a spear mercifully found its mark. He knew the outcome of the battle from the horrible sight that met his eyes. As the opium wore off, he also knew that his father, brother and at least two cousins were dead that afternoon. At his feet lay two boys, he had been playing with that morning. One had been disembowelled. The other, barely alive, bled from a leg that had been mangled by cannon fire. Seeing Bhim standing upright, a number of Maratha sodiers had savagely rushed towards him, only to stop in their tracks at the sound of a curt order. Turning around Bhim saw another group of riders, smartly uniformed and led by someone he presumed was of some importance, for, beside him rode a soldier carrying a fluttering flag he did not recognise. When the riders stopped before him, he saw for the first and only time the French general who led the victorious Marathas, and of whom the Rajputs had spoken of so often.

Benoit de Boigne sat on his saddle, tall, gaunt and breathing heavily. He stared at the child standing amongst the dead, sword still in his hand, tear stricken, and with dried blood caked over the side of his face.

"Let him live," the Frenchman had declared. "The story of Merta must be remembered and told."

And so Bhim lived, perhaps the sole surviver of the battle of Merta. But de Boigne had been wrong. Bhim would never return to the Rathore clan to tell of their defeat. Nothing would have been more dishonourable than to have survived a battle in which every male member of his family had died, save some infants. His mother would anyway commit *sati*, and he did not wish to sully her pride before she died. He was sure he had not been a coward but he carried the sin of having remained alive. And he always questioned why?

So Bhim Singh Rathore left the battlefield and Rajputana, with nothing there to live for, and swearing never to return to the region again. And he never spoke of Merta again.

He spent six years at the holy city of Varanasi, a ragged and impoverished individual contemplating suicide. In those years, however, he also grew extremely religious and learnt to read and write. But he soon realised that religion did not give him any solace. It did not answer many of his questions.

One morning, while he sat at the ghats on the banks of the Ganga, he saw a beautiful woman clad in white, her head shaven descending the steps that led to the water. He watched her filling a small brass vessel before ascending the steps again. A shaven-headed widow was not an uncommon sight in this city. They could be of all ages from mere children to octogenarians, caste out by a social order that proclaimed them taboo. They would live by begging and prostitution, till one day the river would carry their ashes to oblivion.

But the singular beauty of this young maiden made his heart pound and he followed her up the *ghats*. When she became aware that a man was stalking her, she turned around to face him.

"I am sorry, sir. I beg alms but I do not sell my body," she had said, and the virtue of the woman had shone in her eyes.

"Please take pity on a man who has nobody," Bhim had begged of her. "With due respect to your husband now gone, I beseech you to marry me, and we will both once again attempt to live with society."

After a month of persuasion and prayers she agreed, and Bhim married the young Bengali girl, Mandakini, at a shrine outside the city. They moved to Calcutta where Bhim found employment and a place to live. He found happiness, and for some time stopped doubting his life's fortunes, whatever be its strange waywardness.

But his happiness was not without a daub, for the couple remained childless for many years, until once again, those elemental questions of life began to bother Bhim again.

So when Arjun was born six years later, Bhim was overjoyed. The reason and purpose to live grew stronger in him and he strove to work harder and seek more gainful and lucrative employment.

As the years passed, young Arjun grew among the educated and the radical of Calcutta's native youth. Bhim observed with trepidation, how he grew so distant from the boy, how western thoughts and ideas were influencing him. At one point he was sure Arjun would become a misfit in the Bengali society of Calcutta. He questioned the tenets of his own religion and restlessly endeavoured to understand the Christian bible. He had refused to marry and settle down. Nor would his restive nature help him remain in any useful employment for longer than a few months. He spent a considerable time with the foreign missionaries of Calcutta. Fortunately, while he opposed the idolatry of popular Hinduism he equally rejected attempts of Christian missionaries at conversion. Instead he appeared to choose the middle path of the Brahmo Samaj, and became a follower of the distinguished Ram Mohun Roy.

Bhim had been making a modest living working at the dock yard for nearly four years before the two Englishmen, Charles Hutchinson and George Preston arrived at Diamond Harbour.

He had no particular liking for George Preston, under whom he was required to serve. Only his Rajput sense of duty and respect for authority restrained him from ever contradicting or antagonising his superior. He was also increasingly aware of his age and that he would soon be required to retire from service. So when Preston offered him an attractive sum to relinquish his services and join him in what Bhim believed to be official work, he gladly agreed. This was also an opportunity to pluck Arjun out of Calcutta and make a connection with his son.

Only now as he stood outside a tent in Sleeman's camp did those fundamental questions surface again. What was the meaning of his life? What right did he have to guide even his son's destiny? In the weeks that preceded their arrival here, he had tried to impress upon his son the necessity of utilising his education to earn a respectable station in life, and to marry while his youth and energies were at an apex. Yet he wondered if he had any actual control over the boy's future. His own life was a unique and bizarre example.

From the tent behind him the muffled voices of George Preston and the magistrate could be heard, engaged in deep discussion.

In the small valley before him, huddled on the ground, were prisoners in heavy shackles, guarded by a group of alert *sepoys.*

* * *

As he rode, Mohammed Mir Aleem felt sure he had arrived at least within thirty square miles of his quest. It posed a great danger if he was recognised, but the reward would be worth the risk.

It was dusk as he dismounted on the outskirts of Lalitpur, a populated town, which only attracted his attention having heard that a daring rescue of a thug had been followed by a chase through its streets. Aleem was here to try and discover the names of the principal players of that drama of which the entire town was agog. He would have to discern the truth from the rumours, perhaps meet a few witnesses and gauge the general direction that the fugitives had taken. The name of Firengee had been uttered more than once, and Aleem felt an uncontrollable chill creeping down his spine.

He was now at a difficult cross-road in his quest of the Manar treasure. At the end of his trail, he knew he would be up against at least one of these two formidable men. Preston, the enormous Englishman whose race ruled the land, and who could draw resources and protection from the authorities merely for being a white man. Even if entrapped, he was a physically powerful adversary who rarely moved about unarmed.

Of Firengee, the less Aleem thought the better his nerves felt.

Despite this fearful predicament that he now confronted, he had to make a choice. He wondered if Firengee's flight through the town had anything to do with Preston's efforts with the magistrate. If the rumours were to be believed, Firengee appeared to have found a partner too, for it was said he did not ride alone. The choice was daunting, but his conclusions drove him to make it. It was logical. If

Firengee was still roaming free in the neighbourhood, he perhaps still possessed the rubies. This was the only reasonable lead he had to the treasure.

He walked his horse casually down the narrow streets keeping his turbaned head low. The tops of jars containing medicines were clearly left exposed on his saddle. His eye caught two young *sepoys* riding up the street. He paused respectfully to allow a group of bare bodied Brahmins to pass him by before he hailed them.

"Son, has the *haat* been lifted, or does baba have an opportunity to sell his wares there?" he enquired, suddenly acquiring the demeanour and the voice of an old man that he was so skilled at assuming.

The two young *sepoys* reined their horses.

"Are you new around here?" one of them enquired, assuming an official tone.

Aleem chuckled and coughed disarmingly. "At my age, son, one is never new anywhere. I only wish to know if the bazaar has been lifted earlier than the usual time. You see, I was attending to a patient, and did not realise how time had passed me by. Besides, I hear there is trouble. I hear thugs have escaped this way…"

"The *haat* will continue for an hour more," interrupted the *sepoy* impatiently. "You may yet sell some of your medicines."

"Perhaps a thug might fancy them," exclaimed the other *sepoy* laughing mockingly at the old man. "What are you afraid of, baba? We guard this town. The fugitives are on the run, in fear of us lest we lay our hands on them." He held his chest up in an exaggerated show of prowess.

"Son, your presence here is very reassuring," Aleem replied in a grave tone. "Which direction have the fugitives taken?"

"Every and all directions, baba. They were frightened lest we caught up with them. You see the strength in my arms, baba. I could crush them with my bare hands."

"Oh, I am sure you could," exclaimed Aleem in agreement. He felt an urge to slap these loud-mouthed boys off their saddles. "Which part of town did these fugitives finally ride out of, son? Surely your keen eyes could not have missed them."

"They left by the *haat*, on the outskirts, due north. They have to be in the forest. There are no villages for miles in that direction."

"And who might these men be, my boy?" enquired the old man.

"Firengee and another."

"How can you be so sure, son?"

"Go on now, baba!" the *sepoy* replied impatiently. "No other in these parts sports a turban in his fashion. It was Firengee by all description. The prince of thugs. Ha! Frightened and scattered the moment he saw us. Go on, baba. Lest your medicines sour before you reach the *haat*."

With that the duo resumed their patrol down the street. Aleem heard them guffaw as they disappeared in the darkness.

Due north. By the haat. And Firengee it might be. Aleem mounted and rode. Soon he crossed an open field from where he could see the lamps of the bazaar. He did not venture near it. He was headed north by a circuitous route unseen by the crowd that thronged the market place.

When he reached the forest he knew for certain that his memory of these parts had served him right. For, inconsequential and little known to the townsfolk here, there was a small village many miles ahead on the other side of the forest. A village that lay on the route to Ganeshpur outside the authority of this district. A village whose people had long ago helped him gather some of the herbs he used to prepare his potions. The village of Laxmanghat.

* * *

"My guruji always said that most often, life is what happens to you while you are busy making other plans." Salmi sat on her charpoy making gentle rhythmic motions with her thigh to keep the baby asleep.

"Very perceptive, your guruji," remarked John looking out of the window. "We cannot stay here much longer. And speaking of making plans, what do you both intend to do? I have had a hard time explaining to the Sarpanch the sudden arrival of your brother. The birth of the child has fortunately made it possible to explain to them that I needed the help of another man to help us on our pretended journey to Varanasi."

"We *are* going to Varanasi," Salmi replied. "I have convinced Shambu that it as good a place as any other for people in our situation."

"Varanasi was only my ploy to capture the hearts of the villagers here at Laxmanghat. What special fascination does Varanasi hold for you?"

"I had a dream," explained Salmi. "At Varanasi I saw that I would not go hungry. I will name my child after we have had a holy bath in the waters of the Ganga."

"Then the time has come to make preparations for that journey."

"And what of you, Pardesi?" Salmi enquired, her large fawn like eyes looking straight into John's.

"I will accompany you some distance while I make my plan. I feel the need to at least see you both safely out of this district. Out of harm's way. This is a savage region save the infrequent villages and towns where some semblance of civilisation remains. And the authorities will be seeking your brother. This time they will shoot all of us on sight."

"My guruji always said that the test to find whether our mission on earth is finished was this, - that if you're alive, it isn't. Until your time is up nobody can put an end to it."

John sighed. "Man's greatest tragedy is he thinks he has plenty of time. Now where is Shambu?"

Shambu stood outside the village splitting log-wood. He swung the axe expertly but felt discomfort at the string he was asked to wear, to pass as a Brahmin, everytime it got in his way. The tall stranger who had befriended his sister and rescued him had instructed Shambu to speak very little lest he gave away his non-brahmin characteristics of speech and behaviour. So he had used the pretext of gathering firewood and walked beyond the village, deciding to spend most of his time splitting logs.

A long shadow creeping up from behind fell across the splintered log before him and startled him. He had not heard anyone approaching, perhaps absorbed as he was, striking at the wood with his axe.

The old man who stood behind him held a horse that he had walked through the grassy slope which emerged from the forest.

"Pardon my insolence that allowed my unworthy shadow to nearly fall upon you," he said as he bowed. "I did not realise you were a Brahmin. Such is the task you are occupied with."

Shambu was uncertain how he should act. "Ram! Ram! Who is this?" he managed to sputter somehow, hoping it was as close as a Brahmin's reaction.

The old man smiled beatifically. "A healer I am, and have travelled far in search of *jadi-booti* in these forests. Does anyone ail in this village? Or perhaps has the village been blessed with a new-born? I have here balms and potions that are of exceptional strength."

"Nobody ails here," Shambu replied. "Besides, we have our own healer."

"And yet you do not utilise his services," the old man remarked. "Look at you, sir. Your face is injured. May I ask what caused it? It appears to have been inflicted upon you."

Shambu's heart sank, but he managed to keep calm. "I heard the grunting of some wild animal in the forest a few days ago and struck a tree when I ran," he explained, preparing to resume chopping wood, hoping the old man would leave him soon.

"Have you seen any strangers in these parts lately?" the old man asked suddenly.

"Not many," Shambu managed to respond without looking at the man, and trying to keep his calm. He continued to swing his axe. "Nobody has halted here at Laxmanghat lately."

"Then I shall be on my way," the old man bowed as he spoke. "Farewell! Insh Allah, we will meet again."

"Farewell," Shambu replied while busying himself at his task.

* * *

While the interrogation progressed, Arjun kept as much distance from the captives as he could. He stood by Amalie's kitchen trying to distract himself by occasionally talking to the *bawarchee* and the *khitmutgar.* He did not possess his father's strength of heart to watch one human torture another.

His father, the old Rajput soldier, however, did not have much choice in the matter as he was required to remain beside his white master, the stern George Preston, as the magistrate conducted the interrogation.

Bhim Singh Rathore watched as the thugs were threatened and caned by the magistrate's *sepoys.* The task was a slow and sickening one, but one by one the thugs succumbed. Their narratives, as they confessed, were even more dreadful to the ears.

George Preston stamped about impatiently as the *sepoys* tried to wrest information from the lame thug in their midst. The cripple was the most resolute of them all. Blow after blow singed the skin of his back and legs, but he remained on the ground like a mute, his eyes shut, as if in a trance.

"Strip him!" Sleeman ordered his *sepoys.*

As the clothes were torn off the man, Bhim Singh decided he was not going to look at what they were going to do to him. In his heart he wondered which was worse; the torture of this man, crippled in mind and body, or the many innocent lives he was alleged to have mercilessly taken. While he turned around to look towards the tents, he was glad that Arjun did not need to witness this.

Behind him, the sound of a rain of blows from the canes of the *sepoys*, together with an animal-like howl of pain rent the air. But not a word of remorse, denial or confession escaped the wretched man on the ground.

The man cannot take this for long, Bhim thought. He will surely die before he opens his mouth. But Bhim did not wish to turn around to witness the man's agony. He urged to shut even his ears if he could.

Preston meanwhile was reaching a state of delirium. "Damn it! Why doesn't the man talk! Talk! Talk, you fool! Where are the Manar rubies!" He moved his large frame forward to aim a kick at the man, but stopped short at a curt order from the magistrate.

"Keep out of this Mr. Preston. I am the law here!" The keen blue eyes of the magistrate flashed.

"Oh, damn him, Mr. Sleeman! This is getting us nowhere. I have been here for over a week, and I am at my wits end. For whatever strange reason, you chose to interrogate this brigand last of all. And he turns out to be the toughest swine among them!"

"Oh! I do have my reasons, Mr. Preston," the keen eyed man replied. "In a day or so I should receive a reply that will confirm to me which department of the Company sent you here. There is no reason why the authority that sent you to seek this treasure on their behalf should not address me upon the matter if it was true. You see, I am the Company's servant too, and you stand now in my jurisdiction and in need of help. If the reply comes and stands in your favour, I plead guilty of having doubted you. But enquire I must. Such is my nature, Mr. Preston. As you can see, I am not interrogating this wretch to find your fabled rubies. He is guilty of much graver crimes than robbery. I would most appreciate it if you would keep out of the business at hand until that letter arrives."

"Then you doubt my credentials?" Preston stepped back, beads of perspiration trailing down his forehead.

Sleeman faced him squarely looking him in the eye. "At this moment, let's just say that I do."

The monocle steamed up and looked opaque. The enormous figure of Preston seemed suddenly dwarfed by the spare frame of the magistrate.

"Your non co-operation in this matter will go on record," Preston finally uttered in a small voice.

"So be it," replied Sleeman coldly.

At this point, Bhim Singh turned around, attracted by the change of events. The two white men did not seem to be in agreement over some issue and the *sepoys* had stopped whipping the naked wretch on the ground.

But he recoiled at the sight of the naked thug. Lying there, semi-conscious on the grass, his crippled leg in full view, he thought he recognised the man. The man? The boy! Bhim's eyes swam, as he felt dizzy and faint. The memory of that crippled leg mangled by cannon fire! He drew close to the prostrate man and looked at the thug's face.

Behind the lines that marked the years, behind the stubble of his grey beard was the boy who had played *kabbadi* with him, and fought the battle of Merta by his side.

Bhim Singh knelt down and wept, much to the amazement of the *sepoys* around. Still on his knees, he addressed the magistrate. "Sir, I, and only I, can make this man talk."

* * *

George Preston slipped out of the camp that night, walking his horse quietly before mounting it. He had to get out of the district before the inquisitive magistrate discovered he was not an authorized East India Company official. He made his decision after a quiet dinner alone in his tent, pitched a little away from the magistrate's camp. He had waited long enough to note that the lamp had been blown out in the neighbouring tent where Bhim Singh and his son slept. With extreme caution he crawled, dragging his heavy frame towards his horse tethered far from Sleeman's *sepoys* who stood guard mainly in the area of the magistrate's tents.

Preston had decided to abandon the natives and cover the miles required to keep his distance from the magistrate. To evade arrest he had to move alone and under cover of darkness, as he could easily be spotted and described by the local populace if he was seen. His large constitution, monocled eye, his ruddy complexion and English clothes were all too conspicuous. Damn the miserable cripple! Sleeman had, as a precaution instructed his *sepoys* to disarm Preston and his native retainers, and did not allow him to go near the captives or speak to them. Preston knew it was futile to linger there any longer. Damn the magistrate, too!

If only he had one more lead. Aleem, or Nasser, or whatever his name was. If only he could track the old quack down.

He rode swiftly on a well-rested horse, covering several miles under the cover of darkness.

He had one hope left. Ganeshpur, on the edge of the forest. That was where Sleeman's informer had last communicated from. He would make some enquiries there. If he failed he would head for Jhansi one last time. Back to the jewellers, and seek a fresh lead.

As he rode he began thinking once again of the curious sketches of birds he had been shown by Sleeman.

* * *

It was late in the evening.

As Salmi packed food for the journey, the sarpanch of Laxmanghat made his appearance at the door beside the granary along with some of the elders and their womenfolk.

"The *rahukala*, the inauspicious time of the day is still some hours into the morning tomorrow," he remarked. "While you have the time, pray let us know what your needs are. We rarely have people stop by here, and the cry of this baby boy will be missed by us."

John spoke to them, reassuring them that if God willed it, they would see the baby again. "Thank you, we wish to leave early. Perhaps at dawn to best utilise the daylight hours."

The women presented clothes for the baby and Salmi wept as she accepted them.

John raised his hand solemnly in the manner of a Brahmin to bless them as they departed. But he meant every word when he said, "We shall remain grateful to Laxmanghat for the rest of our lives."

"We leave before midnight." He whispered to Salmi.

Salmi stood at the door watching the villagers head for their houses. "I wonder why it had not occurred to them to ask why we were leaving so suddenly and prematurely." She exclaimed.

John did not reply. Instead he addressed her brother. "Shambu, keep watch outside, and don't take your eyes off the entrance of the village. I have a little work yet. Where is my stylus?"

Salmi sighed teasingly. "You really must love this woman greatly to want to write to her at a moment like this."

John made no response as he hurriedly unrolled a sheet of paper.

Salmi folded her clothes and tied them into a bundle.

"Shambu, fill these gourds with water from the well," she requested her brother. "We will need them on our journey." She turned to John. "Perhaps we are panicking unnecessarily. The old *hakim* only asked Shambu a casual question, being himself a stranger in these parts. Many healers travel in this land and they all speak in the same fashion. Perhaps we should not leave this village yet."

When John still did not respond, she playfully peered at his letter.

Salmi looked as startled as John was annoyed.

"I am sorry," she mumbled, then raising her hand to her lips in mock astonishment she exclaimed, "Birds! You are drawing birds at a moment like this! What sort of woman is she who wishes pictures of birds from you so urgently?"

John returned to his writing. He remained absorbed in it for sometime. When he had finished, he folded two pieces of paper into separate envelopes. He wrote the addresses. One in Hindi, the other in English.

"Are we ready?"

Salmi picked up her child as Shambu returned with the gourds of water.

"Discourteous and ungracious as it may seem, we must leave the village unnoticed, and in the cover of darkness." John told them. "We should be miles away when the village wakes up to bid us farewell. I have had to lie to these people again. About having to reach Varanasi on a particular day owing to a vow I had made. Shambu, untether the horses and walk them up to the edge of the village. Do this slowly, as one would lead horses to graze. I don't want to draw undue attention to our intentions tonight. I suspect there could be eyes watching our every movement even as we speak."

Salmi shivered, and covered her child.

Shambu left obediently to carry out his assigned task. But not before John reached into his saddle-bag and withdrew a handful of silver coins.

"You wait here with the baby," he told Salmi, as he left the room to meet a young man he had befriended in a house at the far end of the village. A mere boy, who for a handsome sum had agreed to ride out that very night to deliver the Brahmin guest's letters to a *sepoy* of William Henry Sleeman.

* * *

"He said he was in search of a man, Saheb," explained Bhim Singh Rathore. "A man who was in some large debt to the company."

It was still very early in the morning. The dew lay shimmering on the grass. Sleeman paced the ground to and fro, his eyes wandering about the horizon. The tents were being packed on to saddles and trailers as the camp prepared to move. He regarded the old Rajput standing in attention before him with respect. A survivor of Merta! One who held a sword and watched the slaughter of his entire family and clansmen as a mere boy! He still stood like a soldier, Sleeman noted. Obedient to the end, till his unscrupulous white master abandoned him. Sleeman felt a sense of shame on behalf of the Englishman as much as he felt a sense of pity for the old dock hand. Arjun stood a few paces away in respectful silence.

"Did you know this man?" Sleeman enquired.

"I have met him on many occasions," Bhim replied. "Moin-ud-Din Nasser is his name. A trader who acts as an agent between the in-land districts and the harbour. We have been on his trail for many months."

"And what have you learnt?"

"We traced his movements upto Gorakhpur, sir." Bhim explained, "Then there appeared to be some confusion about the identity of this old man. Since then, I think, we have been tracking an altogether different individual. Their descriptions fit remarkably, but this trader we have known in Bengal appears to be an old healer in these parts."

Sleeman stopped pacing. "A healer?"

"Yes Saheb. A *hakim* by profession, it appears. The man, if he be the same Nasser, goes in this region by the name of Mohammed Mir Aleem."

Sleeman suddenly struck the air with his cane in frustration. "Good God! What a fool I have been!" he exclaimed. "Did this Nasser or Aleem know a certain Mr.Hutchinson at the harbour?"

"Charles Hutchinson!" exclaimed Bhim. "Yes Saheb! And Nasser has never visited the harbour since Hutchinson Saheb was murdered."

"You have served me well today, Bhim Singh!" exclaimed Sleeman in satisfaction. "There is no time to lose, now." He summoned some of the *sepoys* in his charge.

"What about the cripple, Saheb?" Bhim enquired. "If he has recovered, may I talk to the man?"

"Not now, Bhim Singh," Sleeman replied as the *sepoys* stood by for their orders. "We will do that later. I shall keep my word, don't you worry about that. The man will not be tortured and will be given a fair trial. I trust, your gentle approach as his fellow clansman, will do the trick. But he remains my prisoner until then. His wounds will be tended and he will be fed. I shall treat him fairly. If he turns approver, perhaps I could even consider rehabilitating him. But now, I have work to do."

Bhim Singh Rathore felt a sense of relief. He trusted the magistrate's words. Whatever crime the boy he had played with in his childhood had committed, Bhim firmly believed the boy had done only for his survival.

Sleeman meanwhile issued orders, reminding each *sepoy* of the healer they had accosted and failed to arrest on at least two occasions before.

"Aleem. And only Aleem will be our quarry," he told them. "The final pieces of the puzzle will fall in place if we can apprehend him alive. This cardinal and elusive figure in the thugee hierarchy."

As Sleeman prepared to ride with his men, he was informed of the arrival of a *dak* runner. A single envelope was handed over at the campsite, and the runner he was informed had departed on his horse without awaiting the magistrate's permission to leave. This uncustomary behaviour of the runner caused Sleeman to open the letter immediately.

His keen eyes widened as he read the message.

"Talk of the devil, and his whereabouts are delivered up to you!" he exclaimed to himself with an uncharacteristic laugh.

* * *

Mohammed Mir Aleem had been right yet again. His deliberate choice of words had the desired effect on the wood-cutter. It had helped to ferret out the visitors of Laxmanghat, whose presence in the village had only been a wild hunch on his part. As always, patience had rewarded him and the vigil he held at the edge of the forest had borne fruit.

He rode now in the darkness keeping a safe distance, noting that there were three riders. At one point he clearly saw them riding over a crest in the distance, silhouetted against the purple darkness of the starry sky. One of the riders appeared to be carrying a bundle, and their progress, though hasty, was slow enough for him to stalk them without difficulty.

Aleem took great care to ride in the deeper shadows of the night, sometimes dismounting to walk his horse through the thickets off the road. Fugitives and travellers who rode in the night always looked over their shoulders, and he was particularly wary of the tall rider in the group.

He rode without being detected for over two hours, his quarry having stopped only once to attend to the bundle they bore. The faint cry of an infant made him realise why the three made so slow a progression despite their untimely and hasty flight. He also knew now that they experienced a sense of vulnerability and desperation.

He regarded the tall rider against the horizon whenever an opportunity presented itself. Memories of the Sind-mori ravine came to mind and he shuddered. If this was his family, his wife and child, he could not imagine the ferocity with which Firengee would fight to protect them. Aleem would need to exercise extreme caution and guile to bring this man down and retrieve the rubies, if he still carried them. He could not imagine anyone being able to sell them anywhere unless he had access to a very wealthy client. Neither could he imagine how he would ever pin the man down or restrain him if he had to make him talk.

Praise be to Bhawani. Perhaps the woman and the child provided the solution. If indeed they were headed on a long journey to Varanasi, as his enquiries had revealed.

* * *

"Do not halt or turn around to look. I think we are being followed."

They rode at a steady pace in the silence that followed John's announcement. They were now on a curve that seemed to be ascending.

"What shall we do now, sir?" Shambu asked.

"Ahead of us, barely a cannon shot away, the road climbs up a steep slope. Once over the top, and on my signal, we will ride into a thicket that I will determine. Salmi, keep the child calm. Our lives depend upon this moment."

They rode now without uttering another word. Only the hooves of their horses striking an occasional rock betrayed the silence. Salmi held the baby close to her breast in the hope that the warmth would keep him calm. The march up the slope seemed never to end, but finally they were at the top.

"Not yet," whispered John. "Let us ride downhill for a while. We are still visible against the sky."

They descended some distance.

"Now! To the left!" signalled John as he spied a gap in the lush greenery.

Salmi covered the baby as they squeezed in through the foliage lest the branches they brushed against injured or woke him up.

John dismounted. "Here, take this horse Shambu. Walk them all a little deeper into the forest and stay calm, whatever happens."

John crouched behind a bush keeping the top of the road they had just descended in clear view. From inside his robe he pulled out a length of cloth and tied a large knot to one end of it. Then he held each end firmly with the palms of his hand turned up.

Then, while he waited, he breathed slowly and deeply to compose himself into state of preparation. It would take at least five minutes before the rider he had spotted came over the top. It was a bright starry night despite the absence of the moon.

As he sat waiting, he wondered about the letter he had sent Sleeman. He also fervently hoped he would not have to kill the man who pursued them.

Suddenly he appeared, looming large upon his horse, in a slow canter, which became a trot as he descended.

John leapt at the rider. With all the force his body could muster he slammed his shoulder at the horseman's torso, hurtling over the horse along with the man onto the hard road. The startled animal galloped away, kicking the air behind it. The rider grunted in shock and pain as he landed, face down in the dust. John instantly wound the cloth around the man's neck, but he struggled with such strength that John pitched forward from his crouched position on the man's back. Although choked, the stranger tried to lift himself up on all fours nearly shaking him off. John held fast, but before he could press him down again, the man craned his head around in an effort to try and see his assailant's face.

It was John's turn to feel shocked. A shattered monocle lay on the road beneath the man's head, while he stared over George Preston's broad shoulders. Preston tried to lift one hand, clawing about to get his fingers between his neck and the cloth, while he propped himself up with the other. John took this opportunity to slam his knees on Preston's enormous back bringing the man's face down hard upon the road. He now took a fresh hold of the cloth, wound around the fallen man's neck.

"John Penmarric of the West India Dock Company at your service, Mr.Preston!"

"Oh God! The birds…mercy…" Preston began, but as the cloth tightened, he could not speak. His eyeballs were already protruding.

"And this is with compliments from our good friend Robert Pendarrow. Remember him?" John hissed in the man's ear as his clenched knuckles drew the ends of the cloth together.

There was a severe convulsion, followed by a weaker one, and George Preston lay still.

John's hands trembled in the aftermath of his exertions as he sat on the road, wondering how on earth he had come upon Preston after all these years. He turned the corpse over and peered at the face again in disbelief. For the first time in many weeks his thoughts suddenly returned to the rubies in his saddle-bag.

The neighing of a horse alerted him and he sprung up to his feet. Looking about him he could not detect any movement on the road. He removed the cloth from the neck of the dead man and hurried through the gap in the foliage from where he had so dramatically emerged.

The far horizon glowed with a hint of the breaking dawn.

* * *

Aleem stared down at the corpse.

He had witnessed many strangulations in his lifetime, apart from those he had executed himself, and the many he had participated in. He had eaten the *goor* of the *tupounee* following a killing hundreds of times, but he had not witnessed such single-handed skill and strength as that of this lone wolf, Firengee.

Aleem might have ridden into the trap if his ears had not picked up the sound of hooves some distance behind him. As he rode up the slope over which the three riders had disappeared from his view, he had heard the hoof beats behind him grow louder and knew the horseman would spot him when he came around the bend. He had immediately dodged into the undergrowth and dismounted, walking his horse carefully through the pitch-black shadows and prodding it up the slope in a parallel course to the road.

As Aleem reached the top of the slope, still concealed in darkness, the stranger had ridden past him on the road and descended to meet his fate. In mute witness Aleem had watched his death throes as Firengee's unfailing *ruhmal* squeezed the life out of the giant man.

Then he had waited long enough for the three riders to resume their journey before emerging from the darkness to identify the corpse.

The sight of the dead Preston shocked him, but it brought both relief and apprehension. All of Calcutta knew of his close acquaintance with Preston. Rarely did thugs target Englishmen, and the manner of death of this big man could put him under suspicion yet again. At Calcutta rumours in the dock-yard of his involvement in the death of Hutchinson had already put Aleem on his guard. On this night he could not but dwell on the irony of it all: There were innumerable dead bodies in the forests, bheels, ravines and well shafts of the Central Province and beyond which he could be held accountable for. And yet, he feared it would be the death of these two Englishmen in which he had played no hand at all that could have the authorities at his heels.

He decided to drag the body to the side of the road and bury it in the morning light. He would perhaps have to mutilate the body for easy decomposition. Perhaps even stab the face to make recognition difficult. Dismembering and gutting the body, however, did not hide white skin! And English clothes! What manner of predicament was this! The task was not going to be easy and would put his quarry miles ahead by the time he finished.

He would have to locate them again, and overtake them in a circuitous fashion, this time to avoid direct confrontation with that animal Firengee. His only fear was that the Varanasi story might not be true. For, the likes of Firengee, he knew, would never leave a trail. Oh, how he longed to grab those rubies and be gone home to his little boy!

Aleem felt despair. In frustration he violently kicked Preston's lifeless body.

* * *

"Did you kill him?"

Salmi's voice quivered as she enquired again, "Tell me pardesi, did you kill him?"

When he didn't answer, she sniffled aloud. "Was it necessary? How could you do such a thing so easily?"

They rode in silence for many miles. Save for the distraught Salmi's occasional sobbing there was no conversation.

Soon they halted beneath a grove of trees on the outskirts of a town to allow Salmi to suckle the baby and rest their horses. Below them wood smoke from the town of Panna rose lazily in the air.

"Trouble is an inevitable part of life, Salmi," John finally broke the silence. "But to be miserable because of it is optional. If I did not kill him I doubt if I would be alive and riding with you this day."

Dawn had broken and the splendour with which the skies opened up seemed to lift the gloom they all felt. Salmi accepted John's explanation and appeared to be cheering up.

"One day," remarked John, "all this will be behind us. We may, God willing, be better stationed in life. The whole world is seeking happiness. But as much as God provides food for the birds, they have to search for it. Look to your child, Salmi. Your happiness is not far away."

His words soothed the girl and she smiled. "You speak like my guruji now."

"We will ride down to Satna, after which I believe your road lies north to Allahabad and on to Varanasi."

"And you, pardesi?" Salmi asked solemnly. "Where does your road lead?" She handed the sleeping baby to Shambu. A tear welled in one eye. "You are leaving us then, aren't you?"

John tried to smile. "Happiness has no permanent address, Salmi. I have to seek mine elsewhere."

They paused on the side of the road for a long while. Salmi's face as she looked at the glowing horizon was distant and thoughtful. It was a beautiful face, noble and proud, yet soft of contour. Suddenly she searched for the edge of her garment and tore a strip of cloth from it.

"Wherever you are in the world, you shall remain a brother always," she said to John. "Wear this as a token on your arm, and may God always grant you your wishes."

John felt overwhelmed as the girl held his hand and tied the length of cloth to his wrist. "Here, bless my baby," she asked of John, picking up the child from Shambu's arms once again.

John ran a tender hand over the baby's brow.

"And now you will grant me something that I wish," Salmi continued, extending her hand towards him.

John raised his eyebrows.

"My *dupatta*, dear brother." Salmi looked John straight in the eye.

John swallowed hard, transfixed by her gaze. "You always knew...," he whispered almost speaking to himself.

"Its work is over, and I require no explanations from you. But promise me you will never kill again."

John looked at the beautiful girl, a sleeping baby in the crook of her arm, another arm extended towards him. In the first rays of the sun she looked radiant like a native Madonna, he thought.

He removed Salmi's silk *dupatta* from the folds of his robe and restored it to her. He then held the mother and child in his arms for a long while, feeling a curious sense of relief sweeping over his body and mind.

"I promise," he said. "But as the custom of the land dictates, I have as a brother to look to your welfare. I wish you to have some money, nay, a great deal of money to set up your life in Varanasi."

She shook her head and refused to accept it. John then pressed a handful of gold *mohurs* and five pieces of the Manar rubies into Shambu's hand. "Take good care of her," he said. "I have errands at Rewa and Bilaspur before my mission is complete."

Salmi smiled. "Thank you brother. Though neither the money nor the precious stones will be necessary. I know I only need to reach Varanasi. And I also know that in Varanasi, I will not go hungry."

* * *

A hundred and twenty thugs died on the gallows that year, while some four hundred were transported over the *kalapani* to Penang and other institutions overseas. Two hundred and thirty more were imprisoned for life with hard labour. Seven were released after trial, two escaped from jail and twelve died in custody. Seventy-eight were made approvers while some seven hundred awaited trial.

The strange mail bearing the inscrutable sea gulls finally stopped arriving on Sleeman's desk, the last bearing the *dak* stamp of Bilaspur, but he remained grateful for the depth to which this anonymous informer had penetrated into thugee country and gathered the intelligence that had arrived at his office each season. At least a thousand arrests that he had made were directly or in some way connected to the information those letters provided. Thugee was on the ebb and its practitioners were scattered into occupying themselves in more peaceful pursuits. His anonymous informer, Sleeman feared, had perhaps finally been discovered, and had met his fate in some *bheel* or ravine in the hands of the sinister sect he had nearly vanquished.

However, in the corridors and cells of the numerous jails of Hindustan and the many penitentiaries abroad, the name of the renegade and elusive Firengee was still whispered as it was in many towns and villages of the Central Provinces. Many East India Company officials wondered if it was all a fairy tale, a figment of native imagination.

Among the few gangs that still roamed the provinces and in the shelter of princely states, the name was very fashionable. Many young thugs assumed the name of Firengee to gain leadership and spread fear. They hoped to raise the myth to reality!

Only one old man who lay on a pallet in a dark prison cell at Saugor would know the difference between the myth and the truth. He was arrested one early morning by Sleeman's *sepoys* while he attempted to mutilate and bury a large Englishman's body.

But then nobody would believe him for he was either delirious or demented. Sometimes he would rave of rubies the size of pigeons' eggs and of how Bhawani had taken Firengee and the treasure to the burning ghats of Varanasi. Sometimes he told stories to the figure of a little boy without eyes that he drew on the wall of his cell. Of Sindbad, Allah-ud-din, and Ali Baba.

Then there were numerous thugs who were reformed and rehabilitated. Many who turned approvers were put to less violent occupations and grew greatly skilled at carpet weaving and rug making. This suited especially those who were old or crippled.

Arjun decided to study English law as his father now served in a decent and less strenuous position among Sleeman's legal staff at Saugor. Bhim Singh Rathore was grateful for being able to settle close to his native country. One day he hoped to tell his family a secret of his childhood years, and take a small vacation with Mandakini and Arjun to show them the battlefield of Merta.

* * *

They sat on the beach, the lithe guru of *kalari payyatu* and his pupil, the English school master Jack Dawson. The night was warm, but some of the sweat from their bodies evaporated in the cool breeze that blew in from the sea.

The myriad thoughts and emotions Dawson had learnt to quell had still not succeeded in completely stopping the occasional bad dreams he still experienced. Only his fear of the nightmares seemed to have ebbed. And he was able to stand up to the visions stoically.

In between his visits to the *kalari* Dawson had found time to accompany Nandakumar to a few places of worship out of curiosity for the faith of a civilized and disciplined populace. He was not allowed into many temples as they regarded him variously as a Christian, an untouchable and an outsider. Being of the same race that now protected the land he was however treated with respect. But very few and only minor temples allowed entry to a foreigner.

He was however fascinated by the colour and variety of the seasonal festivals, the dance dramas and the thunderous drums of varied percussion and rhythm. He understood little of the stories that were being enacted, but took great pleasure from Kannan and Nandakumar's detailed description of how the various masks and make-up techniques used in *Kathakali* and *Theyyam* were prepared. Even the eyes of the artiste, he learnt, could be made to look protuberant and blood-shot with the plant, *chunda-poova* or *solanum pubesscuce*. He was shown how the *theyyam* performer breathed fire with the aid of a mouthful of alcohol.

Now as they sat on the beach in low tide, the guru spoke to him.

"It has been so many months since you came into our lives. Have you any regrets?" the guru asked.

The master's words were translated by Kannan.

"None gurukal," Dawson answered.

"You have learnt fast. Your inherent physical fitness and your prowess have aided you. You do not indulge in drink or tobacco as most English do. I shall ask you one last time the question that you have refused to answer all these months. What was your purpose in accomplishing what you have learnt?"

"Revenge for an injustice done," Dawson answered. "But I promise that I shall not kill. I shall not take a human life except in self-defence."

Kannan translated.

A silence followed.

The *kalari* guru, a middle aged man, whose physical fitness rivaled the fittest teenager in the region pondered over the Englishman's admission.

"Sweet revenge! How one so easily falls into that trap! Are you not born a Christian? Does Yeshu Christu, not teach forgiveness?"

Kannan translated.

"I shall not grievously harm those whom I wish to take revenge against," Dawson tried to explain. "I only need to teach a lesson to the very kind of Christians you are referring to."

"You cannot break your vows. It will lead to your destruction. Nothing disintegrates your soul psychologically more than not to stick to our vows."

Kannan explained in English as best as he could.

"The bible teaches one to forgive. But I do not wish grievous harm upon my enemies. I only wish them to know that they had done wrong."

The *kalari* master looked mildly irritated, and Dawson grew nervous.

"Don't try to interpret the bible to me," he retorted much to Kannan's discomfiture. "St.Thomas the apostle, follower and student of Yeshu, witness to his crucification, was here in our lands preaching the bible while the English were mere wild tribes on their island. Do as you must, but I warn you, be rid of the disease. As long as you need revenge, the nightmares you complain of will not leave you. Forgive, and you will sleep in peace all your life. Seek revenge by all means, but to reform, not to destroy."

Dawson was not sure he understood everything the *gurukal* said, but he knew he would not return to his job at Saugor. He knew that in a few months he would return to London. Once again to his school in St.Giles, and with a new sense of discipline learnt at Malabar, he would begin to set in order the remainder of his life.

* * *

"John, I have been rejoicing like I have never done before in my life," wrote Lucy Polgarth. "I have not shed so many tears in grief as I have done today in joy.

"Like John the Baptist you have come out of the wilderness. I might sound silly, but your letter, the longest I have received in all these years, has also been the happiest. I am sure I shall be preserving it, to read to my grandchildren a hundred years from now! On reading your letter, you once again sound like the adventurous young man I knew at the breakfast table in London, in the Strand, eating bacon, eggs and kippers, making an enormous and vain effort to impress my father, and disarming me completely.

"That was an extremely long letter, John. And I have read it over and over so many times, I feel quite confident that my grandchildren would most likely be listening to a 'recital' than a reading. Laugh if you must, but it would take only someone who knows you as well as I do to feel the emotions, the pain and the triumph of the years spent in a native Hindustan.

"Do I sound like a tease? Alright, let us call them OUR grandchildren if it makes you feel better. You say you speak many languages - the soft and lyrical Bengali, a constantly improvising Hindustani and many Indian dialects apart from a coded and secret language called Ramasee! It amuses me that it took you such a long letter in the English language to propose to me.

"I shall be aboard a ship within a fortnight. Father has a grand event in mind when we touch port at Calcutta. As for me, I look forward to once again witness the magic of that place, the colours, the odours, the music, the subtle thoughts, ideas, nuances and everything else that makes Hindustan so unique! And to share all this with you, with one who has imbibed it all in a style few Englishmen have. Yes, Mr.Penmarric, I will marry you. I am afraid those tears of delight are trickling down again, and are going to make a muddle of the ink on this paper

"I have made another futile search for your friend Jack Dawson. He does not appear to be anywhere on the British Isles. I discovered that your letters to him lay unopened at the miserable school in St.Giles. Like you John, this man was driven underground, and you may as well vainly search America or Europe, for until he wishes to be seen or heard we can only wait. To quote your own words- 'One can wake up the sleeping, not those pretending to.'

"Father is confident of growing tea in the new English territories in the north-east frontier. We have been keeping abreast of the developments there, ever since the Burmese surrendered at Yandabo. We hear that the condition of the Brahmaputra valley since the expulsion of the Burmese is pathetic. Most of the population has been barbarically killed, and famine, pestilence and civil war continue to ravage the land. Ahom nobles and the Gosains, rulers and chieftains of this land have been displaced, creating an administrative vacuum. Father has a friend in Captain Neufville of the Assam Light Infantry, a corps raised some years ago in Cuttack under the name of the Cuttack Legion, now transferred to the north eastern region. Mr.Neufville once suggested to Dad the idea of bringing an exclusive population of workers from outside to dedicate their energies in the north east to establishing tea plantations. John, you wrote about the famines and the constantly migrating people of Hindustan with such knowledge and clarity. Could a large population of people be moved voluntarily towards industry and prosperity for a change, rather than as a result of fear and starvation? I personally think it is logical.

"John, before we venture forth with our lives, please thank and convey my warmest regards to that Hindu priest Veeru Mahasaya at

Kalighat. Strange are the people and the circumstances that influence ones life. But I now firmly believe you are a better man for it.

"I know you have good reasons John, but is it not going to be difficult for you to behave in the manner of an Englishman who has just arrived from Cornwall? Are you absolutely certain not a soul in Calcutta has ever seen the Englishman John Penmarric before? I sometimes wonder if *being* John Penmarric now would be more of a pretence!

"I have prayed for that girl Salmi you frequently wrote about. Someone I shall perhaps never meet. We have each learnt so much of the other without any communication whatsoever. But even across continents, I feel a strange affinity to that innocent girl who left for Varanasi. I can feel her joys and pains, and somehow John, I know she feels mine too. In my heart it feels like a kinship with a goddess.

"Now I torture myself watching each day go by ever so slowly, until I board a ship to Calcutta. In the meanwhile my dear John, try to become an Englishman again. It has been a long while since you have met that race of people."

* * *

As they entered Varanasi late in the afternoon, the baby in her arms began to cry.

"The time is near. Shambu, hold him for a while," Salmi requested of her brother. They stood in uncertainty in the shade of a grove of neem trees near an old Kali temple above the river.

Before them a teeming multitude separated them from the holy Ganga. Pilgrims from every corner of the continent thronged the ghats, to bathe, to pray, to weep and to burn their dead. As many sought salvation by bathing in the purifying waters of the river.

"Shambu, we need to reach the waters. I will be cleansed and so will my baby. My sins will be washed away. My prayers will then be heard. And we can pray for all those who have touched our lives. Dear brother, find me some way through this crowd."

Shambu walked into the throng, firmly but inoffensively furrowing a path in the human morass with his young body. Salmi followed her brother who carried the child in his arms.

The faint stench of burning flesh drifting in from the distance intermingled with the sweet smell of incense and sandal wood paste. Warm body odours of tired pilgrims blended with the sharp aroma of basil leaf and camphor fires.

They walked down slippery slopes of rock, rutted and polished by the feet of the faithful for centuries. Down well worn stone steps and damp, sandy pathways, arriving near the water as the sun began to set in the horizon. The calmly flowing surface protected by ghat walls heaved with humanity, bathing, dipping, immersing and praying for the miracles and wishes of their lives. Rocks thrown into this shallow part of the river over the years allowed people to stand on them waist-deep.

Handing the baby back to her, Shambu stepped into the water till he was standing in it knee-deep. He held Salmi by the arm and drew her slowly into the river till they were both in waters deep enough to immerse themselves. She handed him the baby. The water was strangely tepid and their clothes clung to their bodies. Salmi covered her nostrils and dipped under the surface for a moment and stood up. Awash, soaked and dripping she stood up laughing aloud, ecstatic and beautiful, her joy and radiance distracting the pilgrims around them.

"Oh Salmi," she spoke to herself. "You are fine-looking in this mortal's body. Only it's time to go!"

Taking the baby from Shambu's arms she performed a quick immersion of the child. The baby shrieked for a while but as she laughed and held him close to her the cries almost instantly subsided. Salmi now waited for Shambu to do the same. The fires of the burning ghats where the dead burnt were now visible far downstream, and she looked towards it longingly.

"I have put you through many a test, dear brother," she said impatiently. "The time has come. Let this be your last one. You have my blessings."

Shambu pinched his nostrils closed and squatted under the surface of the water. The warmth of the water enveloped him as he crouched in its comfort. The soft touch of luke-warm currents soothed him in that foetal position. He did not wish to move. For a moment, it seemed as if he needed to forget Salmi and the baby. He was in a womb himself, protected, unattached and unfeeling. He held his breath feeling a sense of darkness as the tepid Ganga flowed over him. He passed out into blackness.

Finally the image of the girl called Salmi detached itself from his mind to become an insignificant memory, absolving him of love, pain and guilt. He felt at peace again.

His mission was over.

He emerged out of the river slowly, knowing She was gone. With Her baby to the burning ghats of Varanasi where She had materialized from. Where She would not go hungry. He felt the heaviness of his age once again; the boy he relinquished in the river now just a memory. The pilgrims bathing around him were too busy praying for miracles to take notice that a young man, a beautiful girl and a baby had vanished in the river.

So Veeru Mahasaya waded out of the river to climb and retrace his way along the well trodden rocky path to the old Kali temple above. His long hair dripped, sending droplets down his broad back. He felt the refreshing breeze cooling his damp body. He would pray to Her, and sit under the neem tree in deep meditation and contemplation till the break of dawn. The cycle of the Siddhi of *para-kāya praveśanam* had been completed. The pouch at his waist containing gold mohurs and five rubies was proof of his success.

With his eyes shut, he began to slowly chant the hundred and eight names of Kali, reliving the attributes of each form and avatar.

"Durga, Badrakali, Bhawani, Sati, Rudrani, Gauri, Parvati, Lakshmi, Chinnamasta, Chamunda, Kamakshi, Kamakhya, Uma, Meenakshi, Himavati, Kumari, Tara, Shodashi, Bhuvaneshwari, Bhairavi, Matangi, Kamala, Adya, Adi Shakti, Gayatri, Mookambika, Bagla Mukhi, Saraswati, Santoshi, Annapoorneshwari…" Until dawn he would go into a trance, and swim in a mental ocean of divine bliss.

Then he would leave for Calcutta, to the temple of Kalighat to resume his duties there.

* * *

John Penmarric wished Bob could see him now as he stood before a large mirror in a suite he had hired at Spencers, the only luxurious hotel in all Calcutta. It was early in the morning. He wore an expensive suit and a silk hat of the kind Bob Pendarrow would have approved. His shaven face, clean finger-nails and cropped-to-length hair looked almost unreal.

For an indulgent moment, he stood before the full-length mirror and tried to imagine the sinister bearded figure of his former self reflecting in it. The spectre of a long dark robe, cummerbund and black turban, a ruhmal dangling in one hand. Like an apparition, the vivid image he created in his mind seemed to reflect in the mirror, almost taking on a life of its own. It so shocked him, that he had to blink and peek over his own shoulder to make sure the reflection was not of a real man. It made him smile.

Now fully dressed for the occasion, he walked to the large window of the suite. Below him, Calcutta was still waking up. Crows and parakeets flew above a silent city. Wisps of smoke rose from the myriad dwellings, heralding another day. He had awoken rather early, as one was apt to do in the style of his Cornish upbringing…

He closed his eyes and prayed. "Dad! Bless me this day, bless my beloved Lucy, and may you and mother find peace wherever you are."

He pulled a gold watch out of his pocket to check the time. Lucy and her father would be waiting at the church. If he did not arrive on time she had threatened, "All these years and not a minute longer, John! Or I shall certainly turn into a shrew the moment we return from the altar." They had both laughed but he knew she was as anxious as he was to see the ceremony through.

He had more than three hours before the congregation was to begin. And an important errand to attend to in the meanwhile.

He snapped open his portmanteau and raised the stiff leather lid. Beneath his clothes lay a bundle wrapped in a fading black turban. He picked it up and held it in his hands. For a brief moment violent memories of the Sind-mori ravine flashed before his eyes, but he quickly dropped the bundle into a very English leather case and left the room.

He carried the case out to a waiting coach. "To Kalighat," he instructed.

On arrival he headed towards the temple on foot, searching for that very pious Hindu priest he had befriended from the early days of his arrival at Calcutta. In the courtyard outside the temple he found the elderly man, bathed, his long wet hair dripping little droplets of water. He stood amongst a number of noisy children distributing *prasad*.

Veeru Mahasaya turned and waved to him, holding the earthenware containing the *prasad* aloft. "Rama! This is the third time you have stretched your hand out for *prasad*. Do you wish to fill your belly with Her blessings?" the old man playfully chided a boy of barely five.

John smiled at the prancing youngster and greeted the priest.

As he saluted the priest and accepted the *prasad* offered, the holy man enquired, "Do you really wish to relinquish them here, my dear son? Goddess Kali has no use for it." He looked at the faded turban John held under his arm. "In the name of Bhawani, there has been a grave miscarriage of justice. You have accomplished to undo some of it, but she seeks no *bunij* as has been misinterpreted down the ages."

"Perhaps you could sell them, and feed the poor for a generation," John suggested. "They are the fruits of a just war. A war of retribution. I have walked the path you set me upon and my anger is long gone. Burnt in an endeavour for justice far beyond the needs of my own mission. I have already told you what the value of these are and confessed to you how I came by it."

Veeru raised his hand in blessing. "Son, your confession was certainly of great value. But I have spoken to all the priests of the sanctum and they were reluctant to accept anything else, especially articles of so dubious a history into the temple. My son, I am sorry I could not be of much help to you this time." He removed a small cloth bundle from the waist of his *dothi* and presented it to John. A sense of shock and bewilderment overtook him as he unknotted it. It contained a handful of gold *mohurs* and five rubies. "Take these too. They are being returned to you. Do not worry yourself with the lives of those three souls who have departed to Varanasi. They are safe. Take these precious things with you as they are worthless in both these holy places. Do what you will with them. I can see that you do not harbour a desire for them. They cannot harm someone who has ceased to crave. Find some place to invest them." The priest bowed and turned to the children who still pressed about him, jumping up and down and around him in a carefree gambol.

"Rama Krishna! You have consumed enough prasad for a lifetime! Here, let the others eat."

John turned to leave. "I should have asked my friends to throw them into the river when they reached Varanasi," he exclaimed aloud, throwing up his hands in exasperation. "Such wealth! I cannot understand why somebody, even at Varanasi, could not use the money."

"Oh! Don't you know, sir," cried the young Rama Krishna, beaming at John. "At Varanasi, Kali Ma never goes hungry."

The boy skipped about him and laughed.

John smiled at the disarming charm the boy exuded.

"And how do you know that?" John asked, teasing the lad.

"Oh, I do! I do!" the boy replied, still prancing about. "One day I shall see Her. I shall ask Her to appear in my presence. I have a lot of questions to put forth to Her."

"So do I," John nodded solemnly. "So do I."

Removing his shoes, he walked up to the sanctum to pray for his parents and Bob Pendarrow. Strangely, he did not find the image of the Goddess as revolting as when he had first seen Her. Kali, naked, surrounded by decapitated heads, gore, fire and blackness was an apt reminder of the strength and the failings of humanity as he had seen these recent years in Hindustan. The savage inner reality of the human mind in vivid imagery. A latent potential he had learnt to harness in the forests and ravines of this great land.

Then John understood. The inner voice spoke, as the priest had once foretold.

The phansigar resides in all of us. Time and distance do not bind him. When a situation is fertile, the phansigar manifests himself, as he has done before, as he will again.

At the foot of the idol, in a state of tranquillity or defeat, lay a little cloth doll. It had long black hair, a turban, a bearded face, and a bright red tunic. It momentarily rang a bell in John's mind but he could'nt quite remember where he had seen one such before.

As he took leave of the priest, John spoke to his mentor of his bride Lucy, and asked for his blessings.

"Take good care of her," Veeru Mahasaya told John. "One does not ever recover from the pain that one might even accidentally cause one's loved ones. I have known that pain. Take good care of her."

As John waved farewell to Rama, he teased the boy again. "When you see Her, do let the world know."

"That I will, I promise," Rama-krishna waved back to him.

As he rode to St.John's church, he experienced an extraordinary sense of peace and happiness he had not felt for years.

* * *

The regimental band began to play as John stepped out of St. John's Church with Lucy on his arm. The bride wore a diamond tiara in her hair, which her father had presented her that morning. He had insisted it matched the wedding gown she would wear, but Lucy knew in her heart that this was also another of her father's displays of wealth to increase the confidence of some Tea Committee members and investors who would be present at the wedding.

Polgarth had in fact gone to great lengths to invite everybody who was anybody worthy of mention in the city. He had begun by befriending Father Sebastian, and making a substantial contribution to the Church's funds. He had presented a gold chalice to display that day at the altar before Zoffany's "Last Supper". Officers from the garrison, senior members of the church, civil administrators, and most of the prosperous stalwarts of the English trading community were there.

The courtyard outside had been prepared for the reception, and it was a riot of colours. Stewards in white embroidered tunics and scarlet turbans, ladies in exotic dresses and jewellery, and men in uniforms and smart suits. There was drinking and laughter as the brandy, gin and wine corks popped open. Soda water and American ice, a new luxury in these parts, were readily relished along with an assortment of indescribable snacks.

As John and Lucy took the floor to dance, John experienced difficulty smiling at the multitude clapping and singing around them. He had not smiled very often in these many years and his cheeks ached at the prospect of having to acknowledge a gesture from every guest with a smile. Soon others joined in to dance, and he was able to leave the floor and make towards a table for a breather.

"Here, meet an old friend of mine," Polgarth spoke over his shoulder suddenly. John turned around.

"John, this is Colonel William Henry Sleeman, magistrate of the Central Provinces here on a short visit to Calcutta." Polgarth introduced. "And if I may add, also here to be decorated and promoted by his Excellency the Governor General himself."

In an ethereal moment that followed, John took the extended hand the magistrate offered, knowing he would remember this moment for the rest of his life.

"Congratulations, my boy." Sleeman's blue eyes looked at John. "You have a pretty bride there and an astute father-in-law to match." He laughed and jovially patted the old merchant's back. "Put the boy to good use, Mr Polgarth, as I have heard of your plans for new investments here." He turned to John. "Or will your heart yearn to feel the breeze of Cornwall as mine often does?"

"To see real seagulls, yes." John quipped almost absent-mindedly. A confused frown momentarily flitted across the magistrate's face, but it vanished as John continued to speak. "But as you know I am committed to help Lucy's father in his new venture and perhaps see a little of Hindustan, if I could."

Lucy and Amalie joined them with a glass of sherry each.

Lucy was ecstatic. "Hello, Mr. Sleeman. Father just informed me you were here. I am glad you could come, after all."

Sleeman congratulated her and kissed her cheek.

Amalie, dressed in a sleek black dress, congratulated John.

"You have also the colour well suited for this land." Her French accent assumed a teasing disposition. "*Brun fonce*! Lucy, does he not wear it well? In all his years my Henry has not transformed as much as you have on a ship at sea. Have you been sleeping on the deck the whole voyage?" She laughed. "Well, there you are. Tall, dark and handsome. As Lucy aptly described you."

"I blame my past habits for this, madam," John replied laughing. He lowered his voice into a conspiratorial whisper. "*Voir tout en noir*!"

Amalie frowned at John. But it must have been the sherry. Or the Calcutta weather. For her head swam momentarily, and she shivered. She felt better when she left the bridegroom's side and put her arm in Henry's.

Polgarth produced a newspaper from the inside pocket of his coat. "Gentlemen, there are many in parliament who are not happy with our unscrupulous trade practices with China. As we all know now, most of the money needed to buy tea in China was being raised by the opium trade. The Chinese are on the verge of imposing a death penalty on opium smuggling. And they will reject our ventures to buy any more tea there. Read for yourselves. I have great hopes in the possibility of finding the means of growing tea in Assam, now that the Burmese have been routed and we are in firm control." He placed a copy of The Times on the table, published in London, a few weeks ago. "John, there is a great investment here. Take time to read it leisurly."

John made a mental note to ascertain, following his wedding engagements, if five hundred pieces of Hindu standard gold bullion and forty pieces of flawless rubies were sufficient to make an investement that found approval with the Tea Committee. Polgarth should be impressed when he hears of it.

As he casually glanced at the paper, John's attention was however drawn to a singular piece of news that seemed positioned to vie the readers' interest more than any other news on that day. It was dated February 28th, 1838. He picked it up, and it read:

"**Spring Heel Jack Strikes London Again** – The horrifying specter that has plagued London and the neighbourhood since the fall of last year has been reported once again from the Limehouse district.

Lucy Squires a local resident walking near Green Dragon Alley late in the evening was allegedly attacked when the apparition leaped before her and breathed fire in her face. Four people, including her brother William Squire who witnessed the incident told this reporter that they had no doubt that this was Spring Heel Jack, as he bounded away at great speed and leapt over a high fence with great ease. They were unsure whether it merited a formal complaint as the police have yet to decide upon a course of action, having already admitted to not having reached any conclusive theory on the perpetrator of these attacks or his motives. To refresh the memory of our readers we have reproduced extracts from various reports since the first sighting of this dreadful assailant in chronological order. Some of the detailed reports can be found in our older issues.

"15th September, 1837, London - A businessman returning home late one night from his workshop was suddenly shocked as a mysterious figure jumped with ease over the considerably high railings of a cemetery, landing right in his path. No attack was reported, but the businessman's description of the apparition was disturbing: a lean and muscular human male with devilish features including large and pointed ears and nose, and protruding, glowing eyes. The businessman who has since been in poor health following a nervous breakdown did not wish his name to be divulged, but for reasons unknown to this reporter called the creature 'Jack.' The reporter tried to enquire of the businessman if this Jack had anything to say, but the businessman looked demented and unable to speak."

As John read on, he could not help but allow a pattern to emerge in his mind with respect to the location, the names of the victims, or at least a near relative involved. The coincidence was too compelling and increasingly amusing: London, Sheffield, Liverpool, Kensington, Hammersmith and Ealing! There were more victims from Stockwell, Brixton, Camberwell, Vauxhall, Lewisham and Blackheath! They described a devilish creature that could leap like no human being could, over hedgerows, tall iron gates and fences. Spring Heel Jack was described as wearing a shiny oil-skin suit, a peaked helmet, and a black cape. He breathed fire into the faces of his victims, ripped up their clothes, and departed in giant leaps and bounds. Most of his victims were since either mentally shattered or prone to fits, or totally deprived of their senses. They all seemed reluctant to tell much to the authorities or even to the reporters. With a demon in their midst, they all appeared to be suffering their trauma rather privately! Perhaps guiltily?

When he had finished reading the newspaper, John broke into a triumphant and undisguised laughter, much to the curiosity of all who had gathered at his wedding. "Bless you, Jack! You finally got the jury!" he whispered under his breath.

Polgarth beamed in delight at John's joy. "A good investment this tea business eh, John? Wait till you see some of the seeds we have received from our agents in China."

"I cannot agree with you more," John answered not caring for a moment who said what that day. The smile he wore was not going to leave his face even if his cheeks ached and his jaws fell off. He walked across to Lucy and held her hand securely in his.

"Now pick up your drink, my boy," Sleeman, the famous magistrate of Narsinghpur addressed John jovially. "Since you have only just arrived, raw and unaccustomed to this land, let me tell you briefly about Hindustan before you develop a narrow and sadly English view of things. This is a great country dear fellow, and great are the lessons you will learn here. I have been here for quite some years, and have seen the best and the worst of the Indian native which I am willing to share with you. For example, have you ever heard of thugs, my boy?"

Song Of The Phansigar

You who have heard my alluring song,
Now find solace in our privation, our loss.
Could the cult of Bhawani go utterly wrong!
For a little counsel would you pause?

You too have read our history
And know we plead no case.
You believe you have solved the mystery
Of our rise and fall from grace.

But Hark! Do I hear travellers stall
Alone on the road or by-lanes?
Heed not my loss of the charmed ruhmal
The blood doth rush in my veins.

So look over your shoulder, friend,
When you walk on a moon-lit night
For such a night do shadows lend
To this land where might is right.

For somewhere under a peepul tree
Or in the shadow of a door left ajar
One day we'll wait again for thee
To sing you the song of the phansigar.

About the Author

Born in Cannanore, Kerala, Jo Nambiar was an athlete, an equestrian and also holds a Master's Degree in Kung Fu. In the 1980s as a Physical Educationist at the International Youth Centre, New Delhi, his students of unarmed combat included members of the Delhi Police, Indo-Tibetan Border Police, the Assam Rifles and the President's Body Guard. He worked as a Tea Planter with The Assam Company for over a decade. He has acted in Shakespearean as well as contemporary theatre. As a numismatist, Nambiar has one of the largest collections of ancient coins and rare currencies in the country which has global recognition. Nambiar has the distinction of being the Convener of the largest Children's Carnival in the world, the "BALA MELA" for underprivileged children every year at Bangalore. He is also a painter and a sculptor.

Printed in the United States
By Bookmasters